THE AWAKENING

THE SOUL MAGIC SERIES

BOOK ONE

ANNE WILLIAMS

THE PNEUMA PROJECT

Printed in the United States of America

Published by The Pneuma Project

www.ThePneumaProject.com

Identifiers:

LCCN: 2020908754

ISBN: 978-0-578-69493-1 (paperback)
ISBN: 978-0-578-69494-8 (hardback)
ISBN: 978-0-578-69495-5 (ebook)

Available in paperback, hardback, e-book, and audiobook.

Book design by Jetlaunch. Cover design by Debbie O'Byrne.

ACKNOWLEDGMENTS

The creation of the Soul Magic series wouldn't have been possible without all the people who've supported me through this journey. My parents have encouraged me to follow my dreams, no matter how crazy they might be. My two children have cheered me on and showed infinite patience as I toiled for days over ideas in my head and words on my screen. Gary Whitfield has been a beacon of light, an advocate for my writing, a sounding board for my ideas, and a great friend. Billy's Place was there for my children and me after my husband's suicide, and I don't know if I'd ever have found my writing muse again without their love and acceptance during those months of traumatic grief. To everyone else who has been with me along the way, thank you for helping to make this possible, and a grateful thank you to all my readers.

PROLOGUE

The pre-teen and teenage years suck. I haven't met one person who would voluntarily return to those awkward years. Our bodies are physically and chemically changing and are pretty much out of control. All. The. Time. We struggle with raging hormones, pimple outbreaks, the joys of finding our first crush, and the devastation of losing our first love.

Now imagine being thrust into an extraordinary school during these delicate years. Yes, I know you just flashed to the X-Men *or* Harry Potter *movies. Everyone seems to know more about you than you do, every moment fills you with an odd sense of* déjà vu, *and you have to battle all the typical teenage woes and discover your identity—all while trying to keep the entire world in balance.* (Deep breath.)

Yes, that's my story in a nutshell. To understand it fully, though, there's no better place to start than at the beginning. The summer of 2012, to be exact.

Respect the changes that are to come.

Love and balance,
Me

CHAPTER ONE

"I've never heard of this academy," Mr. Jones said without uncrossing his arms.

"Oh, many of the world's greatest minds have attended," the dark-haired woman explained, seemingly unaffected by his cold cynicism. Her fingers flew over the keys of the laptop she whipped out of her bag. "This is the campus," she said, turning the screen toward him.

Emily tried to see the images from around the corner where she was spying, but mostly saw only the back of the strange woman's head.

"Look at those trees, Robert. That reminds me of our trip to New Orleans," Mrs. Jones said and leaned her head against her husband's broad shoulder, gazing longingly at the screen.

"It should. The North Shore Academy is located in Mandeville, Louisiana, which isn't far from New Orleans." The woman continued with her spiel, explaining everything from the uniforms to the enforced curfews and the rigorous curriculum.

Emily wrinkled her nose at the mention of uniforms and curfews. Still, the idea of living away from home—at a school that *wanted* her—made her eleven-almost-twelve-year-old mind do cartwheels.

"So, this is akin to a military school?" Mr. Jones asked as he leaned in for a closer look. Having served in the Air Force, he hoped his children would follow in his footsteps. Unfortunately, complications with Emily's birth made the couple unable to have any more children, and Emily showed no interest in pursuing her father's career path. Besides, he still believed that women were best suited to be housewives and mothers, not warriors.

"I suppose you could look at it like that," the woman said, clearly contemplating the parallel she'd never considered before. "But it's more of a unique education for those who exemplified certain skills on the annual state testing. Emily was one of the few this year who met our criteria."

Mrs. Jones beamed with pride and touched her husband's thigh. "What a great opportunity for Emily."

Mr. Jones held up his hand to gain control of the conversation. "The one thing you haven't mentioned is how much this elite private school is going to cost me."

The woman smiled and nodded as if she was expecting this question. "We do not charge tuition. The students are in a kind of work-study program that assists with their costs. Additionally, our alumni donate generously. Here," she said and reached into her bag again, pulling out a pamphlet. "This provides all the information you'll want about our Academy and others like it around the world. If you have questions, my number and email are on the back. I hope you can appreciate that this is a great opportunity for your daughter."

The woman collected her things and stood to leave. For the first time, Emily got a good look at her. She was a tall, slender woman with a kind face that matched the intonation of her words. She walked gracefully to the door, flashing a smile toward Emily, who was still in spy-mode. *There is something very familiar about that woman,* Emily thought.

"Thank you, Ms."— Mrs. Jones looked down at the pamphlet to find out how to address the woman.

"Please, just call me Maggie."

"Well, thank you then, Maggie," Mrs. Jones said as she opened the door. "We will be in touch."

July came and went, but Emily's parents hadn't shared with her any decisions they'd made about whether she would attend North Shore Academy.

"What do you think about the school that woman came to talk to us about?" Mrs. Jones said to Emily one morning as they were watering plants in their garden.

Emily always enjoyed summer mornings with her mom when her dad was at work. Her mom seemed less stressed during these times. "You mean Maggie?" Emily still felt that strange familiarity. "It sounds alright," Emily said. In truth, since Maggie visited their home a month and a half ago, it was all Emily could think about.

Mrs. Jones set down her gardening tools and looked at her daughter. "Your father is still on the fence, but if you really wanted to go, I'm sure I could persuade him," she said.

"Yeah," she admitted to her mom, "I think I'd like to give it a try."

Emily hugged her mom goodbye for the third time before walking up the brick steps to the front door of North Shore Academy. It was a warm, late summer day, and a small rainstorm had just swept through, making the air smell fresh and leaving little puddles on the steps. The heavy-looking front door was open, and a few adults stood in the foyer to greet the arriving students and direct them to the hall where orientation would begin. Emily took one last glance back at her old life before stepping into her new one. Her mom was standing outside the passenger side of the car while her father was subtly revving the engine, anxious to start the drive home.

"Welcome, Abecedarians. It pleases me to welcome you on your first day at North Shore Academy. I am Theodore, the Headmaster. But please, call me Ted." The tall man at the podium looked at the faces of the twenty new students, studying them as if he was looking for something—or some-one—in particular. His tanned face showed the beginnings of aging but didn't change expression the entire time, so Emily figured he didn't find who or what he was looking for. "The first year at the Academy is the most intense and mentally exhausting of your years, but I'm proud to say we have never had a student leave voluntarily."

The new students looked back and forth at each other, worried and confused by the wording he chose.

He continued. "That being said, we expect a lot from our Abecedarians, and following the rules is not a choice. You will be interviewed by our instructors and counselors and then assigned to a residence hall. From there, you will take your belongings to your hall. Your Hall Director will assign you a room, go over the rules with you, and serve as your mentor, counselor, and leader for your years at the Academy."

The crowd of twelve-year-olds began whispering among themselves.

As Ted held up his hand to quiet the students, a cool breeze swept through the room. It was difficult to suppress a shiver, but it succeeded in getting the students to calm and refocus. "I am looking forward to watching you grow and change."

Ted lowered the microphone and stepped aside for a short, red-haired woman. Emily thought she looked like a pixie or fairy but kept the comment to herself. "Please come to the front when I call your name," the woman said in a chilly voice that didn't match her appearance. "Madison Montgomery," she began. The girl standing next to Emily moved forward and then was taken to another room by one of the adults standing along the wooden walls of the hall.

"Justin Bingham," the pixie lady continued, and a boy from the front of the student group jumped up and was escorted away, just as Madison had been. She kept calling names, and the number of remaining Abecedarians dwindled. Emily felt nervous and looked down at her hands.

"What if this is just like the Holocaust," the boy next to her whispered, "and they're taking us to a death chamber?"

Emily noticeably jerked and blinked in surprise at the boy. "That's a horrible thought!" she declared in a loud whisper as she really looked at the boy for the first time. *Familiar*, she mused and recalled Maggie being that same sort of familiar, which was strangely calming. She tried to play it off cool and added, "Besides, I'm not Jewish."

"Brandon Miller," the pixie woman called.

"Welp, that's me," he said and stepped forward. "Wish me luck."

"Luck, Brandon Miller," Emily said with a grin. *He's cute*, she thought, and sincerely hoped they all weren't about to be gassed.

The few remaining kids were called up one by one until only Emily remained in the echoey hall that reminded her of an empty room in a museum.

"And you are presumably Emily Jones," the woman said, still speaking into the lowered microphone.

"Yes," Emily replied, somehow feeling her voice fill the room, although she didn't believe she spoke any louder than usual.

"Come with me, Emily."

A delicate hand touched Emily's shoulder, and she turned to see Maggie standing there. It felt like she was seeing an old friend. She smiled at the woman who, upon closer inspection, could be mistaken for her aunt or older sibling. Not that Maggie was old. Emily guessed she was maybe in her late twenties. Then again, Emily didn't have much experience guessing people's ages correctly.

"I was glad to hear your parents decided to let you attend," Maggie said. They walked through the doorway into a hall that seemed to be endlessly lined with closed doors. On the walls were painted portraits of people probably long dead whose names Emily didn't know. Again, some of them looked familiar. Emily passed it off as probably having seen them in history books at her old school.

Maggie steered Emily through the last remaining open door into an office. "I think the whole uniforms thing won my dad over," Emily admitted. The room was nice for an office—light furnishings in stark contrast to the dark wood on the floors, walls, and ceiling of the main hall and hallway. There was also a pleasant scent that seemed to be isolated in the office, like fresh-baked cake and cinnamon.

Maggie smiled gently and motioned for Emily to take a seat on the light blue suede couch. Emily was glad to be sitting after being on her feet for the last hour, saying goodbye to her parents, and then listening to Ted speak. "Thank you," she said.

"Would you like a glass of water?" Maggie asked. She began to pour some into one of the two glasses.

"Yes, please." It was humid—more humid than it seemed to get at home—but the hall where they gathered seemed to have better airflow than the office, and Emily hadn't noticed it much then.

Maggie joined Emily on the couch and handed her a glass of water with a lemon wedge and three blueberries floating among the ice cubes. It seemed strange that a woman Emily didn't know—aside from their two-minute walk down a hallway and a passive smile at her home months prior—would know her favorite way to drink water. She was about to ask if her parents mentioned the water when Maggie spoke.

"Do you know me?"

CHAPTER ONE

That was not the question Emily was expecting. "Umm . .
. you're Maggie, and you came to my house," Emily answered
haltingly, unsure what she was really being asked.

Maggie laughed, a soft and sweet-sounding laugh, not
mocking Emily at all. "Yes, that is the obvious answer. Let
me ask it this way. Do I seem familiar?"

Emily felt flustered, frustrated by the questions, and
allowed her twelve-year-old temper to get the better of her.
"Is this some kind of joke? Is this what everyone else is being
asked? How do you know what I like to drink? What is this
place?"

Maggie waited patiently for Emily to finish her outburst
and took a deep breath before responding. "No, this is not a
joke. I don't know what the others are being asked. I will answer
the drink question later. And this is North Shore Academy.
Any other questions before we continue?"

Emily stewed and felt a little embarrassed by her outburst.
She was mentally gathering a list of questions to fire at Maggie
but supposed they could wait until her temper flared again.
She shook her head.

"There are different degrees of knowing people. Do you
agree?"

Emily nodded but remained silent.

"You know the person who delivers the mail, even though
you might not know his name or his favorite color."

"Bob and blue," Emily said.

"Okay," Maggie said with a small chuckle. "What I mean
is that there are strangers you know by sight and with whom
you are simply familiar, and there are people, like family and
friends, whom you know more intimately, correct?"

Again, Emily silently nodded.

"We are making progress." Maggie smiled, still warm and
friendly, and without a hint of frustration. "When you first
saw me, was I a stranger, or did it feel like you knew me? Pick
any degrees of knowing you wish to use."

Emily slid her thumb to intersect a bead of condensation from her glass before it dripped on her leg. "You looked familiar," she finally admitted, "but I don't think I'd ever seen you before."

"Has this happened with other people?"

"Brandon Miller." Emily nodded and bit her bottom lip. "And those paintings in the hallway look familiar. Are they in history books or something?"

"Probably not in any history book you've been exposed to, but they are important people." Maggie paused for a moment and stood, taking a book from the bookshelf that was behind her desk. "As are you."

Emily had flashbacks of being sent to the principal's office in the third grade when she got in trouble for pushing a boy into a mud puddle and was lectured on the importance of how everyone is valuable and should be treated with respect. She let out a long sigh while Maggie thumbed through the pages of the book.

"What about these people? Do you feel any connection to them?"

Emily tilted her head at the picture and then took the book from Maggie to look more closely. Her brows furrowed. She felt a familiarity, yet also something akin to panic that she couldn't remember why. "Yes," she finally admitted but remained focused on the picture that looked like it was taken during World War II.

"This is Ava," Maggie began, pointing at a woman who was probably the same age as Maggie, but somehow looked older—or wiser, perhaps. Emily felt a deep sadness as she looked into the pictured eyes of Ava. "And these two with her are Adya and—"

Emily interrupted Maggie. "Lydie," she whispered.

Maggie smiled and nodded, taking back the book. "Yes, that's Lydie."

"How would I know that? These people probably died before I was born. I mean, this was taken back in the olden days. My great grandparents were alive then."

"You're right. These people were dead before you were conceived."

Emily thought that was an odd way of phrasing it but didn't have time to form a question before she felt something inside her change. It was like a burst of energy or an adrenaline rush. While it didn't make sense, she felt like a part of her had awoken, and she understood.

Maggie saw the change in Emily but didn't offer any explanations. She simply took a drink of her water while continuing to observe Emily, who was pushing the moisture around her glass of ice water. Maggie exchanged her glass for the journal on the table and wrote some notes.

In the silence, Emily fished one of the blueberries out from beneath the ice cubes in her drink and then set the glass on the table beside Maggie's. Emily could've sworn they both had ice water when they sat down, but now only hers had ice remaining. She thought Maggie noticed, too.

"We're almost done here," Maggie said as she set aside the journal. "I just need to ask a favor of you."

With a tilt of her head, Emily responded, "What is it?"

"I'm a little embarrassed, but I've been gone recruiting for weeks and forgot to have someone water my plant. Do you think you could fill this cup from the sink in the bathroom down the hall and water it for me while I have your belongings sent to your new room?"

"Water the plant? With the sink water? Now?" There was so much in the request that confused Emily.

"Yes. Please?" Maggie handed Emily a white coffee mug with the phrase, *This might be wine* written on the outside.

"Alright," Emily said with a shrug and walked out of the office.

Emily had no idea which door was the bathroom down the hall. With most of the doors still closed, she was concerned she would walk in on someone else during their weird interview, so she kept walking until she reached the hall where they began their day. "Hello?" she whispered. No one was in the room, so she continued to the foyer and the building entrance, where she saw the red-haired pixie woman. "Excuse me," she said as she stepped closer to the woman.

"All the Abecedarians are heading to their halls. I think you are . . ."

Emily cut her off, feeling a new panic on being left behind and failing this simple task Maggie had assigned to her. "I'm really sorry, but I just need to find the restroom."

"Oh. It's down the hallway, the eighth. . . ." The fairy woman paused and seemed to be counting. "No, the ninth door on your left. Can't miss it."

"I guess I did." Emily chuckled nervously. "Thanks."

Emily briskly walked back through the hall and started counting doors as she passed them. On the seventh door, she nearly ran into a person stepping out. "Oh! Sorr—" She stopped short when she realized it was Brandon.

He chuckled and held up a candle. "They have you running errands, too?"

"What are you doing with that?" Emily asked, feeling pleased she had run into him again.

"Taking it to Adamina."

"Who?" Emily asked.

"Umm, that short ginger lady who called our names."

"Oh, I thought she would've had a pixie name like Faye or Lily," Emily giggled.

"Huh. She does look like a little fairy or something." He shrugged. "Have fun getting your wine or water or whatever."

"You, too," she replied and then realized it sounded stupid. As they walked in opposite directions, she called out without looking back, "Glad you didn't get gassed."

Emily thought she heard him chuckle as he rounded the corner into the hall. She collected herself and continued counting down doors until she reached the ninth. It looked no different than the previous eight doors, closed and unmarked, so she knocked. "Hello?" After hearing no reply, she slowly opened the door.

It was not a bathroom of the type Emily expected, not that she had put a lot of thought into what the school bathrooms would look like. She assumed they would be just like the bathrooms at her old school, satisfactory enough to do your business, but not really inviting. Girls are stereotyped as clean, which is far from true if you've ever been in a public-school restroom. This bathroom, Emily decided, belonged in a spa for wealthy people. Everything was so clean. It practically had that cartoonish gleam added to bathroom cleaning product commercials. The floors looked like white marble, and there were fresh flowers and lit candles throughout. Emily snickered at the thought that this could possibly be the destination of the candle Brandon was taking to Adamina. The sink was unlike any sink Emily had known. It was more like a water feature in the middle of the room, with flat spouts for the water to fall gently from when you put your hand in front of it. The water cascaded onto a pile of stones with small, leafy, happy-looking plants growing from it. There was airflow in the room, too. It reminded Emily of a spring day when she was a little kid, the kind of day where the sun's warmth kissed her skin and made her light brown hair flutter like a superhero cape behind her.

The best way Emily could think to describe the bathroom was balanced and in harmony. She knew if she repeated the thought to anyone, they'd laugh at her for thinking of a bathroom in that way. Maybe she would use it as a way to talk to Brandon again and see if the boy's bathroom was the same. I mean, he *did* suggest they were marching off to be killed, so at least he had a mind for ridiculous ideas.

As Emily filled the mug with water, she became aware of something she hadn't previously noticed before; the bathroom was void of mirrors. How were girls supposed to check themselves after using the toilet? "Very strange," she muttered and finished filling the mug.

Upon returning to Maggie's office, she realized she didn't ask how much water to put in the plant. She knew from gardening with her mother that it was just as easy to kill a plant by overwatering as it was by under-watering.

Maggie's plant was a beautiful orchid, sapphire blue blooms with two long stems. Emily studied the plant and observed that it looked slightly wilted and sad. Could a plant be depressed? She set down the mug and held the pot in her hands. No, this plant wasn't in the right place, but it wasn't under-watered. Emily looked around the room and decided on the table beside the couch. After setting the plant down, she drew the sheer curtain closed, which allowed the flower to receive the needed light but keep it safe from direct sunlight. Emily added just a small amount of the water and set the mug on Maggie's desk. Before leaving the room, she admired the blue flowers once more and felt like the plant was happier in its new spot.

CHAPTER TWO

When Emily entered her assigned residence hall, it was buzzing with excited girls—some returning students and a few of the girls she had seen in the hall. Despite the noise of the other students, the relaxing sound of water falling seemed to fill the room along with a scent that Emily thought smelled exactly like rain. The walls were painted soft blue, and there were waves of dark blue accents throughout.

"This is more like a resort than a dorm," one girl remarked.

Another laughed and agreed. "My dad practically had to drag my mom home after parents' weekend last year."

"Mine still can't believe they don't have to pay for this," yet another girl said.

Emily barely had time to take in the surroundings of the common room before a blonde woman appeared and called for the girls to settle down.

"Ladies, there'll be plenty of time to socialize once we review the rules, and the Abecedarians are settled in. Now, if the returning students will give us the room, I will conduct orientation. Unless you feel you need a refresher on the rules." The woman looked sternly at all the girls.

The room quickly cleared out and quieted. "I'm Greta, your Residence Hall Director. The four of you have been placed in this residence hall based on the assessment you just completed, and I am honored to have you all here."

As Greta continued to explain the rules in her beautiful southern drawl, Emily couldn't help but wonder what part of the interview with Maggie made her an obvious fit for this dorm. What were the other ones like? Could Maggie really have known which one she'd fit into after their short time together?

"Number four. Uniforms are to be worn during school hours and for school events unless otherwise noted. Number five. Overnight guests are not allowed."

Emily only half-listened to the rules as she observed the room. There was an odd fluidity to it, yet there was nothing moving. She couldn't even find where the trickling water was but could definitely still hear it.

"Does anyone have any questions?" Greta asked and brought Emily's attention back to the group.

A girl with dirty blonde hair raised her hand.

"This isn't a classroom, dear. Please just ask your question."

The girl noticeably blushed and put her hand down. "Can we have sleepovers with the other dorms?" she asked.

"Good question, Ashley. The short answer is no. It falls under the rule of no overnight guests, but there will be times when we have outings with the other residence halls, and sleeping arrangements are less strict. Except there are never co-ed sleepovers."

The four girls all giggled together.

"Any other questions?"

The girls looked at each other and then back to Greta.

"If you have questions later, I'm always available for you to ask. If you'd like, you may see your rooms, but dinner is in thirty minutes. I strongly recommend you not be late." Greta winked at the girls and motioned for them to find their rooms.

Emily peeked into the first bedroom, which was occupied by two of the older girls who had been part of the bigger group that was in the main room when she arrived. They both smiled and waved at Emily before returning to whatever it was they were doing with a glass of water.

At the fifth door, Emily saw her belongings placed neatly on one of the two beds. Between the beds were two desks under a window with a view directly out toward the lake.

"Beautiful, isn't it?" Emily's roommate entered quietly and stood beside her to take in the view.

"Yes, I thought we'd end up in the basement or something. This feels like a dream."

"I know what you mean. I'm Ashley, by the way." It was the girl who asked about sleepovers at the meeting. She was about the same height as Emily with lighter hair and fairer skin. Ashley's eyes were hauntingly light blue in color, a stark contrast to her own dark brown eyes. Again, Emily felt a sense of *déjà vu*, like she was seeing an old friend after a long time.

"I'm Emily." She smiled at Ashley, resisting the unusual urge to hug the girl she'd just met.

"Cool. I guess I'll take this closet, and you can have that one?"

"Sounds good. I wish they'd unpacked for us when they brought our stuff in," Emily joked.

"Oh, not me. I have three brothers and am *very* protective of my things."

Emily blinked, not sure what to say, and then decided to start unpacking. "I'm terrible at putting things away. Just be warned. My mom says I must think the whole house is my room because I leave things everywhere."

"Maybe that's why they put us together. I'm a bit of a neat freak," Ashley said.

Ashley might have been onto something. The two girls were opposite in looks—hair, skin tone, eye color—in living styles, and who knew what other ways they might contrast to each other. Emily couldn't help but think these next six years were either going to kill her or make her into a better person. She hoped the latter.

"I always got straight A's in school, too," Ashley continued. "My momma thinks I'm here because of how smart I am."

"Oh. That's great," Emily replied with as much enthusiasm as she could muster, mentally noting her average grades. "Maybe they *did* pair us because we're so opposite."

Ashley frowned slightly. "I'm sorry. I didn't . . . I mean, I will help you anytime. With anything. Except I won't be your maid. You have to pick up your own stuff."

"Sounds okay to me. I swear I'll try to be neater here."

"It's a deal," Ashley said and held up her right pinkie finger. "Gotta pinkie swear that you'll at least try."

Emily smiled and locked pinkie fingers with Ashley. "I promise to try."

"Glad to see you two getting along so well," Greta said as she poked her head through the open door. "It's time for dinner."

Emily and Ashley giggled and followed Greta out to the dining hall.

"Where do we sit?" Emily asked, surprised by the number of students already seated. No one had plates of food yet, but almost every seat was taken.

"Looks like there are two over there," Ashley replied while standing as tall as she could on her tiptoes.

"I guess we don't have to eat with our residence hall-mates." Emily shrugged and followed Ashley to a table near the far wall.

"It's a little freaky with all these portraits watching us all the time," Ashley remarked as she sat next to an older girl who was busy chatting with the boy on her other side.

"I don't know," Emily said. "I think they're kinda cool. I mean, I don't want them actually watching me, but it's almost. . . . " Emily searched for the right word. "Comforting."

Ashley laughed. "You're weird. I like you."

"Yeah, I thought she seemed a little weird, too, talking about gas chambers and death when we met." A boy had taken a seat across from Emily when she was busy surveying the portraits.

"You were what?" Ashley asked in mock horror as she turned to Emily.

Emily tried to glare but ended up smiling at Brandon across the table. "Hey, that was your theory, you freak."

Ashley looked back and forth between the two for a moment before she shot her hand across the table. "I'm Ashley. And you are?"

Emily could hear the tone in her roommate's voice change from casual to flirting. It took everything in her limited power to not roll her eyes.

"Brandon," he replied and shook Ashley's hand. Emily thought she saw him glance at her when he did it, but she looked away too quickly to be sure.

Ashley continued in her flirtatious tone. "So, how's your dorm?"

"I'd invite you over to see, but we were told having girls over isn't allowed." Brandon finally released Ashley's hand.

"Yeah, that really sucks. I mean, I get it, I guess." Ashley shrugged.

"It's cool. Everything is fiery red and warm, but not hot. It's great."

"Ours is the opposite. Very cool and watery. Peaceful," Ashley added.

"Huh. Like fire and ice-themed. Cool."

Another boy sat in the last empty chair at the table, a couple of seats down from Brandon. "Dude, it's elemental, not fire and ice."

"I guess that makes sense," Ashley said with a smile to the new arrival. "And you are . . . ?"

"Titus," the dark-skinned boy said in a deep voice. He appeared to be older than the other three in the conversation. "I'm a second year, not a noob, ABC."

"ABC?" Emily asked and then instantly regretted it.

"Abecedarian," Titus replied with obvious annoyance. "But even last year, I figured out the elemental shit right away."

Ashley looked at him with doe eyes, obviously impressed by this older—slightly older—boy. "I bet the dances here are magical," she said dreamily.

Thankfully, the first course of the meal was served and broke Ashley out of her trance. The course could have simply been described as a salad, but it was dark green mixed—kale, spinach, and mixed greens—topped with walnuts and blueberries. Emily ate the blueberries first and then picked at the greens until the second course arrived.

"Not a salad girl, huh?" Titus commented as Emily's nearly-full plate was removed.

"I'm not a rabbit," she said matter-of-factly.

"Food is food," Brandon added while grabbing the last green leaf off his plate as it was taken.

"I was vegan for a year," Ashley commented as the server removed her half-empty plate.

Emily fought against rolling her eyes. She understood from her friends back home how easy it was for girls to want to try to impress boys. While Emily herself wasn't against impressing boys, it was never worth the cost of faking who she was. That being said, Emily had also never had a boyfriend.

"They serve protein for the main course, so I hope you can stomach meat now," Titus remarked.

Ashley shrugged and didn't look offended when a chicken breast was placed in front of her. Emily, on the other hand, loved meat of all kinds. Chicken was always a good go-to, and the side of red and purple potatoes and even the asparagus looked and smelled delicious.

"Oh man, this is better than our chef's meals," Brandon commented with a slightly-less-than-half mouthful of food.

"Oh, right. Like you really have a personal chef." Ashley did roll her eyes then, and Emily couldn't help but smile.

"Swear it on my grandfather's grave," Brandon replied, this time *after* he'd swallowed.

Emily mused on how quickly Brandon finished his meal and wondered if he was really making up having a chef at home. He was skinny, tall, and had a healthy glow, but acted like he hadn't eaten in weeks.

As the plates were taken away, Brandon declared to his server, "Give my compliments to the chef!"

The server simply smiled and continued with his work.

"I will convey your approval, Brandon." Ted had wandered behind Emily without her noticing, and she jumped a little when he spoke. "And what about you, Emily? Did you enjoy the meal?"

"Yes, sir. It was fine," she said immediately.

Ted laughed, again startling Emily. "No need to call me 'sir,' Emily. Ted is just fine. How do you like the Academy so far?"

Emily dabbed the corners of her mouth with the napkin and craned her neck to look at the Headmaster. "It's lovely and unexpected," she said formally. Something about growing up with a military dad made her speak differently to adults in charge. She often cringed at how forced the words sounded, but it was how her father demanded that she behave.

"I would like to hear more about what you feel is unexpected, but it seems dessert is being served, and I wouldn't want to keep you from that." Ted nodded at the students whose attention he inadvertently commanded. "Enjoy."

Dessert was a mixed fruit bowl with a square of dark chocolate and a dollop of whipped cream on the side. This was something Emily could definitely get used to. The berries were like a spark of magic to her. In contrast to the other courses, she ate every bite.

"So, you're a dessert girl. Interesting," Brandon observed.

Emily shrugged. It felt natural for her to joke around with Brandon. Their back and forth felt almost natural and unscripted. "It's hard to go wrong with berries and chocolate."

"I've never liked raspberries," Ashley chimed in. "They're too . . . I don't know . . . not bitter, but. . . ."

"Tart," Titus interjected. "Yeah, I've never been a fan, but these ones are grown here and are pretty good."

"Oh," Ashley replied and tried one. While her face didn't show approval, she nodded. "Okay, yeah, these are better than the ones I've had before." Needless to say, she didn't have another.

"So, what's there to do around here besides school and eating?" Ashley asked as she pushed her fruit bowl aside.

"The first month is adjustment month, so the upper classes are doing their thing while you ABCs will be doing your thing. We only have meals and common room time together, but you really won't have much time for that."

"Oh," Ashley replied with a frown, her shoulders slumping slightly.

Adamina started talking to the room on a microphone, almost on cue. "Abecedarians, please join me in the library when you've finished eating. Upper classes are free to go to the rec room or your common rooms. Grounds are off limits tonight."

Brandon was the first to stand. "I guess we're going to the library, wherever that is."

"I was in the library earlier. I'll show you." Ashley pushed away from the table and smiled, first at Titus, and then at Brandon.

"I'll find my way there," Emily replied and remained seated in front of her empty dessert bowl. "I'm going to the bathroom quickly," she added as both Brandon and Ashley looked at her questioningly.

"See ya, noobs," Titus said as he stood and headed in the direction of the others who weren't going to the library.

"Do you think we'll be that rude next year?" Ashley asked, obviously offended.

"Probably," both Brandon and Emily replied.

Emily returned to the bathroom she used earlier to get the water for the orchids. It felt more serene than even her residence hall. As she was letting the water run over her hands, Maggie entered.

"Aren't you supposed to be in the library with the other Abecedarians?" she asked.

"I'll get there," Emily replied, almost dreamily. The thought of a room filled with old books, poor ventilation, and talking interested Emily about as much as attending one of her dad's military functions.

Maggie joined Emily, who was still mesmerized by the water falling onto her fingers.

"Why did you have me water your plant?" Emily asked.

"Because it had been neglected and needed attention. I had something to do and thought you might be able to help."

Emily paused, unsure whether to probe deeper. Finally, she looked away from the water and straight at Maggie. "Because it seems to me that everyone had random errands assigned, and I wondered why that one was mine."

Maggie cocked her head with an amused smile. "So, you talked with all the Abecedarians, and this is the conclusion you've come to?"

Emily's brows furrowed. "Well, not all. No. Not even most. I ran into Brandon when I was trying to find the restroom, and he was on an errand, too."

Maggie nodded. "So, Brandon suggested you were all on pointless errands?"

"No, not at all. I just. . . ." Emily paused, but Maggie interjected immediately.

"It's good you're searching for answers. They will come, but you will be the one to uncover them. You need to get to the library now, Emily. Enjoy your night. I'll see you again soon."

Maggie exited the restroom leaving Emily to ruminate even more over what was happening at her new school. Eventually, Emily dried her hands and joined the others in the library.

"That felt like a waste of good rec time," Ashley groaned at the end of their lecture. "And now we have to go back to the dorms and sleep. This was valuable time we could've used to get to know the upperclassmen better." Ashley threw up her arms and stormed toward the door.

"Where are you going?" Emily asked.

"To find the rec room before everyone's gone."

"Have fun," Emily called out after her, not knowing if her roommate heard her.

"What are you going to do?" Brandon asked.

Emily shrugged. "Go back to my room and attempt to unpack, I guess. Ashley is super organized, and I'm basically a slob. I promised her I'd *try* to be neat."

"That's a silly thing to promise," Brandon remarked as they both retreated to the door.

"Why is it silly? Most people would think it's considerate."

"You don't seem like you care what other people think. So, if you're sloppy, be sloppy." Brandon shrugged and tucked his hands into the pockets of his khaki shorts.

Emily eyed him suspiciously.

"What?" he remarked.

"Nothing," Emily replied. "But I mean, you're the last person I'd expect to say something supportive."

"You don't know me," Brandon replied coolly.

"Perhaps," Emily said with a shrug as they strolled down the hallway of portraits.

Brandon paused and gazed at Emily with a confused expression. "What's that supposed to mean?"

Emily stopped several feet ahead and turned to face Brandon. "It's not supposed to mean anything. You're right. I don't know you. I'm just as confused about why I'm here as all the other ABCs. I suck in school, I don't play sports, I'm not a supermodel or interesting in any way. I'm not rich, and I don't have a chef to cook me meals. In fact, I have to help cook at home, and nothing ever turns out tasting as good as the meal tonight. I have the feeling people know things about me, but every time I ask questions, no one will give me a straight answer." Emily spun away, her face flushed, annoyed at her frustration, and embarrassed about unloading on him.

"Hey!" Brandon called after her, but Emily didn't turn back. He jogged to catch up with her and spoke in a tone she hadn't heard from him. "I get it. I don't understand this place, either. When I start to think I get it, I get mocked and treated like an idiot kid."

"Like what Titus did at dinner?"

"Yeah, like that. But I'm a guy, and we just have to suck that shit up or get bullied." Brandon shrugged.

"That's pretty crappy," Emily admitted.

The two walked silently until they reached the door.

"What are you going to do?" Emily asked as they paused outside, their dorms being in separate directions.

Before Brandon could answer, Titus jogged up and grabbed his arm. "We're starting poker in the common room. C'mon."

"I guess I'm going to play poker. Enjoy your organizing." Brandon pulled his right hand from his pocket and waved at Emily.

"Enjoy your poker," Emily called back before turning to head to her room.

CHAPTER THREE

"Everyone grab a mat and find the empty spot on the floor that speaks to you," Maggie directed as the Abecedarians entered her classroom the following morning. It wasn't a classroom like Emily any had ever seen before. It was maybe closest to gym class on rainy days back home, but this was definitely not a gymnasium. The entire front wall was made of glass with a view of the green lawns surrounding the school and the lake in the distance. Lit candles sat on the wood floor around the nearly empty room. A cool breeze could be felt, but there were no open windows or fans circulating air. Along the back wall on either side of the door were wall fountains, providing the soothing sound of trickling water. In the center of the room, growing up toward an unusually high ceiling, was a tree with pink and white flowers blossoming on the branches, filling the room with a sweet aroma.

"Elements," Brandon whispered to Emily as he snuck up behind her with a mat in hand.

Emily smiled serenely and nodded. "Elements."

The two sat in the middle of the room near each other. The tree stood just behind Emily, and a candle was to Brandon's right.

"How'd poker go?" Emily asked quietly as they waited for the others to find their spots.

"Killed it. How was organizing?" Brandon fired back.

"I hung three shirts and filled one of my drawers."

"Not bad for either of us," Brandon added before Maggie began to speak again.

"I hope you all ate a good breakfast because this morning is going to take every ounce of energy you have . . . and then some."

Everyone looked around with worried expressions.

Ashley, who was sitting toward the back of the room by the fountains, raised her hand. "Can we request coffee in the morning with breakfast? I can't function without coffee." A few of the other Abecedarians nodded in agreement.

"A worthy suggestion, but I promise you that your body will adjust and be better without the stimulant." Ted stood beside Maggie and took the opportunity to answer Ashley's inquiry.

"Oh," Ashley replied quietly.

Maggie smiled and spoke cheerfully to the class. "As I was saying, this class will be exhausting, but one of the most important classes you will take this first year. So, despite some of your natural inclinations, I ask that you do as you're instructed and keep an open mind."

"I also want to emphasize," Ted added, "that you will all progress at your own pace. This is neither a competition nor a race. The results are significant and important, no matter how long it takes you to master. Be patient with yourself and respectful of others. With that said, I will leave you in the capable hands of Maggie."

"Thank you, Ted." Maggie bowed her head respectfully at the Headmaster as he left her side and exited the room.

"Is everyone familiar with the lotus position? Yes, that's perfect, Olivia. Everyone get in lotus position and close your eyes. We're going to begin by learning the proper way to breathe."

Maggie walked around the room and assisted the confused students until all were in the correct position and rhythmically breathing at her instruction.

After several minutes of just breathing, Maggie's soothing voice broke the silence. "There are objects around the room. Some are physical, like the tree. Some are invisible, like the scent of the blossoms or the gentle breeze. With your eyes still closed, find which one calls to you and hold a picture of it in your mind."

Emily was tempted to look around the room. There was so much that called to her, so many objects flashed through her mind. She wondered if others were as confused as she was on which object to focus on or if it was as simple for them to hold one in their mind like Maggie had made it sound like it should be.

Maggie continued to give directions on how to interact with the chosen image. However, Emily was still struggling to keep one image in her mind. As soon as she picked one, another would flash in. She believed the tree was what called to her, but as she held the details in her mind, she was distracted by the blossoms moving with the breeze. Then the invisible fragrance of the flowers would swirl about, commanding her unconscious attention. After that, the water would force itself to the forefront. Emily struggled for the entire morning against the ebbing and flowing of her vision to manipulate the mental object as Maggie directed.

By lunchtime, Emily was visibly frustrated and left for the lunchroom as soon as Maggie dismissed the class.

"That was so relaxing," Ashley commented as she caught up to Emily. "I thought she said it would be exhausting, but I feel so . . . so . . . Zen."

Brandon seemed to follow Ashley's lead and ignored Emily's irritation. "What object did you work with?" he asked.

"The water, of course. I don't know how anyone could focus on anything else with its soothing noise echoing in the room," Ashley chimed in.

"Ha! Was there water in there? I didn't even notice," he replied.

"What are you talking about? Ugh. What did *you* work with then, huh?"

"The fire," Brandon said and tilted his head smugly.

"You mean the candle?" Ashley corrected.

"No, just the flame."

Emily was sure Ashley rolled her eyes, but she practically saw red. "I'm not hungry. I'm going for a walk," Emily stormed off before either of her friends could stop her.

"What's with her?" Brandon asked.

"Dunno. Do you think Titus will eat with us again today?"

Emily was furious but didn't know with whom she was most angry. Was it herself for failing miserably at her first lesson or her parents for sending her to this school? Maggie, for never giving her straight answers and making her do the stupid visualization exercise *all morning*? Ted for running the school? Those ridiculous portraits for staring at her with judging eyes? Or maybe it was the dead people behind the paintings for creating the stupid school in the first place. Her anger shifted between the possibilities almost as quickly as the vision she was supposed to manipulate had changed in class.

Outside the main building where she'd abandoned her friends, she ran. She had no destination in mind and circled the dormitory buildings a few times before she finally ended up under a tree near the dock on the lake. It wasn't the same view of the lake she had from her room, but she barely saw the view as she crumbled under the umbrella-like tree and cried. Hot, angry tears streamed from her blurry eyes as she sobbed.

She didn't know how much time had passed, but when she awoke under the tree, the shadows had shifted significantly. The sun was descending quickly toward the horizon. Emily's stomach growled in protest at not eating lunch, but she was still angry and was determined to do something about it.

While her pace was much slower than earlier, she still made it to her residence hall quickly. Inside, Emily marched past the other girls in the common room, down the hall—without responding to the friendly hellos called out by the girls—and into her room, where she immediately started throwing her belongings into her still half-packed duffle bag.

"Where have you . . . oh my god, Emily. What are you doing?" Ashley entered the room and grabbed Emily's arm to stop her frantic packing.

Emily shrugged off Ashley's hand. "I'm leaving. I don't belong here."

"You can't leave. It's only the first day. What happened?" Ashley asked cautiously, feeling the hostile and unfriendly energy radiating off her roommate.

Emily challenged her. "Are you going to stop me?"

Ashley frowned and stormed out of the room, returning moments later with Greta.

"So, you're going to stop me?" Emily demanded.

"You aren't a prisoner, Emily. Please, stop your packing for a moment and come talk with me in my room."

Emily sighed and hung her head in defeat. She followed Greta's lead, not looking at Ashley as she pushed past the bewildered girl. She had apparently caused a lot of commotion because most of the girls were in their doors, staring as Emily paraded by.

"Go back to your activities, girls," Greta instructed and closed her door after Emily had entered. "Please have a seat, Emily."

"I don't want to sit." Emily paced the room like a caged animal, repeatedly clenching her hands in fists.

Greta's bedroom was about the same size as the other rooms, but she didn't share it with anyone. On one wall, there was a mural of a waterfall nestled in a tropical forest. On the opposite side of the room was a painting of a rainbow with rain clouds around it. The mentor sat on the edge of her queen-sized bed and waited patiently for Emily to slow down.

After several minutes of pacing the room, Emily paused. "Do you have any water?" The anger lingered in her tone, but Greta was pleased she was speaking.

"Of course, I do." She rose from the bed and poured a glass of water for Emily.

Emily held the glass in both hands and gazed down into the clear liquid. "There aren't any blueberries," she lamented and took a long drink.

Greta chuckled softly. "No, I wasn't prepared for this meeting. I'll have some for next time if you'll allow there to be another time." Greta patted the fluffy comforter next to her. "Why don't you tell me everything that's on your mind, and then we'll figure out a way to resolve this together."

By the time the liquid was drained completely, Emily felt regret for the way she acted. "I'm sorry," she started.

"You don't owe me an apology, so who are you saying sorry to?"

Emily shrugged. She was so used to apologizing to her parents when she acted out like this that she never gave any consideration as to what she was sorry about.

After several moments of silence, Greta spoke again. "My first week at the Academy will probably go down in history as the worst first week of any Abecedarian in the history of the Academy."

"Really?" Emily's interest was piqued.

"Really. You see, I grew up in foster homes, shuffled from one family to the next until Ted came to visit my foster family in the summer just before seventh grade. While I don't think I was his first recruit, I was the most difficult and a struggle from the start. My foster family didn't want to lose their state money if I came to North Shore Academy. On top of that, I didn't want to go anyplace I was told what to wear and what I could do. After Ted assured the family they wouldn't face financial issues if they allowed me to attend, they threw my few belongings into a box and dropped me off on the doorstep of this school. I escaped before the initial interview and then four more times during the first week alone. My roommate was reassigned, and I basically picked a fight with anyone who looked at me." Greta chuckled as she reminisced.

"Why did you stay?" Emily inquired.

"First off, the food was better than anything I'd ever tasted."

Emily nodded.

"Secondly, and probably most importantly, with the help of Ted and my mentor, I learned to look deeper than the nothing I'd always been told I was and found my true self. I stopped looking for approval and disapproval from others and eventually found my path, my truth."

"How long did it take?"

"Paths are constantly shifting. They are as fluid as the water that is symbolic of this house. And sometimes as solid or as invisible as that same water, too."

Emily sighed. Another non-answer.

Greta continued. "I don't know why you are upset, but I believe you belong here and will find your truth. Be patient with yourself and with us, too."

"Thank you, Greta. I will think about it." Emily handed the empty glass back to her mentor. "Do you think they have any leftover food in the kitchen? I missed lunch and probably dinner, too."

Greta smiled and nodded. "Take this to Lucas in the kitchen, and he will prepare a snack for you." She handed Emily a small trinket, engraved with a language she didn't know.

"Thank you. And to answer your question, I'm sorry for causing drama."

Emily slipped out of the residence hall and walked to the kitchen, where Lucas did exactly what Greta had promised—made her the best crepe she'd ever tasted.

The following morning, Emily purposely rose before the others and returned to the kitchen. Lucas reluctantly gave her breakfast early but made her promise that she would eat lunch and dinner with the others in the dining hall.

After eating, Emily slipped out of the service entrance of the kitchen. She returned to the tree she'd retreated to the day before. With clearer eyes, Emily admired the beauty of the spot. She sat in the lotus position and closed her eyes, trying to remember the exercise Maggie had talked them through the day before. Emily focused on her breathing and remained calm, but again her mind's eye couldn't hold onto a single image. As the frustration began to bubble inside her, she opened her eyes and refocused on her surroundings, remembering Greta's story. Before she had time to try Maggie's exercise again, she heard voices behind her. It was almost time for classes to start.

It took all the courage Emily could muster to get her feet to deliver her to the classroom. When she arrived, all the students were already seated and breathing with their eyes closed. Emily quietly placed her mat in the far corner to the right of the wall fountain, careful not to disturb anyone. Maggie gave her a nod while she continued to instruct the class.

Emily closed her eyes and released her breath, focusing on being able to concentrate. Despite her continued struggles, Emily didn't allow her frustrations to surface as they did the previous day. While practicing at the lake, she discovered that when she opened her eyes and gave herself permission to rest, she was able to cope with the anger.

Upon opening her eyes for the second time, she noticed the orchid she'd watered in Maggie's office was sitting in front of her. Perplexed, she looked to Maggie for an explanation. Instead, all she got was an encouraging nod.

Here goes nothing, Emily thought and closed her eyes again. The image of the orchid was burned into her eyelids, and she didn't have to concentrate at all to see the flowers. She was so excited by the small victory that her eyes shot open, startling her.

"This afternoon is a free meditation time. While you are given the freedom to find your own spot, if you are caught goofing off instead of working . . . well, let's just say we have an extensive library with some very old books that have collected a lot of dust over the years. Now, go and enjoy your lunch."

Maggie walked over to Emily while she was putting away her mat. "I hope I'm reading your expression correctly. But did the orchid help?"

"Yes. Although I feel like I'm still behind where the others are, it helped." Emily handed the potted plant back to her teacher.

"No, I want you to keep it. Use it this afternoon and bring it back to class in the morning."

Emily held the plant close to her body. "I'll be careful with it. Thank you."

"I wonder if it's flammable," Brandon mused between the main course and dessert as he sat across the table from Emily and Ashley. Neither had brought up Emily's horrible actions the previous day nor her absence at breakfast.

"Leave it alone," Emily protested and smacked Brandon's hand as he caressed a leaf.

"Ow, okay, okay. Sheesh. It was a natural curiosity."

Ashley scoffed. "Yeah, for a pyromaniac."

The two passed glares back and forth while they ate their ice cream. As they were finishing, Titus walked behind Brandon and slapped him hard on the shoulder. "Looks like you were right. Guess I owe you $5."

"What the hell?" Emily asked as Titus strutted away.

"Don't be mad at him," Ashley said. "Most of the school had small pools betting on whether you'd run or not."

Emily growled. "Thanks a lot," she said and snatched up the flower.

"What?" Ashley shrugged as Emily stormed out of the dining hall.

Emily returned to the spot under the tree by the lake with the orchid. Despite her foul mood, she was able to refocus on the plant and make some progress with the meditation lessons. It was strange, she thought, that her image of the potted plant was fluid, like what Greta was saying the night before. Unlike the guided meditation Maggie used, which focused on manipulating a single object, Emily found her manipulation was of the entirety of the plant. It involved the water in the soil and around the roots, the flower, and the aroma wafting from the blooms. She observed how the three aspects of the plant worked together and affected her visualization when she allowed it to be whole.

"Ahem." Someone had walked up on Emily while she was meditating.

Emily sighed involuntarily and turned her head, shading her eyes to see who'd interrupted her.

"Hey," Brandon said timidly.

"What do you want?" Emily responded sharply.

Brandon shrugged. "Just wanted to see if you're okay."

"Peachy," she replied coldly.

Brandon sat on the cool ground and stared out at the lake. "I don't know how to swim," he said after several minutes of silence. "I almost drowned when I was three and have been terrified of water since."

"Your body will naturally float if you're calm," Emily said.

"Easier said than done, I suppose." After several more minutes of silence, Brandon continued. "Look, I didn't believe you'd leave. I even told Titus exactly that as he was joking about it with others in the common room. He told me to put my money where my mouth was. I said whatever and walked away. I didn't bet on you leaving, and even if I was part of some stupid betting pool, I would've been on the side of you staying." Brandon stood and threw a $5 bill down at Emily, which slowly drifted down and landed on her knee.

"I could teach you to swim," Emily said as he started his walk back to the buildings.

"I'm sure there's a lot you could teach me," he said, continuing on his path.

When Emily returned to her room, Ashley was in the process of hanging up Emily's clothes.

"You didn't have to do that," Emily said as she entered her room.

Ashley shrugged and continued to thread a hanger through one of Emily's sweaters. "I figured it would be harder for you to leave if all your stuff was unpacked . . . and your bag was hidden."

"Wait, what? Where's my duffle?"

Ashley giggled. Emily laughed, too, and joined Ashley in organizing her closet. "Thank you for not giving up on me, Ashley," Emily said as they sat on opposite beds, ready to go to sleep.

Ashley casually shrugged. "I told you I'd be good for you," she said with a wink before lying down to sleep.

CHAPTER FOUR

The first month at North Shore Academy was nearly finished, and the entire student body was getting ready for their first dance of the year, the Harvest Moon Masquerade.

"I heard it's a symbolic get-together," Brandon said while making air quotes with his fingers.

"What does that even mean," Ashley said, rolling her eyes.

"You wear masks and celebrate the shift in the elements by dancing and eating lots," Titus interjected in an almost helpful manner. "What are they even teaching you this year? I swear we were already learning. . . ."

"Every year is different, Titus," Maggie curtly interrupted. "Some students' strengths are others' weaknesses and vice versa. This isn't a competition, and you'd be wise to remember that." Maggie was one of the kindest of the staff, but she could also give a death stare like nobody else.

"Yes, Maggie," Titus said apologetically.

"And the three of you need to eat faster. We are covering something new today, and I need every second the clock will spare."

Despite Maggie's warning, Emily, Ashley, and Brandon were the last three to enter the classroom, and they narrowly avoided receiving another of Maggie's death glares.

"Now that we're all here," she paused and cleared her throat, "we can begin our transition lesson. During the first month, you all mentally manipulated an element, specifically the element that identifies with your residence hall. The upcoming dance not only celebrates the change in the season and the changes you have experienced since being here, but it is also a time when the elements literally shift. Can anyone give me an example of how your element will shift?"

The class was quiet for a moment, and then a girl from the earth residence hall said, "Leaves fall from the trees."

"Exactly, Stacy. What else?"

"Winds shift direction and become cooler," a boy from the air elemental house offered.

"Good, good. What about water? What shift do you see there?"

Ashley called out, "It gets colder and starts to freeze."

"Right. And we often start seeing snow in colder parts of the world. How about you fire elementals? What shift happens to yours?"

The class remained silent in contemplation.

"Fire is always hot, regardless of the season. It's a constant," Brandon suggested.

"That is true, but the element still experiences a shift. Can anyone guess?"

Emily had never considered the elements shifting. She'd always just called it a change in the season. The holidays celebrated during the fall were archaic and corrupted by consumerism, something that troubled Emily long before she knew anything about North Shore Academy. "It shifts to be a necessity to keep life functioning."

"Precisely. All of the elements must work and change together to provide balance. Today, we are going to use our elements to manipulate and change the other elements. May I have one volunteer from each elemental group come to the front?"

Brandon looked at Emily, and she looked back at him. They both shrugged and walked toward the front of the room. An older student walked in and handed a piece of paper to Maggie.

Maggie looked down again at the paper. "Good. I'm only going to make one change in the volunteers. Ashley, can you step in for Emily? She's needed in Ted's office."

The class oohed while Emily frowned. Maggie handed her the sheet of paper.

"Meet me at the tree before lunch," Brandon whispered as she walked away.

Emily took out her frustration on the slip of paper as she marched to Ted's office, obsessively smoothing it between her fingers until it ripped. At his door, she composed herself before knocking.

"Come in, Emily," Ted said from behind his large desk. There was already a glass of blueberry infused water waiting for her. She approached and sat in the leather chair opposite the Headmaster.

After she sat and took hold of the glass, Ted began. "Quite a month, huh?"

"I suppose. It's different than I imagined it would be," Emily admitted, still unsure why she had been called to his office.

"How did you imagine it would be? Teachers walking between desks holding a ruler, ready to slap sense into the students as they memorized pages of books to mindlessly recite?"

Emily shrugged. "Something like that. I guess . . . it's just I thought this would be a normal school with normal subjects."

"Why would you ever believe you deserve normal? You are extraordinary—all the students here are—even if you don't see it yet."

"That's just it. I keep getting told vague things like that, but no one has any real answers, just quips that seem to be intended to shut down me asking questions."

"This is your time, Emily. Ask me anything." Ted relaxed back in his chair and rested his folded hands against his chest.

"Oh. Umm," Emily looked down at her hands, fiddling her fingers, "well, I guess first, why was I assigned to the water elemental house?" She looked up from her hands and continued with conviction in her voice. "I mean, I didn't take a test that showed I prefer water over, say, fire. So how was it decided, and who decided it?"

Ted nodded and took a deep breath. "That's more than one question, but I'll answer it simply. You decided."

"See? That's part of my irritation here. Your answer isn't really an answer at all. I didn't tell anyone to place me there, so how can you say that?" Emily's eyes glistened with emotion.

"It isn't always words that communicate, Emily. You should appreciate that just from basic human contact."

"But how did I communicate it? How did Brandon communicate that he wanted to be in the fire elemental house over the wind or earth?"

Ted took in a cleansing breath as he decided how to proceed. "What can you tell me about the day you arrived?"

Emily huffed. "What do you mean? My parents drove me here, said goodbye, and we started the interviews."

Ted nodded. "Yes, now describe the elements on the day you arrived."

Emily took a moment to think before replying, "There was a hot breeze, almost like the wind was on fire. The air was dense with water, making it especially humid. The grass and trees were green, but they were crisper than they are in the spring."

"Better. Tell me about the elements in Maggie's office when you were in there."

Emily closed her eyes to recall the first day at North Shore. "The air in her office was cool and smelled sweet, like cake and cinnamon. The orchids were parched from being directly in the sunlight."

"Yes, the fiery sun. Go on. What about the water?"

"The water inside was cold with ice while the outside of the glass perspired."

"Did the water stay icy cold while you were in her office?"

"Yes, it was the perfect temperature," Emily admitted.

"Did Maggie also have a glass of ice water?" Ted prodded.

"Well, yes, she poured herself a glass, but there wasn't ice in hers."

Ted stood and slowly walked to the side table against the wall, pouring himself a glass of plain water. "I want you to close your eyes," he instructed as he put three blueberries into the newly poured glass of water.

"Okay," Emily said hesitantly. She could feel him approaching.

"I want you to imagine yourself drinking the same glass of water you had in Maggie's office. Can you do that?"

Emily had almost mastered visualization, with only a few moments of frustrating failure. "Alright, I'm picturing it."

"Tell me what you're picturing." He guided her like Maggie did in their classes.

"The water was cold," she began.

"Not was, but is," he corrected.

"The water is cold, the kind of temperature that makes you forget the back of your throat is dry. As I'm lifting the glass to my lips, a piece of ice bumps against my teeth, but the water makes it past. It feels cold and comforting going down my throat, and I feel it all the way until it reaches my stomach."

"Good. Now take a drink of water and tell me what it's like." Ted guided Emily's hand to the freshly poured glass of water.

As soon as the water touched her lips, Emily's eyes blinked open in surprise. No longer was she holding a glass of room temperature water with three blueberries suspended in it; it was now a glass of perfectly chilled water with ice cubes dancing among the blueberries. She almost dropped the glass, but Ted was there to catch it.

"What the . . . how'd you . . . what?" Emily stood from her chair and picked up both glasses she drank from in his office.

"I handed you a glass of water from the pitcher over there. You saw me pour it," Ted explained and returned to his chair.

"Are you saying *I* somehow put ice in the drink while I sat here with my eyes closed?"

"You manipulated the water to create something perfect for you, as you did on your first day in Maggie's office."

Emily rubbed her face, struggling with the concept. "That's not possible."

Ted shrugged. "You also didn't think a school like this was possible, yet here you are. Sometimes to find the truth, you have to put aside everything that's been taught and use what's already inside you."

Emily walked over to the glass pitcher. It was still half full of room temperature water. She closed her eyes and wrapped her hands around it while imagining the perfect glass of water she had just drunk. When she opened her eyes again, a dozen ice cubes floated in the water. Carefully, she placed the pitcher back on the side table and returned to the chair. "My hands are shaking. I don't know whether I'm freaked out or excited about this."

Ted chuckled and nodded. "That's a very accurate description of how all of us felt the first time we discovered our ability to manipulate an element."

"Does everyone else already know this? Have I been walking around as a joke to the student body?" Emily asked in horror.

"No, no. This discovery comes during your first year. So yes, the other students *besides* the Abecedarians are aware. But you are no one's joke. We've all been there."

"So, if the others don't know, why are you telling me now?"

Ted shrugged. "You asked a difficult question, and I wanted to give you the truth. Since you didn't accept my version of it, I had you show you."

"So, Greta can do this, too? And you?" Emily's mind was swimming.

"Yes, we both have water affinities."

"What about Maggie? What can she do?"

"Maggie is . . . different. I'll let her explain when the time is right. But we need to go back to you because there's something else I need to ask you."

"Sure. Anything. What is it?"

"Do you feel a strong connection to water, or is there another element that calls to you, as well?"

Emily pursed her lips. Maggie knew Emily struggled with the visualization and manipulation exercises. Still, she never admitted to anyone the reasons she had a hard time with it. "Yes," she said, drawing out the word. "I mean yes, there is another element. I'm drawn to the earth."

Ted nodded and drummed his fingertips together. "We knew you were unique, and not just at this school. You see, most every student who has ever been through an Academy is like me—attuned to a single element. For reasons I'm not quite ready to share with you, you are what we call a bi-affinate, which is a technical classification for what you just told me. Since we don't have a house suited for bi-affinates, we had to decide which house you'd best fit. And so now, I will if you are happy where you've been placed?"

Emily nodded. She loved her room, the view it gave her, and her roommate. "I'm happy with the water affinity students."

"Good. And now, might I ask a favor of you before I let you join your classmates at lunch?"

"Of course." Emily eyed the pitcher and noticed the ice cubes melting. But no, he could probably make ice easier than she had. He wouldn't ask that, would he?

Ted chuckled, following her eyes. "No, you've made enough ice for today. What I am imploring of you is that you not tell the other Abecedarians about this until they have the formal class on it. Can you keep this a secret for a few more weeks? It's the same thing we ask of the upper-class students, and it's a responsibility we take very seriously."

Emily nodded some more. "I won't tell a soul."

Something about her phrasing made Ted laugh. He rose from his desk and escorted Emily to the door. "Thank you for your candid remarks. Enjoy your lunch and the rest of the day."

Emily arrived at the tree before Brandon and paced with nervous excitement. How was she going to keep this a secret from Brandon and Ashley? She decided to take her newly discovered dual affinities to heart and hugged the tree.

"I didn't think being a tree hugger was a literal thing," Brandon said as he approached Emily.

"It's kinda fun, although a little pokey." Emily brushed bits of bark from her arms and clothes.

Brandon chuckled and brushed a piece from her cheek, causing Emily to blush. He paused for a moment to appreciate the change he caused in her before handing her a blue and red striped gift bag.

"A gift? For me? But it's not my birthday." She could still feel the heat in her cheeks as she smiled at him. "What is it?"

"Open it and find out." Brandon rolled his eyes and stepped back to watch.

Emily reached past the tissue paper to pull out a dark blue masquerade mask. It was outlined with silver glitter and sparkled even more with the bright white rhinestones in the mask. "It's beautiful." Emily was taken back by the gift. "How did you . . . I mean, when did you have time to get this?"

"My mom has a friend with a boutique. I told her about the dance, and she insisted that her friend make me one. I asked her to have her friend make two."

"Connections are nice. I'm sure I could get you a discount at an army supply store or a bed at the VA hospital, but mine doesn't extend much farther than that." Emily leaned in and kissed Brandon's cheek. She thought she saw a little red flash on his skin, but he managed to quickly compose himself.

"There's a catch, though. It's technically a masquerade dance, and we're not supposed to know who anyone is, right?"

"Uh-huh . . . cheater." Emily winked at him.

"I would like to dance with you, so by wearing this to the dance, I'll know who you are and will ask. Promise you'll say yes?"

Emily had never seen Brandon this nervous. They were usually good at playfully throwing insults and snide remarks at each other. It seemed so easy, so simple, how they interacted. This was a different level for them. She nodded with a soft smile. "If you ask, I'll say yes."

That was enough for both of them, and they turned and raced toward the dining hall to join Ashley for lunch.

CHAPTER FIVE

Emily was fascinated by her newfound ability to manipulate water and earth elements. Any free time she had was spent by herself, exploring her gifts. It was eating her up inside, though, that she couldn't share this with her friends. In fact, she had to lie to them about why she was disappearing all the time.

"Found you," Ashley said playfully as she snuck up on Emily on Friday afternoon when she was spending time in the Academy's garden.

Emily was crouched, studying the differences between the leaves of a plant when Ashley startled her, and she fell backward, nearly crushing another plant. "Dammit, Ash! Are you *trying* to kill me before the dance tomorrow?"

Ashley giggled and offered her hand to help Emily stand. "I'd smother you in your sleep if that's what I wanted to do." Her serious voice was accompanied by a disinterested shrug, but then she laughed again. "Whatcha doing out here?" Ashley glanced at the garden.

"I, umm, well, Maggie asked me to bring some of the ashes from your guys' elemental experiments to help fertilize the soil. I guess it's the penalty for missing the in-class work."

Emily shrugged. It wasn't a total lie. Maggie did suggest she bring the burned plant ashes to the garden. Still, it was an exercise for Emily to assist in the earth studies she lacked by not living with the other earth affinity students. For now, Maggie and Ted both explained to Emily, her bi-affinate status couldn't be disclosed.

"That sucks. But hey, you're missing out on picking out your gown for the dance." Ashley tugged on Emily's hand.

It was a gift of the Academy alumni to supply the students with formal wear for the formal autumn dance. It was one of the many perks of going to a school where the former students were among the wealthiest and most powerful people in the world.

"Oh, no! The dress event is happening now? I completely forgot!"

The two girls took off, running toward the hall where their orientation had been. Emily was shocked by the transformation. "It looks like a Beverly Hills dress shop in here!" Emily blinked a few times to adjust her eyes to all the sparkles on the gowns. They were arranged by color, selected to represent each student's elemental affinity. The fire elemental girls rummaged through red and orange dresses while the earth students chose from brown and green-hued ones. The air gowns were silvery and white with wispy accents.

Ashley dragged Emily over to the blue shaded dresses. "Oh, good, it's still here. I thought you'd look good in this one." Ashley held up a dark blue dress for Emily. "Yeah, this will be great. Go try it on already!"

Emily wasn't a fancy girl. The only nice dress she'd ever worn was to her aunt's third wedding when she was nine. Of course, she'd been forced to wear a dress to church every weekend at home, but they were casual dresses, and Emily ripped them off as soon as they got home. She was grateful Ashley had picked out a dress for her because she wouldn't have easily been able to pick one out for herself.

Temporary dressing rooms were set up around the walls of the room. Emily stepped inside an open one and closed the curtain behind her. In the corner, there was a full-length mirror set up for the girls to check themselves out in their fancy dresses. Emily took off her dusty shoes and shorts. She brushed some residual dirt from the back of her leg before removing her shirt and carefully pulling the gown over her head. It took her a minute to muster the courage to look at herself in the mirror. When she finally looked at her reflection, she didn't feel like herself. No, she felt more like a princess. The dark blue color suited her lightly tanned skin. The top had wide straps over the shoulders and came down to form a square neckline which rose appropriately high enough above her girlish breasts. The body was fitted on the torso and flared out into a flowing skirt that stopped just above Emily's knees. Again, she felt grateful for Ashley.

"Are you going to show me or what?" Ashley asked from the other side of the curtain. She tapped her foot impatiently.

Emily pushed the curtain aside and stood like a statue for Ashley to observe. "Well?"

"Oh. My. God. It's perfect! It's gonna look great with your mask." Of course, Emily showed Ashley the mask Brandon had given her. She was afraid Ashley might be mad or jealous because Brandon had given it to her, but she gushed and was excited for her friend.

"I know, right?" Emily giggled. She finally relaxed and did a little twirl, showing off the flare of the skirt. "What about you? What dress are you going to pick?"

Ashley made a little *pfft* noise. "I was at the door when they opened it. I got this amazing dress with a rhinestone empire waist. It's dark blue on the top and softly fades into a light blue," Ashley explained dreamily. "It should go with the mask my mom is sending me from their trip to Rio a few years ago."

"Do I get to see the dress or is this like a wedding thing, and I'm not allowed to see it until the dance?"

Ashley rolled her eyes. "It's not like that at all. The seamstress has to make some adjustments. I won't even get it back until tomorrow afternoon. But don't worry, you'll get to see it as soon as I have it back. Now, get dressed so we can go pick out your shoes."

Emily and Ashley were excitedly chatting about the dance when Brandon sat down unnoticed at the dining table. "Hi?" he said eventually.

Both girls looked at him, then back at each other, and giggled.

"Umm, maybe I'll go sit over there." Brandon started to stand.

"No, stay. Sorry," Emily said, stifling her mirth.

"We were just trying to guess what the guy's area was like today," Ashley explained and then made her voice drop deep. "Oh, look at this one. I'll look like a real prince. Better get shoes to match."

Both girls giggled again while Brandon rolled his eyes. "It was torture, honestly. I have a suit at home that would've been fine. I didn't need some dude measuring my inseam while other guys stood around and watched. Creepy is how I'd describe it."

Bowls of squash soup were placed in front of the students as they chatted.

"So, what does it look like?" Ashley asked Brandon as they sipped the orange soup.

"My inseam?" Brandon asked in horror.

The girls laughed again. "No, silly. The suit." Ashley said.

"Oh. Right. It's black," Brandon replied.

"And?" both girls asked in unison.

"And what? All the suits were black. We were given black shoes and colored ties to go with it." He shrugged and finished his soup.

The girls looked at each other and crinkled their noses. "That's boring. I'm glad I'm not a boy," Ashley commented.

"Me, too," Titus chimed in, causing Ashley to blush and look down, focusing on the dwindling soup in her bowl.

Emily interjected to take the unwanted attention off of her friend. "So, Titus, what are these dances like? I mean, do people really dance, or is it more like just standing around and talking?"

"A little bit of both. The older kids usually dance, and the ABCs are usually the wallflowers. I was out with the older kids last year. Had a blast," he boasted.

Emily shrugged, not knowing what to say. She glanced over at Brandon, who didn't seem particularly interested in participating in the conversation. She wondered if he was having second thoughts about asking her to dance.

There was a strange and uncomfortable energy for the rest of the meal. So, when it was over, Emily stood up and excused herself from her friends.

"I'll see you in the room later, Ash. Brandon . . . have a good one." It was weird for Emily to feel this awkward around Brandon. She didn't know what was going on, but maybe it would go back to normal if she gave the mask back.

Emily dashed back to her room after leaving the dining hall and retrieved the mask from where she carefully placed it on her desk. She held it in her hands, admiring it again, and then glanced over at her dress. It would've gone perfectly together, but it wasn't worth the strangeness that hung between the two of them. She carefully placed the mask back in the bag and left to find Brandon.

First, she checked by the tree where he'd given it to her, but there was no one there. She went to the hall, which had been deconstructed from the fashion boutique, but only found Adamina.

"Excuse me, Adamina?" Emily said, announcing herself to the woman who was busy picking up the remaining discarded hangers and tissue paper from the shoes.

"Emily. What can I help you with?"

While she didn't know the tiny teacher well, she had always appeared to Emily a little cold and unapproachable. "I was wondering if you've seen Brandon?"

Adamina eyed Emily and the gift bag she was holding. "I believe he's in the library."

"Thank you," Emily said politely and left the woman to her work.

She found Brandon in the back of the library, absorbed in reading a thick book that looked more like a dictionary than an enjoyable piece of fiction. Approaching as quietly as she could, Emily placed the bag on the table beside the book and paused to wait for him to notice.

Brandon's eyes shifted from the book to the bag, and then flashed a confused look up at Emily.

Before he could say anything, Emily started the speech she'd been mentally rehearsing since she put the mask back into the bag. "I want things to go back to the way they were before. So, if it means we pretend you didn't give me this or ask me to dance, then that's what I want."

A look of confusion marred Brandon's features. "Fine," he finally said with resolve.

This wasn't the way Emily had imagined the conversation going. "Fine? So, it is because of this we can't hold normal conversations anymore? Well, fine to you, too." Emily's anger bubbled beneath the surface. She was about to slam his book shut and storm out, but as she moved her hand to reach for the book, a gust of wind brushed through the library near them and completed the task, startling her.

"What the hell, Em? I just said fine because it seems like that's what you want." Brandon looked at her, his eyes raging with emotion.

Emily was still startled by the wind and was worried Brandon had noticed she didn't touch the book. This was definitely *not* going the way she'd planned. Emily lowered her eyes from his. "It's not what I want. I just want us to be normal, you know?" Her eyes perused the front cover of the book. She noticed it was one of the legal volumes an alumnus had donated to the library. "What are you reading?"

"Nothing. Just go," Brandon spat and tried to find his page again.

"If you're looking to cure insomnia, there are some herbs in the garden. It would be easier than reading this," Emily said, her tone cautiously playful.

Brandon said nothing and moved his finger along the page to find where he left off.

Emily moved closer and looked over his shoulder to try to glimpse at what was so important to him. "Legal precedence for overturning a felony conviction of a minor," Emily whispered. "Brandon? What's going on?" Emily sat in the chair beside her friend and turned to face him.

Brandon's distressed expression remained focused on the book. "With the masks, my mom sent me papers from the court. I've been found guilty, and I'm not sure if all the attorneys from this school can keep me out of jail."

"Brandon," Emily said. She pushed the book away and took his hands in hers. "Talk to me. What happened?"

"Two people are dead, and it's my fault. The court agrees, and now I'm going to have to face the consequences."

There was so much sadness in Brandon that Emily ached to heal. She wished she could make a flower bloom or create some ice cubes and make it all better, but she knew she was as helpless in this situation as she felt.

"I was just messing around with some friends. We liked going to the old warehouses after school and just doing stuff, you know?"

Emily nodded while continuing to hold his hands.

Brandon went on with his story, his gaze still on the place the book used to be. "I've always been fascinated with fire, so my friends and I decided to burn some old papers in a warehouse. We thought we'd just jump on them and put out the fire. We'd do things like that all the time. Well, there were old oily rags mixed with the papers we gathered. The fire . . . it wouldn't go out when we jumped on it. When it got too big, my friends took off and ran home. I stayed there like an idiot, mesmerized by the flames. I heard the second floor creak and backed away before it collapsed down. Still, I stayed and watched the fire, somehow knowing it wouldn't hurt me. I didn't hear the screams, I didn't hear the sirens, I didn't even notice myself coughing. Next thing I knew, I was grabbed from behind by a fireman and taken to the ambulance for oxygen. My parents arrived, and the police came to talk to me. I wanted to tell them I did it, but my dad told me not to say anything and argued with the police officer while I watched them pull two charred bodies from the smoldering ruins. Apparently, some homeless people used the warehouse for drugs and squatting. They were high and passed out on the upper floor and died because of the fire. My friends let me take the fall. Their parents took them out of our school and sent them to another school upstate. I never saw them again. It's a complicated case because the two guys who died had high levels of meth in their system. The charges I was convicted of are criminal arson and involuntary manslaughter. And now I'm going to have to go back and will be in juvie until I turn eighteen and they decide what to do with me."

Emily didn't know what to say. She was sad for him and heartbroken that he would be leaving. She wasn't aware of how long they sat there in silence, but Brandon apparently was.

"And now you know the monster I am. I should've known things wouldn't be different here." Brandon tore his hands from Emily's, grabbed the bag off the table, and stormed off.

Emily looked after him, dumbfounded and dizzy over everything he had just revealed. It felt like she was glued to the chair and couldn't go after him. Finally, she cleared her mind and ran out of the library to find him. He was outside, walking briskly toward his residence hall.

"Brandon!" she yelled, but it didn't stop him. She had to run as fast as she could to catch up with him before he entered his hall. "Brandon," she said breathlessly as she tried to position herself between him and the building.

When he tried to sidestep around her, she impulsively grabbed his face and pulled his lips to hers. She could feel his element in the heat of his skin and could taste the fire on his lips. Emily never noticed her lips to be cool, but the contrast with his sent tingles through her body.

"Ahem," a voice near them announced. "You both need to get to your halls." The adult (whom Emily didn't know) waited for them to step apart before he continued on his way.

"I don't think you're a monster," Emily said softly. "And I don't think Ted will allow them to take you away. I'll talk to him." She knew Ted would have to understand that it was Brandon's affinity that put him in the situation. He couldn't be the first student who had something like that happen, and there had to be a way around it. She just wished she could share what she'd learned about their affinities with Brandon. If nothing else, it might give him absolution from what he truly believed was an evil act he committed.

"Thanks," Brandon whispered, the sadness in his eyes mixed with the emotions from their kiss.

"We still have some time before curfew. Will you walk with me?" Emily asked.

Brandon looked toward his residence hall and then back at Emily. "Sure. I'd like that."

CHAPTER SIX

Saturday mornings at North Shore Academy were Emily's favorite. They got to sleep in as late as they wanted, and brunch was served buffet style for the students to enjoy at their leisure. But this Saturday morning, Emily had purposely woken up to her alarm, anxious to meet with Ted to plead Brandon's case.

"What? What day is it? Oh shit, I'm gonna be late for class!" Ashley exclaimed as she glanced at the clock.

Emily looked over at her roommate while tying her shoes. "Go back to sleep, dork. It's Saturday."

Ashley rubbed her eyes and sat on the edge of her bed. "What the hell are you doing, then?"

"I have something important to do. Go back to sleep. I'll explain everything later." Emily grabbed her water bottle and walked through the door.

As it was closing, she heard Ashley call to her, "Hey, where's your mask?"

"I'll explain later," Emily said vaguely and hurried through the common room.

During the entirety of the walk to Ted's office, Emily rehearsed what she would say to him to make him do *something* to prevent Brandon from being taken away. Her mind mocked her. *You know how well your rehearsed speeches go.*

Emily tried to quiet her doubts as she knocked on Ted's door. It was probably intended to be closed but was open just a crack.

Instead of the "one moment" which Ted actually said, Emily heard "come in" and pushed her way through the door. Brandon was sitting in the chair where she'd learned about her gifts just a few days prior.

Oblivious to the current conversation, Emily stormed in the room. "You have to help him," she ordered, slamming her hand on the wooden desk. If her initial intrusion didn't catch their attention, her dramatic demands certainly did.

"We'll have to call you back," Ted said as his hand hovered over the phone receiver.

Emily blushed, not realizing they were on a phone call. Brandon looked amused, but still not his usual self.

The man on the other end of the line said, "Alright. I'll get looking into it some more. I should have answers this afternoon. Talk to you then, Ted."

"Thanks, Dave," Ted replied and ended the phone call, his attention not wavering from Emily. He cleared his throat and assumed a relaxed position in his chair, steepling his fingers as he waited for the intruder to explain herself. "Please, take a seat. I can assume by your outburst that you're aware of Brandon's situation?"

Emily nodded as she sank into a chair. "You're going to stop it, right? I mean, there are extenuating circumstances the court doesn't even understand."

Ted shot Emily a warning glance while Brandon looked between the two with confusion. "But I did it, Em. I told you what happened."

Emily stared at Ted. "Tell him," she insisted. "Or let me tell him."

"Hello. I'm sitting right here," Brandon reminded them. "Tell me what? What's going on?"

"I've kept my word. I could've told him last night. I *should've* told him, but I kept my word. It's cruel to let him think this is his fault."

Ted motioned for Emily to proceed.

"Will someone tell me whatever the hell this is?" Brandon sat forward on the edge of his chair.

Emily rose and went to the side table, pouring a glass of water before returning. She held the glass in her hands and stood in front of Brandon with it.

"I already have water, Em. Just tell me."

Emily narrowed her eyes slightly at Brandon. "I'm not telling you; I'm going to show you." She closed her eyes and imaged the most perfect glass of water. Before her eyes opened again, she knew the cubes of ice had formed because the chair Brandon was sitting in squeaked as it slid backward.

"What did you do? What is this?"

Emily couldn't tell if Brandon was angry or just shocked. Still not explaining, she handed the glass to Brandon, hoping her instincts about what would happen next would be correct.

Ted quietly watched the exchange between the two, also knowing what would happen next.

"Take the glass," Emily instructed.

He took the glass by the rim, holding it with only his thumb and middle fingertips. "What's supposed to happen?"

Emily sighed and grabbed his free hand, forcing it to grab hold of the side of the glass. She made his other hand follow suit. She felt the fire in him and was now confident her plan would work.

Within only a few seconds, the ice melted away completely. Brandon nearly dropped the glass, but this time, Emily was there to catch it. He wiped his hands repeatedly on his shorts as if he'd touched something that was covered in germs. "I don't get it. What just happened?" He looked between Ted and Emily for an explanation.

Emily's shoulders sank, and she audibly sighed.

"Try the candle," Ted offered and motioned to the off-white pillar in the corner.

"Alright," Emily said and retrieved it. Like the glass, she held it up for Brandon to take hold of.

This time he wrapped both hands around the middle like Emily had shown him with the glass and stared at the wick. "What am I looking at?"

Emily looked at Ted with confusion. Why wasn't it working?

Ted finally stood and walked around to the other side of Brandon. "Close your eyes and use the mental visualization you've been practicing in Maggie's class," he instructed. "Imagine the top of the candle, dancing with a flame." After a moment, Ted continued. "Now, open your eyes."

When Brandon looked at the candle again, the wick was lit. "This is a trick, right? One of you lit it while my eyes were closed. Ha, ha. Funny joke, Em. Now tell me—"

Ted blew out the candle. "Do it again, only this time keep your eyes open."

Brandon shook his head but did as he was instructed. Despite his brows furrowed with skepticism, within moments, the candle relit. This time, Brandon didn't drop it but tilted his head as he gazed into the dancing flame. "Is this a trick candle?" he asked, his eyes still on the candle.

Ted chuckled and remained standing between the two students. Brandon sat, still focused on the flame.

"Is this the outcome you wanted, Emily? He wasn't ready for this knowledge."

Emily sat again, too. "How do you know when someone's ready?" she asked, ignoring the boy next to her who was too enthralled to pay much attention to her and Ted's conversation.

"We know, and that's going to have to be a good enough answer for now. It's one reason the upper classes are sworn to keep it a secret. Unlocking this knowledge too early," Ted explained as he leaned over the candle, "causes confusion and can make a person reject the truth." He blew out the candle and took it from Brandon, who was left blinking.

"What happens now?" Emily asked, concerned she damaged Brandon somehow.

"What happens now," Ted began, "is you make amends by helping him understand his gift and the rules about it."

Emily nodded. She was happy she would at least have a chance to make it right.

"Now if you two will excuse me, I have other issues that require my attention."

Emily shot up out of her chair and grabbed Brandon's wrist, tugging her dazed friend to his feet. "Thank you," Emily said. "Come on, Brandon. Let's get some food." As the two were exiting, Emily looked back at Ted and shrugged. "I'm sorry."

"Do it again," Brandon said as he ate an orange-cranberry muffin.

The two grabbed a plateful of food from the buffet and took it out to the tree by the lake. It was a lovely day with a mild breeze making small ripples in the lake water.

"Seriously, it's not a parlor trick. You can do it, too." Emily felt more at ease, both because Brandon was starting to understand and accept what he'd just done, and things between them were closer to being back to normal.

"Do you really want me to set the tree on fire? Where would we hang out then?" he teased.

Emily rolled her eyes and formed ice cubes in her water glass again. "You realize that fire isn't just destruction, right? It's also warmth, light, and energy."

Brandon shrugged. He knew, but also enjoyed watching Emily do what seemed to bring a new life to her eyes.

"You're impossible, you know?" Emily jabbed.

"You're wrong," Brandon replied. "I'm quite possible. You see me here, right? Therefore, it's not possible for me to be impossible."

This time Emily smacked his arm.

"Ow," he chuckled with a mouth full of muffin. He rubbed his arm as he chewed and swallowed the bite. "You're not going to hit me at the dance tonight, are you?"

"Depends," Emily said as she pretended to crack her knuckles. "Are you still going to ask me to dance?"

"Probably," he teased and jumped to his feet, running toward his residence hall.

"Cheater!" Emily called after him as she looked at the mess he left behind. She shook her head and chuckled as she gathered the dishes. "And I thought I was the sloppy one."

Ashley walked over as Emily was finishing picking up after the pseudo-picnic. "That's a lot of food for one person." She offered to take the glasses from Emily.

"It wasn't all me," Emily confessed, slightly offended. "Brandon ate most of this."

"Ahh," Ashley said suspiciously. "So, you set an alarm to have a breakfast date, huh?"

Emily found herself rolling her eyes again, something she'd *never* done at home. "No, I had to speak with Ted and wanted to catch him before he got swamped in Headmaster duties or whatever keeps him busy all the time."

"Uh-huh," Ashley replied. "Well, whatever you *were* doing, you *need* to start getting ready for tonight. Speaking of which, where's your mask? It's not on your desk anymore."

"First off, the dance is like eight hours from now. If we get ready now, we'll sit around all afternoon in uncomfortable clothes, anxiously watching the clock. Nope. I'm waiting at least seven more hours to get ready," Emily replied resolutely while piling the dirty dishes in the bins provided. "Secondly, the mask isn't on my desk because I gave it back."

Before she could offer any more explanation, Ashley cut her off. "You *what*?" The few students eating all turned to look at them.

Emily grabbed Ashley's arm and escorted her outside. "I hated how things were between Brandon and me, so I thought if I gave it back, it would make things normal again."

"That was a stupid idea," Ashley suggested. "So, Brandon has it? What are you going to wear?"

"The idea made perfect sense to me. I didn't know what else to do, and Brandon was acting weirder and weirder. But don't worry, we figured it out. I have the mask in the room in the bag. It should be next to my bed. Or maybe it slid under it. I don't know, but stop freaking out on me!"

Ashley exhaled and nodded. "I'll stop freaking out. I'm calm now." But the excitement and energy returned to her voice when she changed the subject. "Do you think Titus will dance with me?"

Emily laughed, and the two walked together with linked arms back to the residence hall.

The start of the dance was timed to begin as the sun was setting. So, as the students entered the banquet hall (a building reserved for special occasions, usually involving alumni functions), the descending sun lit the girls' dresses ablaze with sparkles. The sunset provided a beautiful backdrop to the large room, which had the entire west-facing wall made of glass. Within the glass were several French doors that opened out to a wooden deck, about half of the size of the inside room. A banner reading "Harvest Moon Masquerade" hung above in the center of the room. Small round tables with chairs arranged around them were set up around the outside of the room with lit candles floating in a bowl of water acting as the centerpieces. Taking center stage in the middle of the room, wood flooring had been laid down to create a large dance floor. Earthy, autumnal scents swirled around the room on an invisible breeze that made the temperature inside perfect and gently rustled the leaves of the indoor trees.

"It's magical," Emily whispered to Ashley as they entered the room together. About half of the students were already inside when they arrived.

Ashley had taken nearly the entire eight hours after returning to the residence hall to get ready. Emily didn't have any siblings but had often fantasized about having a sister. It was evident to her that afternoon that she was probably better off being an only child; Emily barely had mirror time to do her hair and makeup.

"I feel magical," Ashley said. "Like a princess entering the ballroom to meet her prince charming."

Emily smiled and couldn't disagree. Ashley looked like a princess in her perfectly-tailored dress. "I hope your prince charming doesn't end up being a frog," Emily commented. She was still not fond of Titus, who she knew was the prince her roommate had in mind.

Even with the masks on, Emily could see Ashley's annoyed expression. "Let's find a table," she said and pulled Emily toward a table by the dance floor. Emily would've preferred one by the glass wall, but hopefully, they wouldn't be sitting at a table all night, and it wouldn't matter anyway.

Two of the Abecedarian girls joined Emily and Ashley at their table—Stacy from the earth house, wearing a cute brown and gold dress with three-quarter length sleeves, and Olivia from the fire affinates, donning a bright red, sleek gown with a low-cut neck that reminded Emily of a nightgown hanging in the back of her mom's closet.

"Isn't this amazing?" Olivia remarked.

"I think it should've been held outside," Stacy replied. "But it's nice enough in here."

"I'm sure you can go outside on the deck if you wanted to," Emily offered.

Stacy shrugged and looked bored. "This is mandatory, right? The boys *are* coming, right?"

"I don't think it's *mandatory*, but according to Titus, *everyone* comes to these."

Emily smiled. It was just like Ashley to subtly mark her claim on the guy she wanted to dance with. Emily only hoped the other girls got the hint as she envisioned a fight in formalwear.

The room filled shortly after the girls sat down, and Adamina walked to the center of the dance floor with a cordless microphone. "Attention North Shore students! Please, everyone, quiet down. We have a few rules to discuss while your first course is served. Then, last year's graduates will perform for you while you enjoy your meal."

A few of the older students chattered, probably excited to see their former classmates, Emily assumed.

"Please!" Adamina insisted, and all whispering stopped. "Rules for the dance are as follows. Your choices for this evening are to be present at this dance or be *in your assigned room* in your residence hall. There will be no walking freely around campus or otherwise. The deck is reserved for people who want to talk, but you must keep the noise outside at a respectful volume. No dancing, food, or drink is allowed to leave this room. Dancing."—Adamina paused and turned in a complete circle to make sure she had everyone's attention. "Dancing may be done alone, with another, or with a group. No wild dancing, no sexual dancing, and no sexual conduct of any kind will be tolerated. Any violation of any rule will be met immediately with harsh consequences."

"Yeah, cleaning those dusty books!" a boy from across the room yelled.

"You would know!" another boy yelled back.

While most of the room giggled, Adamina was not amused and glared. "Don't make this the first year in the history of North Shore Academy that we shut down the event early. Please be respectful and enjoy your night," she concluded.

The servers were already bringing in the first course, but Emily was scanning the room for Brandon. She tried to see him walk in and invite him to their table but had no luck. It felt odd eating without him.

The room was filled with the chattering of students having conversations at their tables until the lights dimmed, and the entertainment began. The music, a sweet melody of minor chords, was hauntingly beautiful. The former students entered in stunning costumes the colors of their elements. The dresses the girls wore reminded Emily of the ballerinas her mom had taken her to see when she was going through her dance phase. The boys wore tuxedos in their elements' colors.

The brown and green clothed people joined together in the center of the room while the others danced around them. "We honor the earth and the changes she will experience. We honor the leaves who sacrifice themselves, so the tree is strong enough to survive. We honor the ground that hardens and protects our roots. And we honor ourselves to stay true to our element throughout every change."

The people dressed in blue took to the center of the floor, while the earth affinities took their place in the surrounding dance. "We honor the water and the changes she will experience. We honor the clouds which change the water to snow. We honor the lakes which harden to protect the life beneath. We honor ourselves to stay true to our element throughout every change."

Once again, the dancers traded places, and the silver-dressed wind affinates took the center. "We honor the wind and its shift in direction. We honor the whispers it brings from other places and the change it brings to our bodies. We honor ourselves to stay true to our element throughout every change."

Emily found herself swaying to the music, absorbing the performers' words and movements. She had never seen anything quite so lovely and moving as this.

The fire elemental group took the microphone and allowed the music to shift, turning low and solemn. "We honor fire for the responsibility she must endure after months of play. We honor the duty she has to keep the earth, wind, and water true and alive. We honor ourselves to stay true to the changes called upon us as the elements remain in harmony."

"In harmony," the entire group repeated and finished their dance.

The lights returned to a normal level, and Emily was surprised to see dessert was being placed at their tables. She barely remembered eating the other two courses and hadn't noticed any servers as they retrieved and delivered the students' nourishment.

"A wonderful homage to our elements. Let's give our alumni the applause they deserve. Well done," Adamina said as she returned to the center. Emily never expected to hear any praise from the tiny woman, as she always seemed annoyed by the existence of the students. Maybe she held graduates in higher esteem?

"The rest of the night is yours," she continued. "Don't forget your respect for your elements, your fellow students, and yourself."

"And the rules!" one of the attention-seeking boys from earlier shouted.

"Yes, and the rules." Adamina handed the microphone to the DJ and took her place with the other faculty who were in charge of chaperoning the dance.

Emily scanned the room again for Brandon, but most of the boys looked the same with their black suits and only their masks and ties identifying their elemental affinity. "I'm going to go outside for some air," she announced to her tablemates.

She was dodging through students already dancing in the middle of the room before Ashley could convince her otherwise.

Emily walked through the French doors and out on the deck. She thought she was alone with only the stars and the moon, but two graduates—a fire and a water affinate—were chatting with a teacher.

"Excuse me," Emily interrupted the trio.

"What is it, Emily?" the teacher asked.

"I just wanted to say that you guys were amazing in there. Thank you." Emily didn't know where this reverence was coming from, but it was how she truly felt. "Do you guys still talk after you graduate? I mean, you'd have to talk to put this together, but I mean . . . I don't really know what I'm saying." Emily stopped, embarrassed.

The girl wearing the red dress laughed and nodded. "Some of us talk, but we are always connected through the school and the elements."

The boy in blue nodded and squeezed the girl's hand. "Some of us more than others. I think you'll be surprised by how the elements really need each other."

Emily understood his meaning from his body language. She never really put much thought into how relationships between the affinities worked . . . or didn't work. At this point, she and the other ABCs were merely trying to wrap their minds around their new environment and new ways of learning to be worried about how they got along—or didn't—with the others. Emily sensed from Titus that the different houses looked down on each other, believing themselves superior. But with her being a bi-affinate and close friends with someone from a separate elemental house, she never really accepted it was how things had to be. It was nice for her to meet this couple who seemed to complement each other perfectly. "I'll keep that in mind. Thank you again." Emily walked to the other side of the balcony and left the three to finish their conversation.

The breeze felt nice, even better than the one inside, and Emily could smell the trees, grass, and water as she studied the newly appearing stars. She thought about her parents for the first time in almost a month, wondering what they were doing, if they missed her, and if they ever felt an element call to them.

"Hey," a voice said from behind her.

"Hmm?" Emily asked and turned to face her roommate.

"You're missing the fun. Almost everyone is on the dance floor. I don't even care if Titus doesn't ask me to dance. I'm having too much fun to let a stupid boy ruin it."

Emily smiled at Ashley and adjusted the girl's mask. "You were having too much fun to worry about your mask being crooked. I'm intrigued," she said and took Ashley's outstretched hand, letting her lead her back inside. "You haven't seen Brandon, have you?" Emily said in a loud voice as they entered the even louder room.

"No," Ashley yelled back and danced her way back to the middle of the room.

Ashley was right. The energy in the room was intoxicating. Emily let herself be almost completely swept away in the euphoric atmosphere, but she kept looking for Brandon.

The first slow song came on, and most of the students left the dance floor. Many of the older students already had plans to dance with someone, and they stayed, quickly becoming coupled. Throughout the song, others would pair up on the outskirts and join the others in the middle, swaying to the slow music like a single-minded group.

Ashley sighed when fast music started again. "He didn't ask me," she complained.

"It was only the first song," Emily remarked but felt Ashley's disappointment. Brandon was nowhere to be found.

Despite their shared frustrations, both returned to the dance party when the music picked up its pace again, sharing in the laughter and fun that was all around them. Before long, the whole room was caught up doing the YMCA dance. Never did Emily expect to dance to songs her parents used to sing to annoy her. The dance floor was a beautifully mixed jumble of all the elemental colors, students laughing, and energy flowing. Yet, Emily's thoughts kept returning to Brandon and him—and thus her, too—missing out.

"I'm going to grab some apple cider," Emily yelled in Ashley's ear.

"Okay!" she shouted back, giving the thumbs-up sign as she continued to dance to the next song.

Emily took off her shoes and carried them with her to the drink table, greedily drinking down one cup and taking a second to sip. She remained there and observed the crowd while drinking the second cup slower, appreciating the crispness of the apple flavor, but also secretly wishing they had a blueberry flavored drink.

"Fun time, huh?" said a boy wearing a brown tie and a lion mask as he got himself a drink.

It took a moment for Emily to realize he was talking to her. "Oh, right. Yeah, this is better than any dance I've been to."

The boy chuckled and offered his hand. "I'm Griff. You're an ABC, right?"

Emily shook his hand and nodded. "Emily and yes, this is my first year."

"This is my third. Pretty crazy stuff, huh?"

"I was expecting a military school. This is far better than I'd hoped."

Griff chuckled and raised his cup. "Here's to far better than expected experiences."

Emily tapped her cup against Griff's before finishing the cider. "I should probably make sure my roommate is still breathing," Emily said. She slipped her shoes back on as the unintelligible "Gangnam Style" song ended.

"Hey, wait," Griff called out to her as the next slow song started. "Wanna dance?"

Emily didn't expect anyone (except Brandon) to ask her to dance. And she'd never been asked to dance by a boy before, so it came as a surprise to her. "Oh, I—" she began.

Griff shook his head and was quickly beside her, leading her to the dance floor. "There's no saying no now," he chuckled and wrapped his hands around Emily's waist.

Emily gave in and set her hands on his shoulders, letting him lead their dance.

"I won't bite, promise," he assured her as he reached up to adjust her hands, so they were draped around his neck.

"Sorry," she apologized. "I've never danced like this except with my dad . . . when I was much younger," she reassured.

"You're a natural," Griff complimented her.

Emily glanced at the masks of the students waiting on the side and noticed Ashley giving her a thumbs-up sign. She smiled at her friend but felt nervous dancing with a boy she didn't know—and who wasn't Brandon.

When the song ended, Emily thanked Griff. "Thanks for being so forgiving of my clumsy feet," she said shyly.

"You did fine. Hey, maybe we can dance again later?"

"That sounds nice, but I was up early this morning and think it's time for me to head to bed."

"Alright," he said, already dancing with a group of students. "Have fun!" he shouted, and Emily wondered if he even heard a word she'd said.

Ashley was grabbing a drink when Emily went to tell her she was leaving. "I'm exhausted. I'm going to head to bed. Stay, have fun," she encouraged her roommate.

"Aww, Em. You looked so cute dancing out there. But okay, I understand. I'll be quiet when I come in." Ashley kissed Emily on the cheek and returned to the rhythmic orgy.

Adamina was standing like a sentry at the door. "Straight to your residence hall, Emily."

"Of course, Adamina," she replied, stifling a yawn.

"There's staff everywhere. We're watching," she warned as if she believed Emily to be lying.

While she wasn't lying, Emily was distracted by a sweet aroma coming from the garden and went to investigate. When she got there, the moonlight was bright enough for her to notice a plant with a flower she'd never seen in the time she'd spent in the garden. It was white with fuchsia lines streaking the petals. Emily brushed the stem and leaned in closer for a smell.

"It's called the four o'clock flower," a voice from behind her said. "Mirabilis jalapa. Known as one of the sweetest smelling flowers in the world, yet most of the world never sees it because it only blooms at night," Ted explained.

"It's lovely." Emily tensed, expecting to be punished for straying and getting caught by the Headmaster.

"Why aren't you at the dance with the others?" he inquired and leaned toward the flower to smell it since Emily was no longer occupying the space close to it.

"I'm tired, so I decided to call it a night," Emily admitted. "I just left, though. You can ask Adamina," she added defensively.

Ted chuckled. "You're not in trouble, but you should find your way to your hall soon."

"I will," she promised and turned to leave. "Have a good night."

"Good night, Emily."

Greta was reading a book alone in the common room when Emily entered. Emily tried to walk past unnoticed, but Greta was keenly aware someone had entered. "It's pretty early. Are you feeling okay, Emily?" she asked with genuine concern.

"Yeah, I'm just tired. I was up early and danced a lot at the beginning." Emily untied her mask and looked down at it sadly.

"Gotta pace yourself," she said lightly. "Did you dance with anyone?"

Emily nodded. "Yeah, a guy from the earth house asked me. I've never slow-danced before, so I'm sure I stepped on his toes about fifty times."

"I'm sure it wasn't as bad as you think. Did you enjoy it?"

This time Emily answered with only a shrug.

"Ah," Greta said, closing the book on her finger to hold the place. "Not the guy you wanted to dance with, I'm guessing."

Emily blushed and looked down at the mask Brandon gave her. "Yeah. But it's probably better we didn't."

Greta tilted her head and leaned forward. "Why is that?"

"It's . . . complicated," Emily explained.

"It always is," Greta offered with a smile. "There are still a few hours left. You could always go back and see if your fortune changes."

Emily shook her head. "No. I don't think he even went to the dance. Besides, this dress is starting to itch. I'm just going to sleep."

Greta smiled warmly. "Okay, Emily. Sweet dreams."

"Thank you, Greta," Emily replied, not masking her sadness this time.

Emily retreated to her room, pulling her dress over her head while crossing the threshold. In Emily fashion, she left the dress in a crumpled heap on the floor where it landed, tossed her shoes in the direction of her closet, and dressed for bed. She thought sleep would come quickly, but instead, she couldn't seem to get comfortable. She tossed and turned, her thoughts returning to the last twenty-four hours and the emotional yo-yo between her and Brandon. First the cold shoulder, the confession in the library, the kiss . . . Emily sighed and touched her lips, recalling the fiery way his lips pressed against hers . . . and then today, with showing him his potential, breakfast alone . . . things felt normal again . . . and the unsaid promise about tonight. She noticed tears streaking from her eyes, making a cold, wet spot on her pillow. She sat up in frustration and flipped her pillow over, wiped her face, and fell back on the bed with the promise she wouldn't think about Brandon anymore. With great effort, Emily recalled the music from the dinner performance. Eventually, she drifted off to sleep with echoes of the words recited at dinner swirling in her head . . . *we honor the change.*

"Oh, Em!" Ashley exclaimed when she returned, not keeping her promise about being quiet when she came in.

Emily groaned. It felt like she'd barely managed to fall asleep and was now awake again. "What's up, Ash?"

Ashley plopped down on Emily's bed. "He danced with me. I mean, I had to ask him, but he said, 'Took you long enough.'" Ashley grabbed one of Emily's throw pillows and squealed in it. "We even danced the regular songs together. Oh, and he smelled so good, and he's not just hot, but he's literally hot, too. It made my skin tingle whenever he bumped against me. Eeee!"

Emily was genuinely happy for her friend and was about to say so when Ashley continued her accelerated talking. "And then he walked me back here. I wanted to kiss him. I thought he was going to kiss me, too, but he kissed my forehead. Isn't that the sweetest thing? Oh, and Brandon is waiting outside for you. But I mean, who would've thought he had a sweet side when he's always so grumpy at meals."

Emily sat up and tried to focus on Ashley despite the bed shaking from her roommate kicking it with excited energy. "Did you say Brandon's outside?"

"Didn't you hear me? He kissed my forehead. Right here," Ashley said, pointing to the spot in the center of her forehead.

"I heard you the first time. I'm happy for you. Really. But Brandon is outside? Here? Right now?"

Ashley nodded, still bubbling with excitement.

"I promise to listen to you tell this all to me again, but I need to see what Brandon wants, or I might not be able to fall asleep again. Okay?" Emily kissed Ashley's cheek before getting out of bed and leaving the room.

"Is that your missing boy outside?" Greta asked from the same spot on the couch while Emily tried again to sneak by.

"Yes," Emily admitted, sounding less depressed than the last time she spoke with her mentor.

"Don't be long. It's technically curfew," Greta warned.

"I won't. I promise."

Emily composed herself before she opened the door. Despite being excited to see Brandon, she was also hurt and disappointed, and yeah, mad at him for ditching the dance. When she closed the door, Brandon shot up from the bench he'd been waiting on and walked a few steps to meet her. He was dressed for the dance, black suit, red tie, and a really amazing mask. It looked like real flames rising from the bottom, wrapping around the holes like the fire was dancing with the soul contained within his eyes. Emily had to remind herself that she was still angry with him and stopped a few feet in front of him, arms crossed.

"Not really how I imagined your dress would look, and you're missing your mask," he joked.

"My outfit is somewhere on the floor. What do you want?" Emily felt the anger in her jaw.

"I'm going to take a guess that Ashley *didn't* tell you where I was tonight?"

Emily shook her head and waited for his explanation. "Come and sit with me for a minute."

"I only have a minute. It's after curfew," Emily said coolly and remained in her rigid stance. "And I prefer to stand."

Brandon sat down and took off his mask. "I know you're mad, Em," he began while he rubbed his temples. "But I swear I had a good reason. Just listen, and if you're still mad, I'll go and leave you alone until you want to be my friend again."

75

"That might be a while," Emily grumbled but knew she didn't mean it. "Go on. Why weren't you there?"

"I was dressed and heading to dinner when Ted pulled me into his office," Brandon began.

"I saw Ted tonight. He didn't mention you were with him," Emily pointed out.

"Does he tell you everything he does?" Brandon fired back.

"Well, no," Emily admitted sheepishly. "Go on."

"So, that attorney, David, who was on the phone when you busted into Ted's office? Well, he is friends with an appellate judge who also graduated from the Academy. Well, after explaining the situation, he agreed to do a telephone interview with me. So, after about an hour of conversation on the record, he said he could reduce the charges, and I'd be able to do service at North Shore to make amends. I'll be on some kind of probation and have to remain on campus for the next two months. But that means I can stay. I'm staying!" Brandon jumped up, expecting a hug or at least Emily to unfold her arms.

But Emily remained as she was, processing everything Brandon had said. "But I ran into Ted over an hour ago. Where have you been?"

"Well, first, I had to listen to my parents lecture me about how fortunate I was and how I can't screw this up. Then, I had to wait for a fax from the judge, sign the paperwork, and fax it back. I think it took me ten minutes to figure out how to send the fax. Stupid machine."

Emily relaxed a little, and as her arms uncrossed and fell to her side, her hand brushed his. "That is really good news, Brandon." And finally, Emily smiled.

Brandon stepped closer and gave Emily one of those hugs people say they wished would never end. She wrapped her arms around him, knowing exactly where to place them, and squeezed him back. He kissed the top of her head. "It's all because of you, Em. Thanks for standing up for me and helping me through this."

"I doubt I had any sway, but I am here for you," she said as she buried her face in his shoulder and absorbed his warmth.

"I think you did more than you realize," and then added, "at least for me." Brandon pulled away from the hug but left his hands on Emily's shoulders. "I know it's past curfew, but since we're already here, how about that dance?"

Emily laughed and looked down at herself in her sheep pajamas. "I'm not dressed for dancing, and we don't have any music."

"You look beautiful," Brandon said with a laugh and pulled his phone from his pocket. He hit play on his playlist, and "Wild Horses" by The Sundays began playing. "Ready?" He held out his hand.

Emily set her hand on his and wrapped her other arm around his neck as they swayed in place. Several of the girls from her house rushed past them to get inside before they got in trouble, but Emily and Brandon remained in their embrace while the song played.

"I'm glad you're here," Emily whispered.

"Me, too," Brandon replied.

The two rocked back and forth until almost the end of the song when Greta opened the door. "You need to be inside, Emily. You, too, Brandon."

"I'll be right there," Emily called back and then returned to the intimate whisper she'd been using to talk to Brandon. "I guess this is goodnight."

"Yeah," he sighed. "When's the next dance?"

"December," she said.

"Will you dance with me then?" he asked.

"Will you show up?" Emily responded.

Brandon chuckled and kissed the top of her head again. "Wild horses couldn't drag me away."

CHAPTER SEVEN

The change in season also signaled a shift in classes. Instead of elemental manipulation with Maggie, the Abecedarians went to Adamina's class in the mornings for "History of the Academy." They then broke off with their elemental groups for an afternoon class lead by the top affinates who were in their last year at the Academy. Once a week, Emily was assigned to learn about her earth affinity with Maggie, but her second affinity remained a secret to most at the school.

"Are you an earth affinate?" Emily asked Maggie one afternoon in mid-November as they harvested ripe grapes from the vines in the Academy's orchard.

Maggie smiled. "I relate to the earth element most, but I am not an affinate. I have no power," she explained.

"Why not? Why are you here if you don't have an affinity?" Emily asked without a hint of rudeness or superiority in her tone.

"That's a very complicated answer, Emily. Tell me about what you're learning in Adamina's class."

Emily sighed, frustrated with another non-answer. "Well, in the past four weeks, we've learned the first Academy was founded in Ireland in 1172 after the Norman Invasions and King Henry II was named as the ruler of Ireland. It was created as a sanctuary of sorts to protect the affinates from the invading Christians."

"Good," Maggie interjected. "Who were the founding members?"

Emily slowed in picking as she tried to remember. "Lucerna, Keegan, and Ava."

"Nicely done. Were any of those names familiar to you?" Maggie prompted.

Emily put more grapes into her basket as she considered Maggie's question, leaving a few unripened ones on the vine. "You showed me the old picture in our interview," Emily finally admitted, "and told me the woman with the sad eyes was Ava, but otherwise, no."

Maggie had stopped harvesting and continued to look at Emily, hoping she would put together what was being hinted at.

"I mean, that was almost 800 years before the picture you showed me was taken. You aren't suggesting . . . no, that's not possible. I don't understand what you mean," Emily admitted.

Maggie shrugged and wiped her hands on her gardening pants. "When you do understand, ask me your question again, okay? For now, you should wash up and join your friends for dinner. I'm going to get these grapes to Lucas to do with what he does best . . . make them even more delicious than they already are." Maggie smiled and popped one in her mouth as she walked past Emily.

"Don't' you find it strange," Emily began as she picked through her salad.

"That we always eat here at this table?" Brandon interjected.

"That we never know what we're going to be served?" Ashley added while skewering a crouton.

Titus chimed in. "That you three always ask stupid questions?"

"Noooo," Emily sighed. "It's just everything we learn about here is so different than our old schools. I mean, I had history class back home, but we learned about the American Revolution and Davy Crocket and stuff. Here, we are learning a history no one else even cares about."

Her friends shrugged, not sharing Emily's confusion over the curriculum.

"Did you ever consider that maybe they're teaching us the stuff that's suited for us to know?" Titus answered, displaying wisdom the three rarely heard from him. "Who is Davy Crockett to you, and why should you care anyway?"

"Are you saying I should care about people who lived 800 years ago in a different country, and they should matter to me simply because I'm at a version of a school they created?" Emily snapped.

"Perhaps," Titus answered as he popped a freshly picked grape into his mouth.

Emily narrowed her eyes at him, wanting him to tell her more than he was probably allowed.

"Great answer, Titus," Brandon said sarcastically and then turned back to Emily. "I don't know, Em. I guess it's important we fully appreciate how we got here or something. I'm sure there's a reason, just like there was a reason for Maggie's class." Brandon's eye widened when he realized he'd promised not to reveal the secret to anyone.

"Don't worry about it," Emily comforted. "Ash already knows—as do all the water elemental students."

Ashley grinned and circled the rim of her glass with the tip of her middle finger, creating frost that splintered down the outside, making her glass opaque in appearance.

Brandon looked relieved. "Yeah, most of the fire guys know, but there are two girls who haven't made the discovery yet."

"Is there ever a time where we all get to openly use our gifts?" Ashley asked Titus.

"If I told you, it'd ruin the surprise," Titus joked. "And I know how much you like surprises."

Ashley blushed fiercely while Titus laughed.

Both Brandon and Emily exchanged questioning glances before looking between their two housemates. "I'm not sure I want to know what that means," Brandon admitted.

Emily, on the other hand, was vastly curious and murmured to her roommate, "I want to hear about this later."

Ashley pursed her lips and nodded.

After dinner, some of the boys started a game of football, which quickly escalated to a school-wide spectacle. Emily, Ashley, and Brandon stood on the sides with their classmates while Titus and some of the upper-class boys crashed into each other and chased a brown ball around the grassy area, which easily converted into a decent football field.

"Isn't this exciting?" Ashley gushed as she followed Titus's every move with her eyes.

"I would've thought the teams would've been element versus element. It's cool to see everyone mixed," Brandon admitted.

"He was wide open!" Emily yelled at the quarterback who'd just thrown an interception. "I swear," she mumbled under her breath, "these guys must've never watched an NFL game in their lives."

Both Ashley and Brandon looked at her with wide eyes.

"It's okay, Em. This is just for fun," Brandon consoled. "Didn't know you were into football."

Emily remained focused on the game as she replied to Brandon's comment. "Watched with my dad every Sunday. It was the only thing we really did together. I'm pretty sure he hated that he didn't have a son."

"I'm sure my mom would be happy to ship him one of my brothers," Ashley said as her head turned to follow Titus, who was running with the ball. "Go, baby, go!" she cheered.

"Baby?" Emily finally turned away from the game to face her roommate.

"Oops," Ashley said and looked around to see if anyone else heard her.

"They all heard you," Brandon said.

Titus looked over at Ashley and winked before he was swarmed by his ecstatic teammates.

"What *is* going on between you two?" Emily asked, now more interested in her friend's gossip than the game, which was practically over after Titus's touchdown.

"You know, we talk and stuff when you two are off doing whatever it is you do," Ashely replied vaguely.

"Stuff," Emily repeated. "So, you're what? Dating now?"

Ashley shrugged. "Nothing official. It's not like you can really date here anyways, but yeah, I guess so."

Brandon purposely excused himself from the girls. It was one thing to be friends with them, but he had zero interest in gushing about boys and relationships and feelings. "I'm gonna go grab a shower before these guys get done. See you in the morning?" he asked and squeezed Emily's hand.

"Yeah, of course," she said distractedly, still curious about the new developments with Ashley. She did squeeze Brandon's hand back, though, still aware enough of his presence to respond to him.

Brandon held Emily's hand for a moment longer and then disappeared through the crowd to return to his residence hall.

"Does Titus realize you're dating?" Emily continued questioning Ashley as the rest of the students started to join the players on the field.

Ashley shrugged and then jumped in the air, waving her arms. "Titus! Titus! Over here!"

It was to no avail, though. Titus was moving with the crowd off the field, still being congratulated with pats on the shoulders and high fives.

Ashley signed in defeat. "I don't know," she admitted finally. "We haven't talked about it. We really don't do much talking at all. We mostly just make out."

Emily looked sympathetically at her friend. She didn't consider what she and Brandon had to be a relationship; they were just close friends who kissed only the one time. Mostly, Emily and Brandon talked, joked, and did tricks with their elemental gifts. "When do you have time for this, and where do you go?"

Ashley smiled. "There's this spot down a little way from the docks. You can't see it from any of the windows." She paused to smirk. "Anyway, all the older kids go there to make out. It's just . . . the spot." She shrugged like it was common knowledge.

"And you're okay with this?" Emily inquired.

"Making out with Titus? Uh, yeah." Ashley replied.

Emily sighed. "Don't you want more? Like actual talking?"

Ashley frowned. "Not everyone has to make goo-goo eyes at each other and whisper to each other over a private brunch every Saturday like you and Brandon do."

Emily blinked in shock. She stood there rooted to the ground and watched Ashley storm off toward the crowd.

Emily was asleep by the time Ashley went to bed. In the morning, when she woke, Ashley was the one still sleeping, and Emily decided to let her roommate enjoy her dreams. Emily had had unsettling dreams and carried the weight of them and her fight with Ashley with her as she met Brandon for breakfast under the tree.

It was rapidly getting colder, but it was nice to have a friend with the fire affinity to snuggle up against.

"Why do we eat here every Saturday?" Emily asked as she absorbed the warmth from Brandon sitting beside her.

"Because we can?" Brandon replied, somewhat confused.

"Yes, but why don't we ever invite Ashley or anyone else to join us?"

Brandon shrugged and took another bite of his eggs. "These are getting cold too fast," he complained and held his hand over them to give them heat again before taking another bite. "Much better. Do you want me to warm yours?"

Emily leaned away and frowned at him. "I'm trying to have a serious conversation with you."

Brandon shrugged and warmed her eggs anyway. "I don't know what to say, Em. We've always just kinda done this. We eat all the other meals with everyone. It's nice to, you know, get away, I guess."

Emily exhaled a hard breath through her nose and shifted her body to face Brandon. She could already feel the chill in the air replacing the warmth he'd provided but remained apart from him. "Are we in a relationship?" she boldly asked.

"Sure," Brandon replied, confusion still lingering in his tone.

"Then why don't we go over to wherever the make-out spot is like the rest of the students?" Emily demanded.

Brandon shrugged. "I dunno. Do you want to go make out with the other students?"

"That's not what I'm saying. Sheesh!" Emily bolted to her feet with clenched hands.

Brandon stood, too, but in a casual, cautious way. "Where is this coming from, Em? I thought you liked eating here together."

Emily could feel the emotion swell in her eyes. "Am I a bad kisser? Is that it?" Emily wiped her eyes with the back of her hand. "Because the only time you ever kissed me was when I kissed you first."

Brandon stepped toward her and brushed away a stray tear from her cheek with his thumb before cupping her cheek in his hand. "You're *not* a bad kisser. I'm sorry if I ever gave you that impression." His thumb caressed her pouting lips. "The only reason I haven't even thought to go to the make-out spot with you is that you're more to me than a girl to make out with—if that makes sense."

Emily swallowed the lump in her throat and nodded.

"And the other reason," he continued, "is because I didn't expect you to kiss me that night. And I want the first time we *really* kiss to be special."

His cheeks turned light pink. Emily thought it was cute and cracked a small smile.

"Are we okay now?" he asked cautiously.

"We're good," Emily replied.

"Would you like me to heat up your eggs again?" Brandon smiled and kissed her forehead.

"Yes, please," she replied as they both resumed their seats under the tree. "I've never had a boyfriend before," Emily admitted as he warmed both their eggs.

"No kidding," Brandon teased and playfully bumped her as she was trying to take a bite.

Emily returned to her room later that afternoon with a plate of warm cran-oatmeal cookies she took straight from the kitchen—with Lucas's permission, of course. He was preparing hors d'oeuvres and snacks for a mysterious meeting that was taking place on campus. It looked too fancy for the usual alumni gatherings they hosted. Emily tried to get more information out of Lucas, but he said, "I'm only the chef. What do I know?" Emily didn't believe him but took the cookies and returned to her room.

Ashley was on her bed looking through a care box her mom sent her. There were open boxes of cookies and snacks surrounding her as she read the handwritten letter that accompanied the treats.

"Hey," Emily said and set the plate of cookies on Ashley's desk.

"Hey." She didn't look up from the letter.

"I brought you a peace offering, but it looks like someone beat me to it."

"Mmhmm," Ashley replied distantly, and then looked over at Emily. "I'm sorry, what?"

"Cookies," Emily pointed to the desk. "Peace offering." Emily gestured between the two of them.

"I'm not really mad at you, Em. I guess I'm just jealous of you and want to have something special like you and Brandon have. But you're so frustratingly oblivious to it and were being a bit judgy to me." Ashley shrugged. "I kinda blew up, ya know?"

"I do know. I was there," Emily replied. "And what do you mean, I'm judgy?"

"You made me feel like I was a—" Ashley paused and bit her lip.

"A what?"

"A slut, okay? You looked at me like I was a slut for making out with Titus. All I've ever done is kiss boys, and only one at a time, so don't give me that look. In fact, Titus is only the fourth boy I've kissed." Ashley looked mad again.

"I wasn't judging you. I honestly felt stupid that I didn't know about the make-out spot. I didn't even know I was in a relationship until today. Brandon and I don't do that. I mean, we kissed once, but I kissed him, and it was a short, impulsive kiss."

Ashley leaned in with wide eyes. "You guys don't kiss when you're off by yourselves? Is he a bad kisser?"

Emily blushed. "No, I thought our kiss was magical, so I assumed *I* was the bad kisser. He said no and that he just wanted the first time he kissed me to be special." Emily shrugged.

"Aww, that's sweet, Em." Ashley gushed.

Emily rolled her eyes and threw a pillow at Ashley, hitting her square on the side of the head.

The two giggled and threw pillows and anything they could find at each other until they collapsed onto Emily's bed exhausted and in tears from laughing.

"I knew I had a good reason to be jealous of you," Ashley said while trying to catch her breath.

"I was jealous of you, too," Emily admitted, equally breathless. "But I'll kill him if he hurts you, Ash. You know that, right?"

"I don't doubt that. You are a water affinate with a fiery soul," Ashley teased. "Don't ever change," she whispered and held her pinkie in the air.

"I won't," Emily replied and locked her pinkie with Ashley's.

If people were animals, Emily would definitely be a cat. Her curiosity was insatiable, and it would likely cost her a few lives—metaphorically, of course. After Ashley and Emily and the rest of the water elemental house residents finished the plate of cookies, Emily returned the borrowed plate to Lucas in the kitchen.

"We're not losing another Elder to this, Eli," Emily heard Ted say while she was taking the long way back to her residence hall. She had never heard her Headmaster have even a hint of anger in his voice, not even when Emily was difficult and impatient.

"We don't have any choice from where I stand, Ted. The dangers in the world are accelerating, and we need to be able to arm ourselves and regain control, or we'll lose it all. Tama's plan is a smart one, and most of the Council agrees," the man Emily presumed was Eli explained.

"You have no experience training those who volunteer to receive this nor to handle what will happen to the donors.

We're not gods, Eli. What happens if they can't handle the power or worse, what if it changes them and we lose control of them? Hell, we're barely able to handle the one student who naturally has that power."

Emily bit the inside of her cheek. *Are they talking about me?*

"Your school's still standing, and no one has died. You're off to a good start, Ted."

The Headmaster took a deep audible breath. "What's being proposed goes against our purpose—to maintain the balance. I can't support this, and I think the Elders need to step back and come up with another plan," Ted explained. The passion remained in his voice, but the anger had subsided.

Emily felt a tap on her shoulder and stifled a yelp that would've blown her cover.

"You shouldn't be here," Maggie whispered, obviously aware of the conversation Emily was eavesdropping on. Maggie motioned with her finger for Emily to follow.

The two quietly walked in the opposite direction from Ted and Eli. When Emily thought they were out of earshot, she asked, "Who was Ted talking to?"

"It sounded like Eli. He's one of the Elders who came here for the meeting," Maggie explained.

"Who are the Elders?" Emily inquired.

"They're kind of like the leaders of all the affinates all over the world. They make the rules and major decisions."

"It didn't sound like Ted agreed with their decision on something. Is he an Elder, too?"

The two strolled toward the lake and began to walk along its shore. A brisk breeze was coming off the water, making both of them wrap their jackets tighter around their bodies.

"No, Ted declined the opportunity to be an Elder in order to remain Headmaster here. But he's close with them, and they still consult him from time to time."

"Maggie?" Emily asked. "Am I a difficult student?"

Maggie frowned and shook her head. "Why would you think that?"

Emily shrugged. "Something that Ted was saying to Eli about having a difficult time with a student, and it sounded like he was talking about me."

Maggie rubbed Emily's shoulder in consolation. "Being different is a gift, Emily. Yes, we've had to make adjustments, but you're far from a problem. We're glad you're here. And I'm glad I get to work with you."

"I'm glad, too," Emily said and then embraced Maggie in a hug. "Thank you," she whispered.

"You're welcome," she replied. "I think you know what I'm going to say next."

"Don't discuss what I heard with anyone, right?"

Maggie nodded with a wink. "I'll see you later."

"Bye," Emily said and took a more direct route back to her room.

CHAPTER EIGHT

The days rapidly grew shorter and colder, but the energy at North Shore Academy was palpable. All the students had transitioned and were able to manipulate their elements, the session of classes was coming to an end. Most importantly, the Winter Solstice Dance was quickly approaching.

"Is this going to be like the last dance?" Ashley asked as she sat across from Titus at dinner. The dance was two days away, and no one had given them an idea about what they'd be wearing.

Titus looked up from the notes he'd been studying between bites. Apparently, after the first year, there were exams taken at the end of each session. "Not really," he replied vaguely.

Emily was grateful they didn't have an exam in their History of the Academy class. They'd barely gotten through the European witch trials of the fifteenth and sixteenth centuries and still had the ones in both Europe and America in the seventeenth century to cover, let alone everything else that happened up to modern times. The Black Death took nearly two weeks to cover completely. While it was not Emily's favorite subject, she found herself enjoying learning the alternate version of history that Adamina taught.

"Oookayyy." Ashley drew out the two-syllable word. "Well, do we get to pick out our gowns, at least?"

Titus didn't look up when he replied, "No, they'll deliver clothes the day of the dance."

Ashley looked at Brandon and Emily for help.

Brandon shrugged. "Don't look at me. I'm just a guy on house arrest who goes where he's told."

Emily laughed. "I know it's been really tough being confined to this huge campus where you can go wherever you please." She stuck her tongue out at Brandon, who grinned in return. "I heard Maggie talking to Adamina about robes when I was in her office last week, so maybe it's a pajama-themed dance?"

"Not those kinds of robes, genius. Robes like judges and graduates wear. We wear normal clothes under the robes for the dance, but for the ceremony, we all wear white robes." Titus pushed his plate away and stood abruptly. "I can't study here with all your chatter. I'm gonna go to the library."

"What are you studying?" Brandon asked before Titus left.

"Civics," he said and bade the group farewell with a backhanded wave as he strutted away.

"He's just stressed," Ashley explained. "He's been studying all week. I've barely seen him."

Emily gave her friend a sympathetic smile. "It'll be better after exams." She looked around the room and noticed a lot of students with their noses in books and papers, mindlessly picking at the food in front of them.

"Hey, Em and I are headed to the hall after dinner to watch *The Hobbit*. You should come with us," Brandon suggested, hoping to cheer up Ashley.

"Yeah, I heard they were able to get it for us, even though it just came out last week. Sure. I've got nothing else to do," Ashley replied half-heartedly.

"Cool." Brandon stood up. "Shall we, ladies?" he asked in a theatrical voice.

Emily giggled and stood in unison with Ashley, who seemed slightly less amused. "You two go ahead and save me a seat. I just have to do something quick."

The two looked at each other and said together, "Bathroom."

Emily shrugged. "Hey, it's supposed to be a long movie. I'll be right there. Get me some popcorn, too!" She briskly walked out of the room, heading in the direction of the bathroom. Once out of sight of her friends, she made a detour to the library.

After several minutes of scanning the faceless students (all their heads were bowed down or buried in a book), Emily located Titus. She marched over and stopped next to him, hands on hips, mustering her best "Maggie glare."

"Ahem," she said after standing there unnoticed for almost a minute.

"If I wanted to chat, I would've said hello when you walked up. Don't you have a pumpkin to pick or weed to pull?" Titus finally looked up to Emily's now-confused expression. "Yeah. Don't think I don't know about you learning all that earth shit. What's your deal, anyway? Can't make ice cubes or whatever it is you water fairies do?"

"My deal…" Emily struggled to form words after the onslaught of insults. "My deal," she tried again, "is that you're being an asshole to my best friend, and I'm not okay with it."

"Okay. Noted." Titus scribbled on his paper, " 'Emily thinks I'm an asshole.' Anything else, mudbug?"

Emily heard her heart pounding in her ears. The rage was growing too quickly to contain. "Yes," she said in almost a demonic tone. With a flick of her hand, Titus's books and papers—along with some other books and documents in her path—went flying across the room on a strong gust of wind, which seemed to come from nowhere. "Go to hell. I'm sure you'd fit right in."

Emily turned on her heel and stormed out of the library, unaware of the audience of stunned onlookers she'd attracted. It wasn't until she was passing by the restroom that she was struck by what she'd done. "Oh no," she gasped and ducked inside the sanctuary of the bathroom. She rested her hands on the sink and tried to slow down her breathing, but she began hyperventilating. Within moments, her eyes rolled back into her head, and Emily collapsed to the white marble floor.

"Em! Emily! Oh, no! Someone help!"

The yelling seemed like a distant echo as Emily convulsed on the floor. She could feel hands touching her and her body moving, but at the same time, she couldn't really connect with the sensation of touch. The world remained black, and her hearing faded into a muted static noise, like an old television station that had lost signal.

"Get her on the bed," Ted instructed. Emily's twitching body was carried to the infirmary by Ashley, Brandon, and Maggie. The trio watched helplessly as the girl was given a shot and finally came to rest.

"Is she okay?" Ashley asked as tears streamed down her face. She'd gone to the bathroom to check on Emily when she found her mid-collapse.

"She will be unconscious for the night," Gaia explained. Gaia was the head of the earth elemental studies at the Academy and the campus's healer. "We'll know more when she wakes."

"I'll stay with her," both Ashley and Brandon volunteered.

"It would go against the rules to allow you to stay, Brandon," Maggie explained sympathetically. "I know you care about Emily, but you'll have to return to your hall for the night. Ashley, you may stay, but only if Gaia doesn't feel you're interfering with her work."

Ashley nodded.

Brandon looked worried and defeated. "Let me know if anything changes," he said to Ashley before leaning over to kiss Emily's forehead. Ted grabbed Brandon's forearm as he was leaving and gave it a sympathetic squeeze. "She's going to be alright." Brandon nodded compliantly and left.

Ted said, "If you will excuse me, too. There seems to have been a disturbance in the library this evening. I'll be in my office. Please let me know when she wakes or if anything changes." He nodded at both Maggie and Gaia.

"Was she okay at dinner?" Maggie asked Ashley.

Ted entered his office to an audience of seven students. "She's crazy!" one of the boys exclaimed as Ted walked behind his desk.

"First of all, we do not call *anyone* crazy at this school. Now would one of you please tell me what happened in the library?"

The boys in the room looked to Titus, and he began.

"I swear she just . . . attacked me." To Titus's credit, he told the truth for the most part, except he turned himself into the victim in the end. The other boys in the room nodded, confirming his story, while Ted listened to the entire explanation.

"Thank you for bringing this to me. We certainly don't condone students attacking other students. I assure you we will get to the bottom of this. You boys are free to return to the library or your residence halls."

The seven boys exited the office, leaving Ted to massage his temples and try to piece together what this could mean.

Maggie entered shortly after the boys were dismissed and sat in a leather chair opposite of Ted. "What do you think?" she asked as she crossed her right leg over her left.

"How much of their story did you hear?" Ted needed to know how much he needed to fill her in.

"Most of it, but I think I can put together the pieces. Basically, Emily walked into the library, lost her temper, and sent books and papers flying?"

Ted nodded. "Yes, but the boys all say she didn't touch anything, just waved her hand. How is that possible?"

Maggie shrugged. "There's no doubt she has earth and water affinity, just like we knew. The air affinity is a new thing altogether."

"If it's even an air affinity, it could've been another student or a coincidence," Ted said slowly.

"The convulsing teen in the infirmary says it wasn't either of those. Which means—"

Both nodded and sighed.

"We haven't seen a tri-affinate since—"

"Ava," they both said in unison.

"Are we one hundred percent positive that Ava succeeded in her Ascension?" Maggie asked.

"Ninety-nine percent positive. There's virtually no way we wouldn't have known if she failed." Ted tapped a pen against the edge of his desk as he thought. "What do we know of Emily's birth? Could you contact Darius and have him get a hold of the hospital records and the mother's OB/GYN chart? There's one other possibility I can think of."

"A twin?" Maggie presumed.

"We'll see," Ted replied.

Brandon returned to his residence hall, feeling the weight of worry about Emily. He was not expecting the welcome he received when he entered, though.

"Your girl is crazy," Titus said as he stepped up to Brandon. The two were about the same height, with Titus perhaps having an inch on him. Titus, however, had muscles that were better formed than Brandon.

"For fuck's sake, Titus. She just had a seizure. That doesn't make her crazy."

Titus tilted his head and pushed Brandon's left shoulder hard enough to cause him to take a step back. "She attacked me with air in the library, bro." Titus struck Brandon again, this time hard enough to make Brandon grab his shoulder in pain. "C'mon, badass Brandon. Show me how you became a felon."

Brandon stood tall, dropping both hands to his sides. He could feel the fingers of fire stretching out on the inside, filling his entire body. As he clenched his right fist and started to swing, he could see the flames extending beyond his skin as it seemed to move in slow motion through the air until it connected with Titus' jaw. To Brandon, it looked like a replay of a boxing match, the ones where you can see the recipient's jaw push out of shape while the beads of blood quivered and oscillated toward the ground.

"That's enough!" Resident Director Huo's voice boomed in the room, returning Brandon's world to normal speed just in time for him to be head-butted in the forehead by Titus. As stars took over his vision and he collapsed to the floor, Brandon felt Titus' foot connect with his gut before the other students could pull him back.

The pain was dulled due to the adrenaline racing through his body, which made it easier for Brandon to regain his footing and stand up to Titus. Huo stepped between the restrained Titus and Brandon (who was still physically smoldering) and commanded an end to the confrontation. "Ted's office *now!*"

"And that's how I ended up here," Brandon explained to Ashley.

"You're an idiot. You two," she said, gesturing between Emily and Brandon, "are both idiots, if what Titus said about

Em is true. Why would you ever attack another student with your element?" Ashley rubbed her tired eyes and propped her head up with her hand while she slouched in the chair beside Emily's bed. "Now, I'm caught in the middle of being pissed at you guys and grateful for you sticking up for Em and me ." Ashley sighed. "Not to mention Titus probably hates me now."

Brandon tried to get comfortable in the adjustable bed next to Emily's. With at least two cracked ribs, however, even breathing caused pain. Shrugging at Ashley's assertion was out of the question. "Sorry, I didn't have a chance to ask him before he kicked the shit out of me."

Ashley pressed her lips together before she said something she'd definitely regret. She may have fallen asleep because the next time she opened her eyes, Brandon had shifted from being on his back to lying on his right side.

"She looks peaceful when she sleeps, exactly how I imagined," he said quietly, obviously noticing Ashley was awake again. Or it was possible he was talking to her for a while and didn't care that no one was awake to respond. "What do you think they'll do with her? I mean, if she really does have two affinities?"

"Didn't we read that Ava had more than one affinity?"

"Yeah, I think you're right," Brandon replied.

"It sounds pretty cool, if you ask me," Ashley admitted. "I just wish she wouldn't have revealed it by attacking my boyfriend." Ashley shrugged.

"Maybe it wasn't her fault. I mean, I didn't go back to the dorm wanting to use fire against Titus. It just kinda . . . erupted." Brandon paused for a moment, reconsidering his next comment, but said it anyway. "You know, Titus is really good at pushing people's buttons."

"And Em is easily pissed off. Yeah, I know; I live with her. I guess I just really wanted what you guys have. I know Titus is a jerk, but he's also an okay guy when he wants to be."

"Everything's so easy with Em, Ashley. I mean, for me. We've always been friends first, which has made things awkward at times, but it's also made it simple. She and I are just ourselves with each other. There's no agenda, no manipulation."

"I can see that," Ashley agreed.

"You know, when I lived at home, I often wondered why my parents were still married. My mom manipulated my dad to get money for shopping, and my dad gave it to her to keep her out of his business. Maybe they loved each other once, but I never got to see it. The last thing I wanted was to come here and meet someone like Emily."

"Did that sound as strange to you to say as it was for me to hear?" Ashley asked.

Brandon's breath stuttered a few times as he attempted to sigh. "Em asked me a couple of weeks ago why I hadn't kissed her again after our first kiss. I told her part of the truth, which is that I wanted the moment to be special. That wasn't a lie, so don't look at me like I'm a hypocrite after telling you about my parents. The other part of the truth is I'm scared things will change, that I'll become my dad, or she'll become like my mom."

"The only thing I've ever seen Em manipulate was water. I don't think you have anything to worry about." Ashley paused but then continued. "But I get it. I always seem to do things to get other people to like me. I like Titus because he doesn't give a shit about who I really am, and there's something safe about that. I'm scared a guy will see the real me and then reject me. It's easier to just be whatever someone needs you to be," she explained.

"Does that make you happy?" Brandon asked.

"On the surface, yes. But just like I know Titus is a jerk, I know deep inside I'm not happy."

"What are you going to about him?"

Ashley released a weak chuckle. "Nothing. I think I'm going to let him come to me. If he doesn't, then I'm okay in knowing he wasn't the right one for me."

"That still sucks," Brandon admitted.

"Yeah, it does," Ashley agreed.

CHAPTER NINE

Emily woke up with a splitting headache in a room she didn't recognize, with her friends passed out on either side of her. "Guys?" she said as loudly as she could without causing herself excruciating pain.

"Uhhh. Is it time for class already?" Ashley groaned.

"I don't know. Where are we?"

"Oh, Em! Em! Thank god!" Ashley practically screamed.

"Shhh," Emily begged and rubbed the sides of her head.

"You're in the infirmary. Do you remember last night?" Ashley said in a quieter voice.

It hurt to think, but Emily managed to recall most of the events of the previous night. "Yeah, I was in the bathroom and suddenly couldn't breathe. Did I collapse?"

"Em, we know about the library and the whoosh, whoosh stuff, too." Ashley waved her hands back and forth to represent the wind gust.

"Oh, god. That really happened? I thought it was part of a bad dream."

"Oh, it happened," Brandon chimed in. He groaned as he pushed himself up to sit.

"Why are you groaning? What happened?" Emily's brows furrowed as she watched Brandon struggle. "What happened to him?" she asked as she turned back to Ashley.

"Just a little bruise. Don't worry about me. How are you?" Brandon stood with only a twitch of his eye to expose the pain he was in. He took Emily's hand and sat on the bed next to her hip.

"Have you ever been run over by a truck and then have it back up to run you over again?"

Brandon shook his head. "Can't say I've had the pleasure."

"Good. That's how I feel."

"About what I'd expect," Gaia said as she entered the room. "Glad to see you're finally awake, Emily. I brought you some peppermint tea. It should help with your head. Ashley, you should probably go back to your residence hall and get changed. Ted is going to address the students in an hour." Gaia turned to Brandon. "Ted wants to see you now in his office. Don't do anything strenuous for the next few weeks, and the ribs should mend themselves. There's really nothing else that can be done for them."

"Ribs mend? Will someone tell me what the hell happened?" Emily demanded.

Brandon squeezed her hand and slowly rose from the bed. "I'll tell you everything later. Thanks, Gaia."

"Mmhmm," the forty-something-year-old woman with gray streaks in her auburn hair said.

"I'll talk to you later, Em. We have a lot to talk about," Ashley said and joined Brandon as he left the room.

"Fantastic." Emily groaned as her friends left. Turning to Gaia, she asked, "What exactly *did* happen last night?"

"Medically, you had a seizure. Everything else is frankly none of my business. Have you ever had a seizure before?" Gaia asked.

"No, never," Emily admitted.

"Did you hit your head or eat anything out of the ordinary last night?"

"Not that I can recall. I walked into the bathroom and suddenly couldn't breathe. That's the last thing I remember."

"Alright, that's all for now. I'm going to keep you here for at least another day to make sure you don't have a repeat seizure," Gaia explained. "Ted will be by sometime today, but he's got a busy morning ahead of him. Try to rest and finish your tea. We'll work up to food as soon as I'm confident you're stable. There's a bell next to the bed. You can ring if you need anything."

"Do you have anything quieter than a bell?" Emily asked, practically wincing at the thought of a bell ringing.

Gaia chuckled. "I'm afraid anything quieter would defeat the purpose of getting my attention. I'll be checking in on you periodically."

"Thank you," Emily said and brought the cup of tea to her lips to drink.

"Ted?" Brandon stepped into the Headmaster's open doorway.

"Come in, Brandon, and close the door," Ted instructed.

Brandon positioned his hands on the arms of the chair and lowered himself to sit.

"I'm left with a dilemma with what to do with you, Brandon," Ted began.

Brandon nodded, expecting this was how their conversation would go.

"On the one hand, you clearly violated the conditions of your sentence. If I report this incident, the court will respond harshly."

"I'll accept whatever the consequences are," Brandon interrupted. "Just please don't expel Em."

Brandon thought he saw Ted's mouth twitch and start to smile, but the man quickly composed himself, and the solemn expression returned. "A noble gesture, but what Emily will or won't face for consequences is not your concern." Ted cleared his throat and continued. "On the other hand, you've been compliant for all your service, have performed exemplarily in your classes, and haven't tested the boundaries of your confinement."

Brandon nodded and remained silent.

"So, after conversations with Huo and several other members of the staff, I have decided not to report this to the court, but to revoke your privileges to leave campus over the winter break. Having you in an environment that isn't equipped to help you control your elemental ability could put others at unnecessary risk. You are also assigned to weekly sessions with Maggie to retrain you on how to keep your fire from erupting with your mood fluctuations. Do you have anything you'd like to say before we sign the agreement?"

"I just want to say again that I didn't pick a fight with Titus. Technically, I was defending myself—and Emily's honor."

"Regardless, Brandon, you have to be able to control yourself and your elemental abilities—no matter what anyone else says or does. *You* are responsible for *your* actions. Remember that."

"I will, Ted. Thank you for not filing this with the court." Brandon stood slowly and signed the new contract, which pretty much guaranteed he'd never step foot off the campus until graduation.

"I have to address the school now. I expect to see you in the audience."

Brandon nodded and took his leave from Ted's office.

"Good morning, students. I wish I could say I was glad to see all your faces here, but I'm afraid the reason for our meeting is less than pleasant. As some of you are aware, we had a couple of situations last night, with students misusing their gifts. I want to make it clear to every one of you that this type of behavior will *not* be tolerated at North Shore Academy. Each of us holds the ability to do tremendous harm with the gifts we've been granted. North Shore Academy is a place to learn how to use those gifts to bring balance, not cause chaos. It is why the number of affinates in the world represents an elite fraction of the population. As some of you upper-class students have already learned—and the rest of you will soon learn—an untrained or unstable-minded individual with these gifts can cause tremendous devastation. Some have caused incredible damage throughout history. If anyone in this room is struggling to control their affinity, the staff is here to give you the extra assistance you need. Please see to your Resident Director, Maggie, or me if you have any questions about what I've said today or if you need extra help. I hope the rest of your day will be more pleasant than this morning has been."

Brandon stood in the back of the students while Ted addressed them. He could feel eyes scan for him during the speech and felt ashamed for losing control. As soon as the students were dismissed, Brandon quickly exited the room and darted into the dining hall, hoping to grab a plate from Lucas in the kitchen and leave before too many people entered.

He *almost* made it out the door when he heard Titus call his name from across the dining hall. "Yo, Brandon!"

The students in the dining hall collectively tensed and watched as Titus crossed the room.

Before Brandon could say anything, Titus began. "It took pretty big balls to stand up to me last night."

The room seemed to inhale in unison. Brandon saw some teachers making their way toward them, too.

"I can respect that," Titus continued. "We good?"

Brandon almost laughed but kept it in. "We're good, Titus," Brandon replied, and the two bumped fists.

"Cool." Titus wandered to a table to eat with his friends.

"I know, Mom, but really, there's nothing to worry about. I've been studying hard for exams, and I guess I overdid it," Emily lied as she sat propped up in her bed talking to her mom on the phone.

Gaia, who had brought the phone to Emily to call her parents, silently prodded the girl to ask the vital question.

"We don't have a history of seizures in our family, do we?" she asked and chewed on the side of her bottom lip while listening to her mother's response. "Okay, good. I'll let them know. How are you and Dad?"

Emily listened some more to her mom gossip about trivial things happening in her absence. "Uh-huh," she occasionally interjected.

Gaia left the room to allow Emily some privacy to talk with her mom.

"Yes, Mom. I'm fine to come home for Christmas. I'll let you know if they tell me otherwise." Emily paused. "No, Mom. Please don't worry. I told you I'm going to be fine." Emily listened to her mother say goodbye. "Yeah, I love you, too. See you soon. Bye."

Maggie entered the room as soon as Emily finished the phone call. "Let me guess. Your mom was worried and wanted to come to take you home today."

Emily shrugged with one shoulder. "Pretty much. I told her I was fine, but I honestly don't know that's true. What happened to me?"

"We're trying to figure that out, Emily," Maggie reassured her. "How long have you known about your air affinity?"

Emily appeared shocked by the question. "I have an air affinity? But I thought you said I was earth and water?"

Maggie nodded. "Yes." She sat on the chair beside Emily in which Ashley had spent the night sleeping. "Can you tell me more about what happened last night?"

Emily recounted the events from dinner until the library for Maggie. "I was so angry and completely lost control. I wanted to throw Titus's things across the room and then . . . I just did. I moved my hands, and it was like an explosion of air. I wasn't even sure I did anything until I got to the bathroom. I could feel it then," Emily recalled. "There was too much air, and I just collapsed. Ash said she found me."

"Has anything like this happened to you before?" Maggie inquired.

Emily thought for a moment and then remembered back when she was mad at Brandon, also in the library, and slammed his book shut. "Yes. Once," Emily began and told her the story. "I honestly didn't think I did anything, though. I didn't *mean* to."

"I know you didn't, but this is why we slowly introduce affinities to the students and then have them learn how to use them in a very controlled environment. It's why you and I meet every week, so you can get the training with your earth affinity. Adding a third to your repertoire just means we need to adjust your schedule so you can get help with it, too."

Emily thought Maggie looked exhausted. "Do you think they'll let me go to the dance tomorrow?" Emily asked after a moment of silence.

Maggie smiled. "That's up to Gaia. If she thinks you're strong and stable enough, then I don't see why not. Which means," Maggie said as she stood, "you need to get lots of rest. I'll be back later to check on you, okay?"

"Okay," Emily said sadly. She liked Maggie's company and felt isolated and helpless, stuck in her bed in the infirmary.

"I'm sure your friends will be back to see you after their classes, so try to rest up before then."

"Thank you, Maggie."

Brandon picked up lunches from the dining room and joined Emily in the infirmary. "We jumped ahead in History of the Academy class today. Did you know the worst maritime disaster was caused by a fire affinate, *and* it wasn't even reported as news? More people died on the Sultana than on the Titanic. I don't know how they do it, but the Academy and its alumni are *really* good at covering things up."

"Oh," Emily replied, picking the blueberries out of her fruit salad. She knew she was hungry but didn't have an appetite. "Why were you talking about affinate-caused disasters in class today?"

"I'm sure Ted and the teachers are trying to scare us about misusing our powers in light of yesterday's events," Brandon replied casually.

Emily froze and looked down at the blueberry she held between her thumb and first finger. "So . . . everyone knows what I did?"

Brandon nodded. "And what I did, too."

Emily tilted her head to look over at Brandon. "What *did* you do?" she asked coolly.

Brandon forgot she didn't know what happened after he left the infirmary the night before. "The short version is I punched Titus with a flaming hand."

Emily blinked in surprise. "What's the long version?"

Brandon set his gyro on his plate and recounted the night to Emily. "I'm lucky I didn't get expelled," he admitted after concluding with the meeting in Ted's office and the speech to the school that followed. "But everything's cool between Titus and me now." Brandon shrugged.

"And your ribs? They're broken?"

"Cracked, at least that's what Gaia thinks. She can't know for sure without an x-ray. I'd have to go to the hospital, and then there'd be a record of it which could get back to the court, and I'd end up someplace I really don't want to go," Brandon explained. "My lungs are fine, and I'm not pooling blood anywhere, so Gaia just told me to come back if I felt anything other than the usual pain for the next few weeks."

Emily placed both hands over her face and slowly rubbed it. "I should've just gone to the movie with you guys. This is all my fault," she complained into her hands.

"Hey," Brandon said and touched her forearm. "It was probably bound to happen anyway. You're a good friend to Ashley, Em. Besides, now you know you have another affinity. What's it like to have two?"

"Three," Emily admitted, her face still buried in her hands. She felt Brandon release her arm.

"You have *three* affinities? What's the other?" he asked in surprise.

"Earth," Emily replied and let her hands drop to see if Brandon's expression matched the hurt in his voice.

"Wow." He slowly leaned back to press his shoulder blades against the back of the chair. "How long have you known? And why didn't you tell me?"

"A couple of months. I've been working with Maggie to learn how to use my earth affinity. I wasn't allowed to tell anyone . . . haven't told anyone until just now. Titus knew I think, but I don't know how. Listen," she implored, "from what I've discovered, it's very rare to have more than one. They don't really know how to accommodate my so-called gifts because they can't exactly have me living in two houses at the same time, learning everything from both at the same time. I guess they thought it was best to keep it on the down-low."

"Three houses now. I don't know whether to be envious or scared of you," Brandon joked.

Emily didn't find humor in it, though, and melted back into her pillow. "I don't even know if they'll let me stay here anymore. From what I overheard Ted telling an Elder the other day, they're barely able to handle me . . . and that was when they thought I only had two affinities."

"I don't think they'll kick you out, Em. That would be stupid. I'm sure they'll come up with something," Brandon replied sympathetically and mindlessly started to play with the charm on a necklace Emily hadn't seen him wear before.

"What's that?" she said, eyeing Brandon's neck.

"Oh. It's a birthday gift from my parents. Something that's passed down through the generations when a boy turns thirteen."

"Your birthday? When is it?" Emily blinked in surprise and then unconsciously realized no one seemed to celebrate birthdays at the Academy. Hers was in June, so she'd never be at school to worry about it.

"Today," he said sheepishly.

Emily's eyes widened, and she sat up again. "You're kidding. Oh my god, happy birthday! I would've gotten you something if I'd known."

Brandon shrugged with a smile. "What? You'd go to the store and buy me something with your invisible money? No, I didn't want it to be a big deal. I've pretty much got everything I want." He reached out and squeezed Emily's hand.

She rolled her eyes in response. "That was cheesy."

"I know," he grinned.

Emily laughed. "Regardless, I'm going to find a way to give you something. What does the charm say?" Emily squinted as she tried to read what looked like handwriting stamped on a flat piece of silver.

Brandon looked down and read it upside down. "Don't be afraid to give up the good to go for the great. It's a quote by Rockefeller, I think. My great-great-great-grandfather or something worked with him before going off on his own to make his own fortune. Anyway, it's supposed to thrust all the Miller men into the greatness of the past generations." He shrugged and tucked the necklace back under his uniform shirt and slowly rose to his feet. "I have to get going to class. I'll be back tonight for dinner, okay?"

"Hopefully, I won't still be here," Emily called after him.

"Feeling better, are we?" Maggie said as she entered as Brandon left.

"Yes, I feel fine," Emily admitted.

"Gaia is teaching a class right now, but she'll be back to determine exactly how good you're really feeling afterward."

"Maggie? Why don't we celebrate birthdays at this school? At my old school, even the loner kids got their name read on the announcements when it was their birthday."

Maggie's face screwed up the way it always did when Emily asked her questions.

Emily interrupted before Maggie could say anything. "Let me guess . . . it's complicated, and I will understand at some point in my lifetime." Emily was sour.

Maggie's expression softened as she smiled. "Something like that. We just don't celebrate birthdays in the way you're accustomed to. You're more than welcome to celebrate with your friends, though."

"Yeah," Emily replied. "It looks like I'll be borrowing a bottle of ibuprofen from Gaia and some gauze to wrap it in."

"Speaking of which," Maggie said, "I'm sure Brandon filled you in on the events of the day?"

Emily nodded. "So, everyone knows I have more than one affinity now."

"Yes, but they only know about the water and air affinities. For now, we're going to continue with your earth studies as they were, without adding that to the shocking announcements."

"I think Titus already knows. When I was in the library, he said some things about knowing about my earth studies and then proceeded to insult me."

"Hmmm. I'll have a talk with him. But let's stick with my plan and not share that knowledge with anyone else for now, okay?"

Emily flinched.

"You told Brandon, didn't you?" Maggie assumed.

Emily nodded sheepishly. "I didn't know it was still a secret. But Brandon won't tell anyone. He's not a gossip, but I'll let him know when I see him for dinner."

"Good. I've got some things to take care of. Are you okay for now, or do you need anything?" Maggie asked as she rose to leave.

"No, I'm fine for now."

"Okay, Emily. We'll talk again later."

Maggie was at the doorway when Emily spoke up again, "Hey, are they gonna kick me out of the Academy?"

Maggie paused and looked back at the worried girl. "Of course not. We just have to make some adjustments. There's no place better for you to be."

Emily nodded, relieved by the reassurance. "Thank you again."

CHAPTER TEN

The air elemental affinates stepped to the center of the circle of white robed students and faculty. As they lifted their arms in unison, a whoosh of wind whipped around and blew the students' hair backward. After a moment of the elemental whirl, they recited, "With the air, we cleanse ourselves."

The fire students were next. They stretched their arms forward and flexed their hands, so their palms were all facing the center of the inner circle they created. Once in position, a small fire appeared in the center. Emily could feel her cheeks warm while she sat in the chair that Gaia insisted on and watched Brandon play his part. "With the fire, we cleanse ourselves," they all said. As they lowered their hands, the fire dissipated.

Emily watched in wonder as the groups rotated again. She loved interacting with the elements. While intimately connected with three of them, the fire element was also special to her because of Brandon. The earth students formed their inner circle next and moved their arms in a low sweeping motion, palms to the ground. The leaves they sprinkled on the ground as they entered the ring swayed with them. "With the earth, we cleanse ourselves."

"We're next," Ashley bent down to whisper to Emily.

"I know," Emily whispered back. Gaia held onto Emily's upper arm and helped her rise to her feet. She hadn't stood for more than a few minutes since her collapse in the bathroom two nights prior. She was lucky to be attending the ceremony at all, Gaia reminded her. Emily's headaches hadn't subsided, so they were wary of risking her having another convulsing episode.

The water group took longer than the others to form their circle because they had to wait for Ashley to walk slowly with Emily. Emily nodded she was ready to Greta, who was leading their part of the ritual. The group raised their arms straight up with their facing palms upward and then lowered them with palms facing down. A light mist sprinkled the group of students. "With the water, we cleanse ourselves."

Ashley helped Emily halfway back to her chair, and then Gaia took over. Emily hated this treatment and hated it more that they weren't going to allow her to dance.

Ted entered the center of the group of students and faculty, turning slowly as he addressed them all. "The winter solstice is a time when we reflect on the changes of the past year and welcome the ones to come with the rebirth of the sun. We cleanse ourselves here tonight to make amends with our elements, our fellow affinates, and ourselves, and to restore balance. You have all done well tonight in honoring your elements and yourselves. Please remember that while you go and enjoy your dance. For those of you leaving to spend the winter break with your families, please have a safe journey and make happy memories. Be sure to leave your robes with your Resident Director. You're free to go and enjoy the festivities. Happy winter solstice, all."

The solemn atmosphere of the ceremony quickly dissipated as the students disrobed and ran toward the hall where the last dance was being held, laughing, and talking along the way. Emily was joined by Brandon and Ashley, who assisted her and Gaia in taking off Emily's white robe. "I hate this," Emily grumbled and sat down in the chair again.

Gaia had already heard enough of Emily's complaining and took the girl's robe to be collected while Brandon and Ashley hovered over Emily. "You guys should go and enjoy the dance. I'll probably just have Greta take me back to my room since they're finally allowing me to be in my bed again." The last part she said loudly and in the direction of Gaia.

Ashley frowned down at her friend. "C'mon, Em. You can still *go* to the dance. You just can't—"

"Dance?" Emily asserted. "Isn't that the whole point of a dance . . . to dance? Sitting there and watching everyone else enjoy the night is not my idea of fun. Go on without me."

"I have an idea," Brandon said and took off running. "See if you can find us a table, Ash. We should be right there," he called back to them.

"Go and have fun, Ash. I hope it's a magical night for you." Emily wanted her friend to have a good time, meet a new guy to gush over, and even wake her up when she came back to the room talking way too fast about the great things that happened. It had only been two days since she told off Titus, and despite not sleeping in the same room as Ashley, she knew he hadn't talked to her. Emily could see her friend's sadness.

"There was this cute upperclassman I bumped into at breakfast this morning." Ashley schemed. "If I could get him to dance with me." Emily could see the wheels were turning in her head. "Maybe it'd make Titus jealous enough to ask me to dance. Yes!"

Emily smacked her forehead with the palm of her hand. "Just go and have fun already."

Ashley skipped off toward the building while Emily shivered, feeling the cold air affecting her in the absence of the robe and Brandon's heat.

Brandon came jogging back and placed his warm palms on Emily's knees, leaning down to talk with her. "Okay, they agreed to allow me to *walk* you to the dance if you promised to stay sitting in there. You wouldn't be in this chair. You won't have Gaia hovering over you. But we could go, chair dance together, and devour as much food as we wanted." Brandon stood and held out his hand to help Emily stand.

Emily remained seated and narrowed her eyes at Brandon. "That sounds a lot like me going to a dance and not dancing. How is this supposed to be something I'd agree to?"

"I *said* we could chair dance together." Brandon sighed, feeling defeated. "Look, Em. You're leaving to go home tomorrow for two weeks. I want you to remember this as a happy place, so you'll come back."

Brandon gave Emily his best puppy dog eyes impression until she finally gave in. She held up her hand for him to help her stand. "What exactly is chair dancing?" she asked as they slowly walked toward the festivities. Despite his own injuries and discomfort, Brandon supported almost all her weight with his arm around her waist, and she draped an arm over his shoulders.

The room looked completely different than it had at their last dance. The lights were off, and the room glowed a soft white and blue with the light strands draped around the trees and a snowflake disco light, which gave the appearance of snow falling in the room. Candelabras held long, white candles with blue flames dancing on the wicks. Sweet cinnamon, peppermint, and wintergreen scents invisibly swirled through the air as the students jumped and moved in rhythm with the music the DJ played.

"Music should be named an element," Emily said to Brandon as she tapped her foot to the beat of the song.

Brandon chuckled. "Not as bad as you thought it would be then?"

Emily shrugged playfully. "This chair is *slightly* more comfortable than the other one."

"You're ridiculous. You know that, right?" The two had been holding hands since they sat down. He gave her hand a gentle squeeze and bobbed his body in time with the music.

"Do you want to dance with everyone else? You don't have to sit here all night with me," Emily said.

"You want to dance, you said?" Brandon flashed a mischievous grin and stood as a slow song began. "If I remember correctly, you promised me a dance. Are you a liar, Em?" Brandon tugged on Emily's hand.

"I'm not supposed to," Emily said with a crinkle of her nose but stood anyway.

Brandon pushed his chair aside with his foot and wrapped Emily in his arms. "Don't worry," he whispered through the curly wisp of brown hair hanging in front of her ear. "I've got you."

Both of Emily's arms circled his neck as the two rocked slowly back and forth. It barely felt like she was standing—more like floating on air—as they danced with their foreheads touching.

"You doin' okay?" he asked. "Need to sit?"

"I'm perfect right here," Emily replied while staring into his beautiful brown eyes. As her gaze lingered, she felt a tingle spark in her, like she'd been there before, and it was exactly where she belonged. "What are you thinking?" she asked as they swayed.

"Do you really want to know?" he replied.

Emily nodded her head, happier at this moment than she'd been in a long time.

"I was wondering if the gyros for lunch yesterday were lamb or beef."

The dreaminess faded, and she sighed. "I think I'm ready to sit again," she said, even as the song still played.

"What?" he asked innocently. "You said you really wanted to know."

"I did. You're right. I just feel a little light-headed," she lied.

"I'll go grab you another sparkling cider." Brandon made sure Emily wasn't going to fall out of the chair and said, "Don't go anywhere."

"You're hilarious," she said sarcastically but doubted he heard over the bass pounding when the next song started.

Emily looked around the energetic masses for Ashley. She spotted her near the center of the dance floor, surrounded by other students who were all dancing and laughing together. *Good*, she thought. *At least Ash is having fun.* She also noticed Titus talking with Brandon at the drink table, and her mood soured again.

"How are you feeling?" Maggie startled Emily as she sat in Brandon's chair.

"Tired," Emily admitted. "Is it safe for me to go home tomorrow?"

Maggie nodded. "I talked to your mom this afternoon. She knows you need to take it easy while you're home. So, no painting your room or shopping sprees, okay?" Maggie smiled, obviously in the same good mood as the rest of the room.

Emily wished Ashley's attitude was infectious. She felt like a burdensome, fragile, party pooper.

"You have my number, right? If anything happens with your affinities or anything, call me right away. I'm spending the break here at school," Maggie explained.

"I got it. There won't be any trouble, though. Promise." Emily was tempted to hold up her pinkie finger to swear it like she and Ashley did all the time but folded her hands in her lap instead.

"You're full of surprises, Emily," Maggie said in a good-hearted way. "I just want you to know I'm here if you need me." Maggie waved at Ted, who was across the room trying to get her attention. "I mean it, Emily. Anytime."

"Thanks, Maggie. I know."

Two more songs played and ended before Brandon returned with her cup of sparkling cider. "Oh, good. You're still here," he teased. Brandon's eyes were watching the students dance while he tapped his hand on his leg.

"You know, you can go dance if you want," Emily suggested again.

"I'm good here," he replied, but he continued to watch people dance.

Emily watched him watch other people for a few songs before speaking again. "I think I need to call it a night. My head's pounding," she said and pointed at her head for clarification.

Brandon nodded and helped Emily to her feet.

"Everything alright?" Adamina asked as the two neared the door. Emily thought the tiny woman made an awful sentry, but it seemed to be her duty to stand at the door at dances.

Emily nodded.

"I'm going to walk her to her hall. Greta said she'd help her inside when we got there," Brandon explained.

Adamina gave a single nod, but recited her exit speech, "Straight to the residence hall. There's faculty watching the campus."

"Straight to the hall. Got it," Brandon said, and the two were allowed to exit.

The walk to the dorm took a while at Emily's slow pace. For the first several minutes, Brandon attempted to make small talk, but when Emily's replies were half-hearted, he stopped. "Okay, what's wrong?" he asked.

"Nothing. It's just this headache," Emily lied.

"BS, Em. Your body tensed up when we were dancing, and you've been grumpy ever since. What did I do? Or not do?" Brandon was obviously clueless and fishing for answers.

"I said there's nothing wrong. You've been great tonight. It was fun. Yay dance," Emily said dryly. "Is that what you wanted to hear?"

"I wanted the truth, which you aren't able or willing to tell me. So fine. You're great. We're great. This is the best night of your life." Sarcasm was thick in Brandon's voice, as was his frustration.

Emily's expression was a mix between a frown and fury. "What were you and Titus talking about?" she demanded.

"That's what you're pissed about? Because I was talking to Titus?" Brandon rolled his eyes dramatically to make sure Emily saw.

"No, I'm pissed because you were thinking about a stupid sandwich when we were slow dancing. I mean, who does that?" Emily pushed away from Brandon and started walking alone.

"Every guy does that! Geez, Em. What's your problem?" Brandon easily caught up with her.

Emily turned with her finger pointed at him and poked him in the chest. "The problem is that you don't see any problem with it. I'm going to walk by myself for the rest of the way. I'm pretty sure I can manage the fifty feet left."

Brandon stared after her with a dumbfounded expression but watched from where he stood to make sure she made it in the hall okay before returning to the dance. Emily might not have had a good time, but he'd be damned if the first dance he got to attend at North Shore was going to end on that note.

Ashley returned to the room quietly, but Emily wasn't asleep. She was throwing some of her belongings into her duffle bag to take home with her since she had been confined to the infirmary during the time she would've ordinarily packed. She also knew it would be a miserable drive home if her dad had to wait for her to pack in the morning.

"Hey, Em. How ya feeling?" she asked sweetly.

"Fantastic," Emily spat at her friend, instantly regretting it. "Sorry, Ash. I'm just angry. Don't worry, I'm not going to go elemental on you or anything." It felt like everyone was watching Emily now, waiting for another eruption of some kind.

"I didn't think you were," Ashley said, keeping her calm demeanor. "It's just when Brandon came back to the dance without you, I kinda wondered if something happened."

"He went back?" Two girls returning from the dance looked in with wide eyes as they passed by Emily and Ashley's open door. Emily breathed in deeply through her nose and slowly out again, holding her hands up in resignation. "No, I'm not going to be like that. I'm glad he went back and danced." As she said that, a nervous knot formed in her stomach. What if he danced with another girl? Emily knew she was a complete bitch to him.

"Em?" Ashley set her hand lightly on her roommate's shoulder.

"Yeah?" she replied, all emotion drained from her tone.

"He was moping for most of the rest of the dance. Maggie went and chatted with him, and then he finally joined us for the last three songs. What happened?" she asked cautiously.

"He said he was thinking about sandwiches when we were dancing!" Emily could hear the emotions rising in her voice, so she took another calming breath.

"That was a stupid thing for him to say, even if it was true. My oldest brother did something stupid like that once, too. He learned *really* quick that telling a girl he was with that he was thinking about anything *other* than her was an invitation to be slapped." Ashley giggled, recalling.

"So, it's really a guy thing to be such an idiot?" Emily asked.

"Duh. All guys are morons. Why we put up with them, I'll never know." Ashley shrugged. "Well, I *do* know, but still. What were you thinking about at that moment?"

"How completely wonderful and happy I felt like I was exactly where I was supposed to be." Emily rolled her eyes at her own romantic notions.

Ashley gave Emily a much-needed hug. "Titus didn't ask me to dance. I was a little disappointed, but then I decided I wasn't going to let boys make me feel bad anymore."

"And that worked?" Emily asked in amazement.

"Kinda. Not really. But it worked enough to keep me dancing with people who were just there to have fun."

"What about that guy from breakfast?" Emily zipped up her duffle and sighed as she finally allowed herself to sit and relax.

"He has a girlfriend," Ashley said with a grin and a shrug.

"His loss," Emily yawned and curled up in her bed for her last night of the year she'd sleep there.

CHAPTER ELEVEN

Emily never realized how long two weeks could feel. She'd left North Shore early Saturday morning without saying goodbye to Brandon, something she started regretting on the second day home with her parents. So much had changed with Emily over the previous four months— things she couldn't share with anyone back home—and yet everything back home stayed exactly the same. Emily watched her parents have the same conversations they had every year at the holidays. They went to the same service at the same church they'd always attended and even sat in the same pew.

The two things about home she did miss were the snow and being a normal kid with her ordinary friends. A tradition she had with her friends from her old school was going to the mall on Boxing Day. Even though Emily had promised Maggie she wouldn't go on shopping sprees, she decided the fresh air and a little walking would do her good—or at least improve her mood. She promised herself, though, that she'd take it as easy as possible.

"So, what's your new school like, anyway?" Crystal asked as the four girls browsed the mall for after-Christmas deals . . . and boys.

"It's cool, but lots of rules. And I have to wear a uniform," Emily responded vaguely.

"I think what Crystal *really* means is how are the boys at your new school?" Jenny corrected, and the three girls giggled and nodded.

"Do you have a boyfriend? Jenny's dating Jason," Katy bragged.

"Jason? Really?" Emily scrunched her nose in disapproval.

"He kinda grew out of his awkward looks and is totally hot now," Jenny said defensively and pulled out her phone to show Emily a picture. "This was us at the winter formal a few weeks ago. See? He's a total babe now."

Emily nodded. "Yeah, it's definitely an improvement from last year."

Katy smacked Emily in the arm with her purse. "You didn't answer my question. Do you have a boyfriend?" she asked again, annunciating each word.

"Yes. No. Kinda?" Emily shrugged.

"Girl, spill. Did you bring pictures? Is he hot?" Crystal asked in rapid succession.

"It's complicated. We had a fight before I left, and I haven't talked to him since. No, I don't have a picture because we're not allowed to use our phones on campus," Emily explained.

"That sounds like torture. What do you do for fun? Is there a mall close by?" Jenny asked.

Emily could feel herself get dizzy. It had only been a week since her seizure. "Tell you what . . . let's take a break from shopping to get something to eat, and I'll answer any question you want. But I want to hear all about what's been happening with *you* this year, too."

The girls split into pairs; Katy and Crystal going to Panda Express while Emily and Jenny stood in the Subway line.

"Now that the other two aren't here, let's *really* talk about boys. So how far have you and . . . what's his name?" Jenny began.

"Brandon, and what do you mean, how far have we—?" Emily looked at her friend, unable to translate this new language she'd picked up since the summer when they last saw each other.

"Like what base have you gotten to? Jason and I are *comfortably* at second base. He wanted to go to third, but I'm not really ready to you-know-what."

Emily didn't know what you-know-what was, but she tried to play it off as best as she could. "Well, umm, we've kissed," she said, omitting it had only been one kiss *she* instigated. "It's not like we have anywhere to go and do more than that. We live in dorms that don't allow non-residents inside. One of the *many* rules."

Jenny scrunched her nose. "Sounds like hell. Is it a military school or something? My mom said your dad told my dad it was a military school."

Emily shook her head. "No, thank god. It's just a private school."

The two ordered their food and then joined the others at the table where they were already eating. "Look at that one," Crystal whispered but pointed at a guy who looked to be about seventeen and was looking straight at them.

"Don't point!" Katy smacked her friend's hand and then shook her head.

The entire time they ate, the three friends gossiped about people walking by and rated the boys they saw. Emily found her thoughts drifting back to the Academy and how things were better there. While getting ready to go out with her friends, she thought she missed this life, but seeing what her life would've been if she hadn't gone to North Shore Academy made her feel . . . elite.

"What's wrong, Em? You've barely touched your sandwich. I thought you said you were hungry," Crystal observed.

"Wait, lemme guess," Jenny interjected. "You guys have some kind of weird diet at your school. Are you anorexic?"

The three girls inspected Emily and concluded she wasn't skinny enough to be anorexic.

"Thanks, guys," Emily said sarcastically. "No, we don't have any weird diets there. In fact, our meals are prepared by a gourmet chef and served to us." She realized after she'd said it how snobby she sounded. "Anyway," she continued, "I just haven't had fast food in six months, so it tastes weird. That's all."

The girls looked at her like she was an alien for a moment and then got distracted by a cute guy walking by. Emily missed North Shore, she missed Ashley, she missed Maggie, and she really missed Brandon.

After they'd had enough boy watching and eating, the four returned to shopping. "Oh! Can we run in this store really quick?" Emily asked as they passed the window of a store that sold swords and medieval-looking clothing and figurines.

"Ew, Em. I think my nerdy brother shops in there," Katy remarked.

"I think my grandpa shops in there. Yuck. You go ahead. I'm going to go next door to see if any of the clothes are discounted," Jenny added while the others nodded.

"Oh," Emily said. "I guess I'll catch up with you in a minute."

Despite their fight, Emily hadn't forgotten Brandon's birthday. She hoped to surprise him when she returned with a gift, and he'd have missed her so much that everything would be back to normal.

"I'd like that one," Emily said to the salesclerk as she pointed to a red dragon perched on half a geode. The middle of the rock was red, like lava—or fire—and while she didn't know if Brandon liked dragons, in particular, the whole figure symbolized fire. It would be much better than buying him a necklace or bracelet, which were her fallback gift ideas.

After tucking her change into her purse, she picked up the bagged gift and went next door. She browsed between the racks looking for her friends but didn't find them. She even tried looking under the dressing room doors but was politely invited to leave. She checked a couple of the surrounding stores before surrendering to the idea that she'd been ditched.

While not as hurt as she thought she should be, she still felt a sting of humiliation as she called her mom to pick her up. Emily had to be *very* careful not to let her crappy old friends get the better of her, or she might lose her temper and do something horrible.

She pulled out her phone and dialed another number.

The phone was answered after the second ring. "Hello."

"Maggie. Thank god you're there. I'm trying really hard to keep my cool, but my so-called friends just ditched me at the mall."

Emily kept Maggie talking on the phone with her until she saw her mom's car pull in. "My mom's here now. Thanks for talking with me."

"Anytime, Emily. I'm glad you called."

"One more thing, Maggie." Emily bit her lip and then asked really quick before she lost her courage. "How's Brandon?"

"He's been busy, but I think he's doing well. I'll see you when you return next week, okay? And call me again if you need to talk."

"I will. Thanks. Bye."

Emily phoned Ashley that night after her parents were soundly asleep. "What does that mean, 'I think he's doing well?' I mean, isn't she supposed to know those things? What wasn't she telling me?"

"Just a guess," Ashley started, "but it sounds like he's fine, and you shouldn't be worried about him."

Emily melted into her bed with the phone to her ear. It was comforting to hear Ashley's voice again. The two chatted about their Christmas gifts and how it felt to be home, both concluding that they felt out of place in their old lives and really couldn't wait to return to North Shore.

"Another week, Em. We just have to suffer through one more week, and things will be back to normal," Ashley reassured her friend.

"Normal. It's funny how the meaning of that word has changed in just a few months, huh?" Emily mused.

"Yeah," Ashley agreed. "Hey, I have to get going. My brothers want a rematch in "Dead or Alive." So, I gotta go kick their asses again."

Emily had no idea what "Dead or Alive" was but assumed it was some video game since she knew Ashley's brothers were obsessed with their PS3. "Alright. Talk to you later, Ash."

"Night, Em."

Curled up in her bed, Emily fell asleep reading *The Fault in Our Stars*, a Christmas gift from her parents.

"It would be great if you could spend time with your friends from church," Emily's mom encouraged her.

The *last* thing Emily wanted to do was spend New Year's Eve at her parents' church, praying to a god she realized she never really believed in. She was a dutiful daughter growing up, going to church with her parents every Sunday and every holiday. She'd spent at least nine of the last twelve New Year's Eves at the church, celebrating with the other kids there. While Emily never considered herself religious like her dad was, she didn't feel disenfranchised from her faith until her affinities awakened. Life, balance, and spirituality were so much more complicated than the over-simplified lessons her parents' church preached as law. Emily didn't have all the answers, but she had new clarity.

One of the pastors joined Emily as she sat alone in a pew while the other kids were blissfully enjoying games and food. "You seem troubled, child."

"I'm just thinking," she said politely.

"This is a good place to come for answers. The Lord has brought you here for a reason," the man said wisely.

"That's just it, though," Emily began. "Your lord didn't bring me here; my parents did."

The pastor looked shocked. "He's your Lord, too, child. And His will guided your parents on their journey."

Emily thought that sounded like a load of crap but decided maybe she could better understand her own beliefs by talking with him. "How do you know your lord and god are real?" she began, careful not to show any disrespect.

"The Bible tells us so," the man explained simply.

"What if you had never read the Bible? How would you know?" Emily had, in fact, read the Bible in her Sunday school classes, so it wasn't as if she was asking out of ignorance.

"His works are everywhere around us; you just have to have open eyes and an open heart."

"So, you mean you just have to have faith in something even if you don't have proof of its existence?" Emily couldn't help but feel like this paralleled the way Maggie and Ted kept telling her the answers she was looking for would reveal themselves.

"The proof of God's existence and love is all around you. You just have to open your heart to Him, and you will see."

Emily's mind flashed to the book she'd just finished reading. "How can you put your faith in a god who allows children to suffer from terminal illnesses?" It wasn't intended as an attack, but the pastor's face revealed to Emily that she had clearly offended him.

"His ways are mysterious, and we must have faith in His plan. Now, if you'll excuse me, Emily, I have to get ready to lead the midnight prayer."

Emily grumbled something in the pastor's wake. If there was a god, she would've been struck down where she sat. If nothing else, that night, Emily deepened her faith in herself, in her abilities, and in a forgotten knowledge inside herself.

CHAPTER TWELVE

The tension in Emily's house grew following her conversation with the pastor, who apparently had a long conversation with her father the following day. Emily spent two days grounded in her room until her father finally drove her back to North Shore Academy two days ahead of schedule. When Emily's mother stayed behind, she feared the entire car ride would be a continuous lecture. Instead, her father didn't say a word until he parked at the Academy.

"When you return for the summer, we're having you baptized. Whatever ideas the devil has put inside that mind of yours will be washed away."

Emily blinked in surprise as she stood outside of the car, peering in at her dad. "Yes, sir," she whispered compliantly and then slammed the car door shut. Her dad didn't wait for her to walk inside before he left. She wanted so badly to make it hail and ding his precious car; she could feel her temper starting to flare out of control.

Just as she was about to do something regrettable, she felt a hand on her shoulder. "You're back early."

Emily followed Maggie inside to her office. "Want to talk about it?" Maggie asked kindly.

131

"Not really," Emily replied, plopping dramatically onto the suede couch. "I mean, he thinks he can just order me around like he does my mom, and I'll mindlessly go along with whatever he or his stupid church says. He honestly thinks I'll let them *baptize* me?"

Maggie's eye twitched. "What do you mean, baptize you?"

Emily rolled her eyes. "So, I *respectfully* asked the pastor questions about why he believed in his god, and now my dad told me I'm getting baptized when I return home this summer. Something about Satan in me or who knows."

Maggie approached the topic delicately. "You'll be thirteen this summer, correct?"

Emily nodded.

"Perhaps you will be able to make your own choices by then and express them *calmly* to your parents," Maggie suggested.

"Or maybe I won't go home at all," Emily replied and crossed her arms while a sullen expression governed her face.

Maggie smiled at the rebellious child. "You certainly have your own mind, Emily. And the summer is still a long way off. You can't know how you'll change between now and then."

Emily was still grumpy but was starting to calm down. "I still won't be what he wants for me to be." *A son*, she thought.

"On the brighter side . . . we have a new student at the school who I'd like to introduce to you. I think you'll find you two have a lot in common," Maggie said with a warm smile.

Emily perked up a little. "A new student? What do I have in common with her or him? Or is this another one of those things I have to find out for myself?"

Maggie laughed. "No, this one, I'll tell you." Maggie pretended to look to see if anyone else was around and then whispered, "She's a bi-affinate."

Emily nodded slowly. "Oh. But aren't I called something else now?"

Maggie nodded. "You're technically a tri, but for the time being, we're going to keep the earth affinity our secret. Would you like to meet her?"

Emily shrugged. "Sure."

The two walked out of the office and toward Adamina's classroom. "She's been practicing her fire affinity with—"

Maggie didn't have to continue. As soon as they stepped in the doorway, Emily saw Brandon doing some kind of fire juggling for a girl—a woman, really. She was the attractive-even-from-behind kind of girl sitting on a desk with her back to the door. Her whole cute body shook when she giggled, including the perfect rings of blonde hair spiraling halfway down her back.

"Show me how to do that," the new girl said between giggle-snorts that even sounded adorable.

Brandon took her hands and started to explain when Maggie cleared her throat. "It's good to see you both so focused in here. I'd like to introduce you to our other bi-affinate."

The color seemed to drain from Brandon's face, which only Emily noticed as the girl-who-was-adorable-from-behind hopped off the desk and walked toward Maggie. Emily was supposed to get along with this girl who looked like she stepped out of Elle Magazine and was flirting with *her* boyfriend?

The new girl was all smiles and dimples as she bounced her way over to meet Emily. "Hi, I'm Myra," the shapely beauty said as she held out her hand to Emily.

Emily couldn't deny this girl with a womanly figure was stunningly beautiful. She recalled the cartoonish gleam she imagined the first time she went into the Academy's restroom and envisioned a similar sparkle coming off Myra's perfectly white teeth and deep blue eyes.

"This is Emily," Maggie finally said and nudged Emily to shake the girl's outstretched hand.

Emily forced what she believed to be a pleasant smile onto her face as she shook Myra's hand. "Pleasure," Emily managed.

"Oh, sorry. I'm sure my hand was hot. Bran volunteered to help me with my fire training over the break, and I've been trying to create little fireballs all morning. He's such a great teacher, though. I'm still such a novice with fire." Myra giggled.

"Bran?" she repeated and was promptly elbowed by Maggie. *She has a nickname for him?* "My hands are just naturally cooler because of my water affinity," Emily explained. She tried to inject a little inflection into her voice to keep the rage she felt from being blatantly obvious. She glanced toward Brandon, who was still on the far side of the room, purposely not making eye contact with Emily. "I should take my things to my room. I'm sure I'll see you again, Myra." Emily turned on her heel and left.

It wasn't until Emily was at the door to her residence hall that Brandon finally caught up with her. "Hey, Em. I wasn't expecting you back for a couple of days." He smoothed the side of his hair with his right hand. "Did you have a good break?"

"We haven't spoken since the dance. You didn't even *try* to contact me. I come back to find you flirting with some fire bimbo, and you didn't even say hi when you saw me. Now you want to know if I had a good break?" Emily blinked several times at Brandon before reaching into her bag. She pulled out the wrapped present and thrust it at Brandon. "Happy late birthday," she said and walked inside the sanctuary of the water elemental house.

"Why are boys so stupid?" Emily asked as she helped Greta rearrange the furniture in the common room.

The Resident Director laughed lightly. "If you find out the answer, I know women everywhere would like to know." Greta stepped back to admire the new look of the common room. "What do you think? Does it feel more Zen?"

Emily only felt grumpy and had barely paid attention to how they were rearranging the room. "Sure," she said flatly and sighed as she flopped onto the couch.

Greta handed Emily a hot chocolate and then joined her on the sofa. Both stared out the window and watched the raindrops sprinkle against the glass. "Is it possible you misread the situation?" She quickly threw her hand up in surrender, though, when Emily shot her a death glare. "Or maybe it's exactly how you thought it looked. Regardless, whether you're in here being mad or enjoying yourself is all your doing."

"How long has Myra been here?" Emily asked, not bothering to react to Greta's words of wisdom.

Greta sighed, defeated. "Ted arrived with her five days ago. Apparently, he was charged with her training since we're the only Academy which has a bi-affinate."

"So, what you're saying," Emily began, "is it's my fault she's here."

Greta chuckled lightly. "It's not a fault situation. It's an opportunity for *you* to connect someone who will likely face the same struggles you do with trying to balance multiple affinities. It's all about how you look at it, Emily."

Emily stopped herself from saying what it looked like when she walked in on Brandon and Myra and nodded instead. "You're probably right. I'll try to keep an open mind." She knew she didn't mean it. "I'm going to go finish unpacking my stuff now. Thanks for the hot chocolate."

"Anytime, Emily. And thanks for helping me move stuff around here. I really think this opens up the room," Greta mused.

"One of us won't be alive by then," Emily explained after her roommate told her it would be another day before she got back to the Academy.

"Em," Ashley warned over the phone. "Don't kill her before I can get there and can help."

It felt like the first time Emily had smiled in weeks. Between her old friends, her dad, Brandon, and Myra, she felt like all her happiness had been sucked out of her.

"Is she really that pretty?"

"I didn't say she was 'pretty.' She's *gorgeous*," Emily restated.

"What are you going to do until classes start? Are you going to stay in the room for the entire two days?"

"That's more or less the plan," Emily agreed.

"Em, you gotta eat and stuff. Maybe you should talk to Brandon?" Ashley suggested cautiously.

"You're probably right, but I don't have anything nice to say to him, so I'm just going to continue to get my meals from Lucas in the kitchen and avoid the two of them altogether."

There was a knock at Emily's door. Greta stood in her doorway, waiting for her to finish her phone call.

"Hey, Ash? I have to run. Greta needs to talk with me, and I have to run grab my dinner before it's served in the dining hall. Have a safe drive here. Miss you."

"Miss you, too, Em. And I can't promise the safe part; my brother is dropping me off on his way back to college. I'll see you soon, though."

Emily hung up her phone and tossed it on the pillow before turning to Greta. "What's up?" she asked, feeling a little more relaxed after talking to Ashley.

"Ted has asked to see you in his office before dinner," Greta explained.

"Alright." Emily stood and put on her jacket before leaving to meet the Headmaster.

"Welcome back, Emily. We weren't expecting you back for a couple of days. How was your break?" Ted began as Emily took her usual seat across the desk from the Headmaster.

"Yeah, I seemed to have surprised everyone with my arrival. Sorry," she shrugged. "Break was . . . trying," Emily explained.

"No apologies needed. And trying? How so? Did you have issues from your seizure?" Ted sounded genuinely concerned.

"Not really, although I felt a little weak at times. It's just my dad. He's angry with me, thinking I'm Satan's spawn now or something." Emily shrugged.

"You've changed a lot since you saw him last. And from what I know of your father, he's not a man who accepts change easily. I'm glad to have you back here, though. I heard you met Myra earlier."

"Yes, the new bi-affinate you brought here." Emily could hear the sourness in her tone.

Ted chuckled. "Yes, well, the Council thought this would be the best place for her. Myra has had a difficult past. During her first year as an earth affinate at the White Mountain Academy in California, she was in a car accident, which caused her to be in a coma for over a year. When she awoke in November, she had a new affinity."

"Fire," Emily interrupted. "Yes, I saw her practicing it when I arrived." She tilted her head, curious about how Ted explained Myra's story. "Do people usually wake from comas with a new affinity?"

"To be fair," Ted began, "it's not every day an affinate ends up in a coma. But to directly answer your question, no. The circumstances surrounding Myra's new affinity are unique."

While Ted answered Emily's question directly (for once), the way he explained it seemed like there was more to the story than he was sharing. "What do you need me to do? From what Maggie told me, my earth affinity is being kept as a guarded secret. So, I have no known affinities in common with her."

"We're still working out the details, but we'd like to have a class for the both of you where you become more skilled at working with two elements simultaneously. Our thought right now is we'd like to work up to you both balancing each other out while using both affinities. Together, you encompass all four elements."

"It seems like it's going to be a lot of work for me to continue to fake only having two," Emily pointed out.

"Depending on how things go, we may reveal to Myra in your sessions you have three. We're in uncharted territory here, Emily. I'm asking for your help specifically because you have more control over the elements than Myra right now. We need to make sure she doesn't get . . . overwhelmed."

"You mean you don't want her to seize out like I did," Emily stated plainly.

"Yes, well, since she's been unconscious for so long, we're not certain how much strain her brain can handle. We want you both to be safe, as well as the other students." Ted set down the pen he'd been twisting between his fingers and leaned forward. "I know it frustrates you to hear this, but you're an extraordinary soul. I'm delighted you're at my school."

"I'll try not to let you down," Emily replied with equal sincerity.

"We'll talk again soon. You should hurry and grab some food before dinner's over."

The disappointing part about dinner already being out, even though it was just a buffet because most of the students weren't back yet, was that students weren't allowed in the kitchen during meals. Technically, they weren't supposed to be in there at all, but at least you wouldn't get an earful of Italian outside of dining time. Needless to say, Emily didn't make it to the dining hall before dinner was served, so she was stuck. Either she could grab a plate of food and make a run for it in the rain back to the residence hall, or she could eat in the dining hall. She chose the latter, picking a table on the far side of the room from the buffet line where there were only a couple of upperclassmen eating.

Emily intended to nibble on a few pieces of fruit and maybe a chicken breast because the day had left her without much of an appetite, but as soon as she tasted the food, she was reminded of one of the many reasons she loved North Shore.

"Mind if we join you?" Brandon and Myra stepped to the empty seats in front of Emily with plates of food.

Emily shrugged. "I don't think those seats are taken." *Of course, they came in together*, she grumpily thought. She pulled her plate in closer, making sure they had enough space for theirs.

"So," Myra began. "Everyone kept talking about you when I arrived. I'm glad to finally meet you." Myra was very polite, but it didn't stop Emily from wishing she'd get a piece of spinach caught in those perfect white teeth.

"Well, here I am." Emily was horrible at small talk. Even if Myra turned out to be the nicest person in the world, she didn't feel a connection to her like she did with Brandon and Ashley. And at the moment, the connection she had with Brandon was hidden behind an angry wall deep inside.

"The food is better here than at the hospital. I barely remember what it tasted like at White Mountain Academy."

"Yeah, Ted told me about your accident. I'm sorry to hear that." Emily shifted her gaze between her food and Myra, childishly pretending Brandon wasn't there.

"Crazy story, huh? I'm not sure I'd want to be in a coma just to wake up with another affinity, though," Brandon remarked.

"So, are you from California, Myra?" Emily asked.

"Yes, but Southern California. White Mountain was a lot farther north. It seemed like a completely different state."

"That's cool. My parents took me to Disneyland when I was four. It was fun, I think."

An awkward silence hung in the air, only interrupted by the occasional crunch of an apple.

"Thanks for the dragon, Em. I really like it." Brandon was trying hard to make amends with Emily for the run-in earlier in the day.

"No problem," she said, finally looking at him and offering a fake smile. "I think I'm going to go finish unpacking. See you guys around," Emily said and left the table. For all the idiotic things boys did, this was the stupid thing girls would do, testing boys to see if they would run after them. A month ago, Brandon would've chased her down to make sure she was okay, but a lot had changed in a month. Emily even walked back slowly in the pouring rain, but all it got her was cold and soaked. She practically ran to her empty room once she was inside, slammed the door shut, and collapsed onto her bed in tears.

CHAPTER THIRTEEN

Emily awoke the next morning with puffy red eyes, which looked more green than brown, and blotchy cheeks. She might have continued crying even after she'd passed out. She decided a nice hot shower might help and took a much longer-and-hotter-than-usual one. With her robe wrapped around her body and towel holding up her wet hair, she casually shuffled back to her room, feeling marginally better.

"Hey," a deep voice said as she stepped inside.

Emily flashed a terrified look at her visitor, down the hall to see if anyone was within earshot, and then closed the door, wrapping her arms around her body. "What the hell? You can't be in here," she scolded in a whispered shout.

"You're avoiding me, won't make eye contact, won't even respond to me . . . what choice did I have?" Brandon almost sounded amused, but the emotion didn't reach his eyes.

"You always have choices, *Bran*," she remarked sarcastically.

Brandon flinched. "I probably deserve some of this anger, but *you* left without saying goodbye. *You* didn't reach out to me, either. Not that *anything* happened between Myra and me, but what did you expect? You bring me a gift, and every-thing is fine?"

Emily plopped on the bed opposite of the one he was on, careful to make sure her robe didn't open and reveal anything. "Yes," she said matter-of-factly with a shrug. "I had a *horrible* time at home, and the only thing that kept me going was coming back here to you and Ash."

"Ahh, and there it is."

"There *what* is?" Emily inquired, hearing the confusion and frustration in her tone.

"You wanted to come back to your *friends*, not your *boy*-friend. Let me ask this. Did you get Ash a gift, too?"

Emily could see where he was going with his train of thought but answered truthfully anyway. "Yes, I got her a snow globe." She shrugged. "So?"

"So . . . my assumption is correct." Brandon stood and walked to the window. "I think we need to go back to how things were before."

"You mean before I kissed you?" Emily could feel a lump in her throat.

Brandon nodded and lifted the window open. "I proba-bly won't see you around for a while. Things are going to be awkward. Take care, Emily."

The way he said her full name made her flinch. Emotionally-charged tears formed in her eyes and spilled down her cheeks. She didn't think Brandon saw them before he jumped out the window, tucked his hands in his pockets, and walked away without looking back. She slammed the window shut, collapsed onto Ashley's bed, and sobbed.

"Em?"

Emily was woken up by a gentle nudge and the sound of Ashley's voice. It took a microsecond before Emily had her arms wrapped around her best friend and was sobbing again.

Ashley tried to comfort her friend, stroking her stringy hair, which had dried while she was passed out.

"Oh, sweetie. You're a mess. Why don't you tell me what happened, although I think I can guess."

Emily stuttered and sputtered her way through the story, hiccupping throughout.

When she was done, Ashley sighed and squeezed her friend in a giant bear hug. "The only thing we need to do right now—aside from getting you dressed and brushing your hair—is to go and bother Lucas in the kitchen to give us some of his stash of ice cream."

Emily sniffled and nodding. "That would be okay."

Brushing her hair didn't help, though, because Emily had fallen asleep with it wet and scrunched in a towel. So, Ashley threw a baseball cap on her roommate's head, and they walked to the dining hall, looking around like spies to make sure they didn't run into Brandon.

"Where did you even get this hat?" Emily asked, still suffering from random emotion-induced hiccups.

"My brother brought it back from college. Thought it'd look cute on me." She rolled her eyes. "Or else he knew it'd look stupid and just wanted to laugh at me. Either way, it's serving a good purpose today."

Lucas was directing the kitchen staff when the girls walked in. His usually tense expression softened when he saw Emily's face. "What is this?" he said with his thick Italian accent and motioned to the distressed girl.

"She's having a bad day, Lucas. Do you have any ice cream we could devour?" Ashley asked sweetly.

"Ice cream? No, no. Lucas will get you something better." The olive-skinned man wandered through the kitchen, correcting his staff, who were apparently preparing something incorrectly. He disappeared from the girls' sight, but they could still hear him somewhere in the back by the freezer.

Ashley and Emily hopped up to sit on one of the stainless-steel countertops, mindlessly kicking their legs as they waited.

"What could be better than ice cream?" Ashley wondered aloud.

Emily shrugged. "Maybe a glass of wine?" Both girls giggled.

It took about five minutes, but Lucas finally returned with two white teardrop-shaped plates with what looked like ice cream with a drizzle of chocolate on the top and a mint leaf for color. Each took one with a curious head tilt.

"This looks like ice cream, Lucas," Ashley commented. Emily nodded in agreement.

The Italian chef scoffed. "Not ice cream; *torrone semifreddo*," he explained with animated gestures. "Taste," Lucas invited the girls.

Emily and Ashley exchanged confused glances, and then each took a small taste of the white, ice-cream like dessert. "Mmmm," they said in unison and went in for a bigger spoonful.

Lucas smiled and left the girls to enjoy while he returned to his duties.

"Do you think it's weird for the kitchen staff to work at a school like this?" Ashley pondered and licked her spoon.

Emily shrugged. "I'd never thought about it, but yeah, it's gotta be a little strange. I mean, they have to know we're . . . different."

"Hey, Lucas," Ashley called out as he scurried past them.

He made a detour to return to the girls. "Is good, yes?"

"Yes, delicious," Emily replied.

"We were wondering," Ashley started, "if it's weird for you to work here with all us affinates."

Lucas yelled something in Italian over his shoulder in response to a crashing noise. "Weird? No, no. *Sapere è amare*," he said passionately.

"Separate Mary?" Ashley asked in confusion. Emily was thinking the same thing.

Lucas laughed. "No, no. *Sapere è amare*," he repeated, enunciating each syllable.

"It means 'to know is to love.' *Sapere è amare*," Maggie explained as she joined the trio in the kitchen. She greeted Lucas with a kiss to each of his cheeks. The two spoke briefly in Italian to each other while the girls listened, not knowing what they were saying.

After a slight bow of his head to Maggie, Lucas turned to the three of them. "Buongiorno," he said and returned to his duties.

"Bon journo," Ashley said with a thick American accent, poorly imitating the word Lucas had said.

Maggie chuckled. "What brings you two to the kitchen for—" she paused to inspect the nearly-licked-clean dishes. "—torrone semifreddo?"

The girls nodded, glad she guessed correctly because they wouldn't have been able to repeat the dish's name.

"Hmm . . . that's Lucas's special stash. Must be something serious going on," Maggie suspected. "Let's go to my office to talk about it, so we're not in Lucas's way."

The girls hopped off the counter and followed Maggie to her office. They passed by Adamina's classroom, which Emily walked by quickly, not wanting to know if Brandon and Myra were in there "practicing."

"How'd you learn Italian?" Ashley inquired as the three entered Maggie's office and closed the door.

"Lucas taught me," she said with a slight blush appearing on her cheeks.

Emily noticed it, but since Ashley didn't spend much time in Maggie's office, she was busy looking around.

"How long have you known Lucas?" Emily asked and curled her legs under her on the couch.

"It feels like lifetimes," Maggie replied with a dreamy smile.

The girls exchanged surprised glances. It was hard enough to keep track of which student was dating whom, but they had never really considered the faculty having relationships.

"We're not here to discuss me," Maggie interrupted the silent conversation between Emily and Ashley. Maggie sat on the arm of the couch with her warm cup of tea while Ashley continued to look over the volumes of books on the shelves around the room. "That's a good one there," she commented as Ashley passed over a specific one. "Now . . . what sent you two to the kitchen for soul food this morning?"

"Brandon ended things with Emily," Ashley explained as she sat down with the book Maggie suggested.

Emily was grateful that Ashley spoke up first because she could feel the lump returning to her throat. She managed a shrug when Maggie reached over and squeezed her shoulder.

"I know this isn't going to help much now . . . but you already know just by being here for a few months how quickly everything can change. We ask ourselves to respect the changes in the elements, so is it too much to expect we do the same for the changes in ourselves and others?"

"Who are these people?" Ashley interrupted, tilting her head curiously as she stared at a picture in the book.

Emily was happy for the distraction and peered over at what her friend was looking at. "That's Adya, Ava, and Lydie," Emily explained.

"Huh," Ashley replied, still looking at the three women in the old photograph. "Why do they look familiar?"

"I know, I had the same reaction," Emily commented. "I don't know, and Maggie only has cryptic answers." Emily looked directly at Maggie.

Maggie refrained from responding and sipped her tea.

Emily tried to consider what Maggie was saying before Ashley interrupted her and thought back over all the ways she'd grown and changed since September. But mostly, she felt the absence of Brandon, which was an emptiness she felt deep inside. "Why does this change feel so . . . so—" Emily struggled for the right word.

"Wrong?" Maggie suggested.

"Yes, wrong," Emily agreed.

"As water affinates, you can appreciate better than many how fluid life is. Not all change is for the better, and not all change is permanent, either. But every change allows you to grow and shift." Maggie sighed softly. "To borrow from Rumi, 'Life is a balance of holding on and letting go.' The Academy is a place to help teach you how to create balance with the elements. Life is the ultimate school where you have to discover what things you need to hold onto and what things you need to let go to find *your* balance."

As Emily sat and contemplated what Maggie was saying, she narrowed in on another Rumi quote framed on Maggie's wall. She read aloud. "These pains you feel are messengers. Listen to them."

Ashley finally broke the silence as only she could. "You realize we're practically teenagers, right? Our hormones usually don't care what's logical or what will create balance."

Maggie chuckled softly and nodded. "Fair point, Ashley. Perhaps I should make sure Lucas has plenty of raspberry leaf tea for the next time you need some comfort food." She turned back and addressed Emily. "Are you feeling any better?"

Emily shrugged. "A little. I mostly feel drained and empty," she admitted. "Maybe I'll go for a walk in the garden or around the lake."

"Getting in touch with your elements is a great way to help you heal. You're going to be okay, Emily."

"Thank you again, Maggie. I don't know what I'd do without you here." Emily acknowledged internally that the woman felt more like a sister than a teacher.

"Hey, can I borrow this book?" Ashley asked, mindless to most of the conversation around her.

"Of course, you can. Please bring it back when you're done," Maggie said with a smile. As the three stood, Maggie advised, "Don't forget classes start tomorrow. Enjoy your last free day."

CHAPTER FOURTEEN

After breakfast the following morning, the students went to their new schedule of classes. Instead of breaking out by elements in the afternoon, the Abecedarians started their day grouped with their own affinities, taking their first class of elemental healing.

"I bet she's in the fire class," Emily grumbled as she and Ashley sat beside each other in their designated classroom. There were seven water affinates in the Abecedarian class: four girls and three boys. Greta led the course with Lir, the Resident Director of the boys' water elemental house.

Ashley elbowed Emily in the ribs. "Remember what Maggie said—balance," she whispered and sighed as she added, "I miss Brandon, too."

"Water is one of the most critical elements in healing," Lir began. He had a subtle Irish accent, deep blue eyes, and dark brown hair that looked like a Hollywood hairdresser had styled it right before he entered the classroom. Most of the girls at the Academy had a crush on him, but Emily hadn't paid much attention to him the first part of the school year because of Brandon. While she couldn't guess his age, he was certainly young, and perhaps a recent graduate. "Our bodies are roughly 60% water. Without water, life itself wouldn't be possible," he continued.

"He's gorgeous," Ashley whispered.

"Do you have a question, girls?" Lir asked, addressing Emily and Ashley. The problem with having such a small class was you couldn't get away with anything.

"I was just wondering if we need to be taking notes," Ashley lied while Emily's face appeared red.

"Notes are optional, but not mandatory, Ashley," Greta chimed in, narrowing her eyes at the two.

"May I continue?" the blue-eyed man asked.

Ashley and Emily nodded.

"Good. Can anyone guess what one of the first things we consider when we begin healing with water?"

"If there's a deficiency?" Xander, one of the quieter Abecedarians, volunteered.

"Yes, but more specifically, whether or not the body's water is in balance. Since men and women have different body chemistries, we're going to spend a great deal of time in this class switching between same-sex and opposite-sex partners."

There was a low murmur between the students while Greta and Lir spoke privately for a moment. "Because there is an odd number of you in here, I will step in and act as one of the partners," Lir explained to the class.

"For the first exercise," Greta began, "I want you to pair up with a same-sex partner." Emily and Ashley immediately scooted closer together.

"Xander, you will work with me," Lir said. "Everyone stand and face their partner."

The students shuffled to their feet and stood facing their chosen partner.

"Now hold your hands out in front of you, like this," Lir continued. He held his arms at rib height with his elbows bent and his palms facing opposite directions.

"No, your left palm is up and the right down." Greta walked the room, making corrections as needed.

"Now, you are going to connect your palms with your partner's." Lir and Xander demonstrated while the rest of the class mirrored them.

Emily could feel the natural vibration coming from Ashley. It was familiar since they were used to having contact with each other.

"Good. We're going to call this the baseline measurement since I hope you are all well hydrated. You can drop your hands and find a new partner of the opposite sex." When the students hesitated, Greta moved around the room and paired up the students. "Emily, come up here with me," Lir instructed.

Emily gulped but did as she was told. When she held up her hands in the starting position, she noticed they were shaking.

"Don't be nervous. I'm not as scary as I look," Lir said quietly to her with a grin, which made her feel more relaxed.

When their palms merged, the experience surprised Emily. As nervous she was, she was expecting something shocking when she touched him as it had been when she and Brandon would touch. But it turned out to be . . . ordinary.

"Do you feel how different it is?" Lir asked the class. Everyone nodded in agreement. Emily nodded to go along with the class, but it didn't feel much different if she was honest with herself.

"Everyone stay with your partner while I pass out glasses of water. When I say, drink the water and repeat the exercise," Greta said. When everyone had their water, she said, "Okay, drink."

Lir watched the class as they drank, but Emily watched him. She wondered if she was broken, like maybe somehow Brandon had shattered her ability to feel anything. I mean, she *should* feel at least butterflies while basically holding hands with one of the hottest guys she's ever seen, right?

Emily finished her water just after Lir finished his. "Ready?" he asked her.

With a short nod, she pressed her palms to his again.

"Can anyone tell me what differences you notice?" Greta asked as she paced the room, observing.

"It's heavier energy," Julius volunteered as his palms were merged with Ashley's.

"That's a great observation. Anyone else? Emily?" Lir encouraged.

"Umm," she started. "I guess heavy is how I'd describe it, too." Others in the room nodded in agreement with her.

"Fair enough. Now switch back to your original partners and feel how different it is now," Greta instructed.

Emily returned to Ashley, whose eyes were already asking what it was like to hold Lir's hands. Emily flashed her friend a look and shook her head ever so slightly, and the two completed their exercise.

The lecture about the basics of water healing continued for the remainder of the morning. At the conclusion, Greta said, "You all have an assignment to complete outside of class over the next week. Each day, I want you to do this exercise in the morning and at night with your roommate. You'll write your observations in these journals Lir is passing around. Next week, we will discuss your findings."

"Thank you," Ashley smiled as Lir handed her the journal.

"You're welcome, Ashley," he said and moved on to Emily. "I'd like you to stay after for a few minutes. Don't worry, I won't keep you long."

Ashley kicked the toe of Emily's shoe when she didn't respond right away. "Sure," Emily said and took the journal.

"Sure?" Ashley asked in astonishment after the teacher had moved on to the next group. "I swear I need to give you lessons in flirting."

"He's our *teacher*," Emily whispered in an angry voice and then sighed. "Just wait for me to get lunch. I'll catch up with you, okay? I'm not ready to walk into the dining hall alone."

Ashley nodded. "See you in a few. And don't be afraid to flirt a little. Sheesh!"

Emily walked to the front of the room to speak with Lir while Greta picked up the empty glasses around the room and took them to the kitchen. "Did I do something wrong?" Emily asked.

"Wrong? I wouldn't say that. But why did you lie when I asked you about your observation?"

Emily nervously played with her fingers as she clasped her hands in front of her. "Because I felt stupid for not feeling anything," she admitted.

"Isn't that a valid observation, too?" Lir insisted kindly. "I can't tell you I understand what it's like to have more than one affinity, but I had a theory about what might happen with you doing this exercise in class today. You see, multiple senses are activated when we do something as simple as touching someone else. It involves feeling, seeing, and even smelling. Your affinities are like senses, too, so when you touch someone, all of them are engaged. Does that make sense?" Lir asked while his eyes looked for the truth in Emily.

"Yes," she agreed.

"That means to be successful with one affinity, you might have to focus harder to temporarily shut out the others. I don't mean for you to ignore them. Hmm . . . let me think about this for a moment." Lir paced and quietly contemplated his theory while Emily watched. "Okay, let's try something. Describe this room."

Emily recalled when Ted had her do a similar exercise in his office the day she discovered her water affinity. She looked around the room before answering. "It's warm but dry. The wood floors are shiny, like they were just waxed. It's bright from the overhead lights and the sunshine coming from the windows. There are only two of us here. You're wearing a navy polo and khaki pants. I have on my uniform."

Lir nodded approvingly. "Now close your eyes and describe the room to me again."

Emily complied and closed her eyes, taking a minute before she answered. "One of the lights is buzzing," she began. "There's a breeze coming from the hallway, subtly mixing with the warm air. I can see your shadow moving and can smell an earthy, almost spicy scent in your wake. Cologne, maybe?"

"Anything else?" he asked when he touched her shoulder from the opposite side of where he had been standing when her eyes were open.

"You don't feel heavy at all," she admitted. "You feel . . . fluid, balanced." Emily opened her eyes and turned to face him. "I get it," she said. "But there's a lot of . . . noise . . . I guess you could say."

"I would like to continue to work with you in class and outside. I have a couple of different ideas on ways you can help quiet the noise," he offered. "But this is enough for today. Try to use this technique when you do your daily exercise, okay?"

Emily nodded and left with her journal to catch up with Ashley for lunch.

The two girls assumed their usual spot in the dining hall, which was thankfully not where Brandon and Myra had picked to sit. They were several tables behind Emily, so she was spared seeing the two interacting.

"Of course, they're eating together. Only goes to show I was right about them all along," Emily grumbled angrily into her panini.

An adorable laugh followed by a snort echoed in the hall—or at least that's what it sounded like to Emily—which turned into Myra's voice teasing Brandon. "I thought you were going to boil all the water away."

"Forget about them, Em. Tell me about what you and Lir did after class," Ashley said with an insinuating tone.

"You got to spend time alone with Lir?" a girl behind Ashley turned around and joined in on the conversation.

Emily was horrified and probably turned fifty shades of red, but Ashley leaned in and whispered to her, "Watch this." She turned to the girl and said, "Yeah, Emily had a *private* lesson with Lir." She added a little eyebrow wiggle, smiled, and turned back to her food.

Emily had buried her face in her hands. "I can't believe you just did that," she said with a muffled voice.

Both girls could hear the gossip spread throughout the dining hall.

"I'm going to kill you. I swear, I am." Emily was so embarrassed and a little hurt her best friend had just started a rumor about her. The truth was, and Ashley knew it, there was nothing hot or gossip-worthy about her time in or out of class with Lir.

"Nononono." She held up her hand. "Wait for it." Ashley circled her finger in the air. "And now— "

Almost on cue, a chair scraped across the floor, and a server dropped the desserts he was carrying. The entire dining hall, including Emily, turned to see what happened. What they saw was Brandon stand up and crash right into the server who dropped everything. In his scramble to help pick up, Brandon glared over at Emily with narrow, angry eyes.

Emily slowly turned back to face her food, and a small smile tugged at the corner of her mouth. "How did you know that would work?" she asked Ashley when they were both enjoying dessert.

"I just know the game, Em. They were playing it, so we joined in," Ashley said smugly. "And we won."

The only bad part of Ashley's plan was they had afternoon class with all the Abecedarians—including Brandon and Myra. Emily felt the dread in the pit of her stomach when everyone turned to look at her come in. Shortly after, though, she was getting hounded by questions from envious girls, so by the time Brandon walked in and took a seat at the back of the classroom, Emily was enjoying her mini-celebrity status, vaguely answering the twenty questions she was being asked at once.

"Really, it wasn't that big of a deal," Emily tried to explain.

"Settle down, class. We have a lot to uncover in these next few months and don't have time for all this excess chatter."

Adamina commanded the attention of her students for the remainder of the afternoon, allowing Emily some much needed time for self-reflection.

"You're not a horrible person, Em. Technically, *you* did nothing wrong. Rumors have a life of their own, and I'm sure by tomorrow, the only person who will remember any of it is Brandon." Ashley tried to comfort her friend, but somehow hurting Brandon didn't make Emily feel very good anymore. "Besides, if it stops her from doing those obnoxious giggle snorts, then everyone wins."

Emily couldn't argue with Ashley's logic. "Alright, are we ready to do this exercise for class?"

Ashley held out her hands. "Ready."

CHAPTER FIFTEEN

As January raced by and Valentine's Day loomed on the horizon, students started coupling up at an astonishing rate. Even Ashley started dating Xander within a couple of weeks of classes beginning.

Ashley's ingenious plan to make Brandon jealous ended up backfiring, though, because, by the end of the first week of classes, the two new lovebirds were walking everywhere, holding hands. Emily, unfortunately, caught them kissing each other goodbye at the start of her and Myra's bi-affinate class, so after that, she made it a point to enter the class *after* whatever teacher was in charge of them for the day.

"Is there any version of this universe where I fit in?" Emily complained to Maggie one afternoon when they were tending to the garden.

"You fit in fine here. What do you mean?"

"Where do I begin?" Emily said dramatically. "Let's see, I have one friend, and she's constantly with her new boyfriend. The only boyfriend I've *ever* had refused to kiss me when we were dating and is now publicly sucking face with the girl who can't even tell you what 2010 was like."

Maggie threw Emily a warning glance. "It's *not* okay to talk about Myra like that. Besides, I thought you two were getting along well and making good progress together."

Emily stopped pruning the rosebush to put her hands on her hips and scowl at Maggie. "If by 'progress' you mean everything is an ultra-competition with her *all the time*, or that she's constantly trying to overpower my affinities at every turn, or by coming across as the miraculous do-gooder, then yes. We're making great progress."

"Perhaps I meant Ted is telling me he's seeing tremendous growth in you and thinks it's helping *you* a lot to be working with Myra. Have you considered maybe your jealousy of Myra is skewing your perception?"

Emily returned to her bush and sighed. "Or maybe it's because I don't see myself as ever being good enough and am surrounded by constant reminders of that fact."

"You're also surrounded by constant reminders of how amazing, special, and unique you are," Maggie countered.

"Ow!" Emily shouted.

Maggie jogged over to see the large gash on Emily's first finger she received from a thorn. It stretched from her fingertip halfway down her finger to her second knuckle. "Oh, that's a bad one. Come over here. We have calendulas in the garden for just this reason." Maggie guided a cursing Emily to the yellow and orange flowering plants, which looked almost identical to marigolds. "We just need to—"

Before Maggie could instruct her on how to use the plant, Emily had already knelt down beside it. She closed her eyes while she manipulated the flower's healing capacity to work on her cut. Maggie looked on with awe. "Case and point," Maggie said as Emily stood with a healed finger. "You've had zero earth elemental healing classes, yet you just healed yourself."

"I don't know how I knew how to do that," Emily admitted.

"Hold on a second. Let me record this," Maggie said teasingly and pretended to write in an imaginary book. "Emily amazed herself and realized she's good enough."

"You're hilarious. Maybe you should teach comedy classes instead of earth elemental studies." Emily dramatically rolled her eyes, but then genuinely smiled at Maggie. "Thank you."

The start of February marked the beginning of the commercialization of love, even on the campus of North Shore Academy. The sixth-year earth elemental students were trying to raise money for an expansion of the garden, so they decided to sell roses for Valentine's Day. The flowers were to be delivered with a note (or as anonymous) on the fourteenth.

Emily hated seeing all the signs posted on the campus, feeling worse and worse about her singleness with each happy poster. "At least there isn't a dance scheduled," she commented to Ashley. They passed a sixth sign on the way from their dorm to the water elemental classroom on the Tuesday before Valentine's Day.

"I heard some students were going to try to throw an unofficial dance on Thursday anyway," Ashley buzzed.

She was happy for her friend finding a guy who treated her well. Still, it stung a little that the closest thing she got to affection from the opposite sex was her extra tutoring lessons with Lir. Not that she would ever complain about spending time with her hot teacher, but there was nothing remotely romantic about their relationship. He was fun, insightful, and Emily felt very comfortable in his presence. "I'll be sure to officially miss that unofficial dance if it happens."

"You're so dramatic," Ashley teased. "Besides, everyone knows the best place to meet available guys is at weddings and at Valentine's Day dances."

"I think you're making that second one up," Emily said suspiciously. "I'm okay, really. I just don't need to be reminded of how lacking I am in love every ten feet." Emily pointed out the seventh sign for roses hanging outside their classroom door.

As the girls took their seats, Lir came over to them. "Emily, Ted needs to see you in his office after class today." Lir looked unusually solemn as he gave her the message.

"Okay . . . do you want to meet later for our lesson?" Emily inquired.

Lir nodded as he turned his attention to the class and began his lecture on water memory.

"I don't think another is wise," Ted explained to the person on the other end of the phone line. Emily wasn't eavesdropping, but the hallway leading to his office was long and empty. Apparently, his door wasn't all the way shut.

"Yes, she is showing significant progress, but it's still too soon to know for sure." His tone was pleading as Emily knocked lightly on the wooden door to get his attention. "Look, I have to go now. Stall the Council's vote until I have a chance to get there and make my case in person." He paused. "Yes, I'll talk to you soon."

Ted hung up the receiver and stood to meet Emily at the door. Usually, he just motioned for her to come in. "What's wrong?" she immediately asked.

There wasn't even a play at making light of whatever Ted had called her into the office to discuss. "We should go for a walk," he suggested.

"If this is about the posters that were allegedly ripped down, I promise it wasn't me," Emily said defensively.

"This isn't about posters or anything you did or didn't do. Humor me, for once, and walk."

The two walked silently outside, Emily continuously looking over at Ted with a worried expression.

"Can you feel how close I am to doing something we both don't want?" Emily didn't mean it as a threat, but she could feel something inside her that wasn't going to result in flowers blooming or ice cubes forming.

"I received a phone call this morning," Ted began. "From your father."

Emily's hand balled into a fist, but Ted grabbed her wrist.

"I need you to breathe and calm yourself." Ted motioned to the building, and within a moment, Maggie had joined them.

Emily felt Maggie's hand wrap around hers and her meditative words whispered into Emily's ear.

"Emily, your father called. Your mother had a stroke." Ted knew if he paused for too long, he might lose whatever control they'd helped Emily regain. "She's in the hospital, and I'm taking you to see her today," he explained.

Emily's face lost all color, and she leaned on the two adults as they half-carried her to a nearby bench.

"I just saw her. She was fine. This is a mistake. She's going to be alright." Emily's skin was ice cold, and she was rocking as she sat there. "She can't die. I can't lose her. I won't. I can take her some herbs and heal her. I can balance her body. I can—"

"Please go get Rai, Lir, Adamina, and Gaia quickly. They should all be in their classes right now," Ted instructed Maggie and sat with Emily to help as he could.

Lir and Gaia showed up first, followed shortly by Rai and Adamina. Ted lifted Emily in his arms while the four teachers stood around them in a circle and chanted softly.

Elements we ask of you
Bring Emily balance through and through
Enrich your child in this time of strife
And be a source of strength in her life.

The color slowly returned to Emily's skin, and Ted gently returned her to the bench. The six adults stood around to make sure Emily remained in balance. After several minutes, Ted gave the nod, and each teacher took their turn with Emily.

"The fire will light your way and keep you warm," Adamina began.

"The earth will keep you grounded when it feels like you're falling," Gaia added.

Lir stepped up to Emily and rested their palms together as they'd been practicing in class. "The water will carry you gently down the path."

Finally, Rai leaned in and whispered, "The air will keep you standing and will surround you with happy memories."

Shortly thereafter, the four teachers returned to their classes while Maggie and Ted sat with Emily.

"The elements will give you the strength to get through this, but you have to trust in them," Maggie encouraged. "I'll be here when you return." She kissed Emily's temple.

"When are we leaving?" Emily finally managed to say.

"Go pack a couple of things. The helicopter will arrive shortly," Ted explained. "I have a few things I need from my office. Maggie? Will you stay with Emily?"

"Of course. Come on, Emily," Maggie said kindly and helped Emily stand.

Maggie did most of the packing while Emily watched in a daze. "I don't understand. She was fine at Christmas. Why can't I heal her?" She pleaded with her eyes to Maggie.

After a deep breath, Maggie stopped packing for Emily and sat beside her. "You can heal what is out of balance. You cannot stop a soul from releasing from the body. If it's her time—"

Emily nodded in understanding and stood to grab a few more things. "Can you tell Ashley?" She managed a small smile. "I'm ready."

The two walked out and met Ted on the field where the spontaneous football game was played months prior. While the students were kept safely inside for the arrival of the helicopter,

Emily could see faces looking through the windows, watching her and Ted climb on board.

Given another set of circumstances, this would be a dream for Emily to ride in a helicopter. But in her current state, while she was calm, she was also tired and fell asleep for the ride.

Emily felt the dread in her chest as the doors to the elevator opened to let her out on the ICU ward. Machines up and down the halls beeped, there was a sterile smell to the air, and nurses rushed past her. She paused outside her mom's room and slowed her breath and heart rate before stepping in.

Her mom was lying flat on her back, IV tubes connected to both arms, and a heart monitor quietly keeping track of her mom's remaining beats. Emily's father was in the chair beside her, eyes fixed on the TV, which was airing a muted basketball game.

"Hi," she said softly as she stepped closer.

"She's not able to speak anymore, the doctors said," her dad said distantly.

"Oh," Emily replied and sat on the bed beside her mom. She took her mom's hand in her left hand while she brushed a lock of hair out of her mom's face. "Do they think she'll recover?" Emily asked quietly, her eyes studying her mom.

"C'mon!" her dad shouted at the game. Emily shook as she was startled by his outburst and swore her mother's heartbeat picked up a little.

"Dad!" Emily demanded. "Is she going to recover?"

"Is that how you speak to me?" Her dad growled and stood up. "I'm going down the hall to the waiting room where there's actual sound on the TV."

Despite her dad's lack of an answer, Emily knew already. When she was sure they were alone, Emily leaned down and rested her head against her mother's chest. "I love you, Mom. You didn't deserve the life you had, and I'm sorry for all the difficult moments I caused." Silent tears streamed down Emily's face, but somehow, they gave her strength. "I wanted to heal you, but I can't. I just want to be with you now and let you know you mattered."

Emily's mom opened her eyes and pointed to the pen and paper on the side table. Once Emily figured out what she wanted, she placed them both in her mom's hand. With effort, her mother managed to write a few shaky words. The words *I know* and *my eyes* were scribbled on the paper.

"I don't understand, Mom. What do you mean?" Emily pleaded.

Her mom tapped the pen on the paper over the words *my eyes*.

Emily didn't understand, but taking a guess, she leaned forward and gazed into her mom's eyes. They looked tired. And then she saw past her mom's eyes to something deeper. She saw her mom's memories of teaching Emily to tend their garden and felt her mother knew it was important to her. Emily wondered if it was her own memories surfacing or her mother's. In those final few moments staring in her dying mother's eyes, Emily witnessed lifetimes, but it wasn't her mom's life or any life that Emily recognized . . . and then it was quiet, like the light illuminating the unseen knowledge was simply turned off.

"Mom, no," Emily pleaded, but she knew her mother couldn't hear her anymore. She closed her mother's eyelids, kissed her forehead, and whispered, "Thank you," before folding her mother's note and leaving the room.

Emily wasn't terrified or angry; she was determined. Something inside her sparked to life with her mother's death. She realized that with her last bit of energy, Emily's mom had given her soul a gift, and it awoke something fierce inside Emily.

While nurses and doctors hurried down the hall to attend to her mom and the beeping machine in her room, Emily rushed past them and hit the elevator button.

"Where do you think you're going?" Emily's father barked from the orange vinyl chair in the waiting room.

"Mom's gone. I'm leaving," she said plainly to the man who still couldn't pry his eyes away from the insignificant game on TV.

"Like hell you are," he said, finally rising from his seat. Few things could motivate her father like the opportunity to exert dominance over Emily or her mother. With her mother gone, that meant Emily would be the target of his full force.

Emily wasn't going to stand around to be forced to bend to his will. The elevator was taking too long, so she pushed open the stairwell door and descended the stairs. She could feel the air around her carrying her, each step grounding her energy, and the tears on her cheeks, strengthening her.

Outside, it was a chilly night. There was old blackened snow pushed to the edges of the parking lot. Ted was on his cell phone outside the entrance when Emily exited the building and grabbed his arm, pulling him toward the car that had brought them from the airport to the hospital.

"I should be there by tomorrow at the latest. I'll call you when I have an ETA."

Ted barely managed to get out the last sentence before Emily grabbed the phone from him and hung it up. "Did you know about this?" Emily demanded and thrust her mom's note at him.

He read it and handed it back to Emily. "What did you see?" Ted asked calmly.

"No, we're not doing that right now. Did. You. Know?"

"Yes," he said simply. "It's not something you can tell someone," he continued. "You have to allow the knowledge to be awakened in you."

Emily showed she accepted his answer by answering his question. "I saw many confusing things in her eyes, or maybe I saw them within myself. I don't know, but I saw myself in my mother's womb. There was another with me, a brother. He died and became a part of me."

Ted nodded. "His soul, yes. It's the reason you have three affinities." Ted learned about this when he had Emily's mother's medical records pulled after Emily's sudden emergence of the air affinity.

Emily's brows furrowed. She still did not know her entire truth. "My mom showed me she knew, too. She could see him in me, and she could see my special connection to the earth. I bet my father took that away from her," she spat angrily.

"That's not how it works. No one has the power to take something from you unless you are willing to give it up." Ted paused for a moment, considering something, and then continued. "When we return to the Academy, I think you should have a conversation with Maggie," he explained.

Emily was confused but nodded. "I feel like there's so much more inside me that I don't know and don't understand. It's like I've opened my eyes for the first time, but don't know how to see yet."

Ted could hear the change happening within her just by how she was talking. He knew she'd entered the Awakening. "It will take time, just as it takes time to understand your affinities. Can I ask something of you?" Ted implored.

"Let me guess . . . don't tell anyone?" Emily said curtly, sounding again like her twelve-year-old self.

"I thought that one was obvious," he replied with a smirk. "Yes, but can you be patient with yourself? Being fully Awakened to your truth will take time. I promise you it will come."

Emily gazed out the window to the city lights that glittered below the helicopter.

"We have to make a stop before we return to the Academy," Ted explained as they flew toward a destination unknown to Emily.

"Stop the Council from doing something?" Emily asked casually. In response to Ted's surprised look, she added, "I may not understand everything, but I do have ears."

Ted nodded. "I wish this was a social call, and I could introduce you, but that will have to wait for another time."

The flight to their new location took about four hours. Emily hadn't expected to be *at* the destination when they landed, but the helicopter landed in a grassy area off to the side of the main house. Both she and Ted got off. The moon was just a sliver in the sky, which made it difficult for Emily to see the details of where they landed, but she could feel the elements all around.

"Where are we?" she asked as they walked toward a house.

"This is Elder Tama's estate on St. John's Island," Ted explained.

"We're on an island?" Emily questioned as they walked by an oak tree. Her idea of an island was tropical plants, sand, and an ocean nearby, which were all obviously lacking in their current locale.

Ted smiled with amusement. "Yes, and you're free to explore the property while I meet with the Elders. Like I explained earlier, this isn't going to be a good time for introductions." Ted seemed more determined than usual. His tone lacked the relaxed cadence Emily associated with him, and she quickened her steps to keep up with his pace.

The two parted in the courtyard in front of the primary residence. "Try to stay nearby," Ted advised before entering the house.

Emily glanced through a window without moving closer to the house—she was curious, not creepy—but she couldn't make out any significant features of the seven adults who greeted Ted as he entered. She scanned the dark landscape and could see another smaller house a little way ahead with a lit swimming pool in front of it, providing minimal visibility. As she walked by the pool, she crouched down and touched the water, which was surprisingly warm. She giggled, a sound remarkably out of place with her mourning her mother, as she imagined the adults inside throwing a pool party.

Facing the back of the smaller house as she walked around the pool, she could feel a larger body of water off to her left, which somehow felt freer than the water in the pool. Emily felt that up until that night, she'd been warm, safe, and protected, like the water in the pool. Now she felt akin to the larger water, both more natural and mysterious.

As she reached the back entrance to the smaller house which faced the pool, she put her face up to the glass panes on the door and looked inside. It was unoccupied, so Emily tested the door to see if it was unlocked. To her surprise, it was—Emily's dad would never have allowed an external door to remain unlocked—and she invited herself in. Immediately, she was overwhelmed by the smell of old things, like a museum except not as stuffy and definitely dustier. While she couldn't locate a light switch, she managed to feel out a candle, which she lit with a box of matches that was next to it.

Emily walked with cautious curiosity as she explored the house with her little candle illuminating tiny sections at a time. Between the three bedrooms, study, and living room, there were enough volumes of books to fill the library at her old school. Not the Academy library, of course—that was *much* larger than the house she was exploring. The unhung portraits seemed to watch Emily as she investigated the numerous antique relics in the living room. A draft from the fireplace swirled around Emily as she passed by, causing her an unexpected chill. She looked between the fireplace and her candle, shrugged, and attempted to light it.

Several minutes, half the box of matches, and one singed finger later, a gentle fire was adding heat and ambiance to the room. Emily grabbed a book from the fireplace mantle and curled up on the nearby couch while the fire crackled softly. She carefully opened the brittle pages of the book she'd chosen and released a giant yawn. It had been an emotional, mentally challenging, and in general, very long day. The nearby clock chimed twice, and Emily realized it was less than twenty-four hours away from the dreaded Valentine's Day. This small house felt like a good place to mourn the loss of her mother and her first love. She hoped the meeting would last long enough to do that. Trying to put those thoughts aside, she rested her head on the arm of the couch and began reading.

October 5, 1810
I visited the tree this morning, but Justus didn't come. I know he is busy upholding the pretense of this life he's living with his new wife, but it makes my soul ache to not get to share these days with him. There is little comfort to be found in our initials carved into the tree, and I know I will eventually need to help the tree heal . . . as soon as my heart has.

December 23, 1810
Justus swore on the elements that he would join me to celebrate the solstice. I waited for him beneath the tree that is now known as Angel Oak until this morning's sun rose. Not even my fire could warm my soul as it appears that the façade I believed Justus to be putting up has become his reality now. A poor soul enslaved to work on his plantation joined my solstice observance briefly and told me his Master was preparing for a joyous Christmas celebration with the governor. I will endeavor to carry forward in this life without the part of my soul that is his.

Emily sighed and rested the journal against her chest. With the fire crackling softly beside her and the diary of a woman who had to accept a love lost, she couldn't help but let her tired thoughts drift to Brandon. It was among those thoughts that Emily finally succumbed to sleep.

Emily awoke to bright sunshine on her face and a blanket covering her up. The fire had long burned out, and the journal that had lulled her to sleep with reminders of unrequited love had been returned to the mantel. On the coffee table was a teapot along with an empty mug that held a fresh bag of herbs. After stretching, she poured the hot liquid into the cup and walked to look at the view from the front of the house she'd explored the previous night. A path led from the front porch down to a wooden dock built over the water's edge. Sitting in one of the two chairs on the dock was a woman gazing out at the scenery.

"I hope the water is still hot," the woman said without looking back as Emily approached.

"It's the perfect temperature," Emily replied as she admired the lake. In the back of her mind, she was still expecting it to be the ocean since they were on an island.

"Please join me," the woman said and invited Emily to sit in the empty chair.

"Is Ted around?" Emily asked as she tucked a leg beneath her and sat.

"I'm sure he's still arguing with the others. I grew tired of the bickering hours ago and came out here to recharge."

"So, you're an Elder?" Emily realized as soon as she asked it that it was a stupid question. She was likely the only one there who *wasn't* an Elder . . . besides Ted.

"I'm Tama," the woman said and finally looked over at Emily.

Emily studied Tama's face, and one of the first things she noticed was the sadness in her eyes. It reminded her of the photograph of Ava. However, Tama looked at least a decade older than Ava appeared in the photo. Tama's gray-streaked hair was pulled back into a bun, and her face was graced with age lines that suited her and made her look wise, Emily thought. "I'm Emily," she said politely.

"Yes, I know. I have a slight advantage over you, I suppose since I knew you were coming with Ted. Did you enjoy reading the journal last night?" the Elder inquired.

"It was sad," Emily admitted. "I hope it's okay that I was reading it. I needed to get my mind off other things."

"Your mother," Tama interjected with a nod. "It's a truth of life that is unavoidable."

Emily thought it was an odd thing for this woman to say, but she nodded dutifully. "I'm grateful I got to say goodbye, at least."

The two sat quietly for several minutes, sipping their tea and looking out over the lake. Tama finally interrupted the silence. "I understand you have three affinities now. Are you having any difficulties balancing them within yourself?" She set down her tea and turned her full attention to Emily.

This wasn't a question intended as small talk, Emily realized, but the woman had an agenda in her questioning. "It isn't easy," Emily admitted. "I see others with one affinity master lessons with ease while it takes me time to figure things out. Lir, my water elemental healing teacher, explained that my affinities are like senses. And the same way you can hone in on a single sound in a loud room or taste different ingredients individually in a dish, I can tune into the affinity I need to use. I'm still working on it, but I seem to be getting better."

Tama smiled softly. "That's an excellent way of looking at it. Do you see Myra struggling like you are?"

Emily paused and bit the inside of her cheek. Tama had no way of knowing what a sore subject Myra was for her, nor did Emily know how to answer the question in a way that she didn't come across as a jealous child. "Well," she began slowly, "Myra seems driven to master her affinities and to be strong. It's different for me, though. I'm more aware of the need for balance than she seems to be." Emily was proud of how unemotionally she explained that.

"Do you think there's a danger with her seeking power instead of balance?" Tama probed.

"We learn at the Academy that we have our affinities to balance the elements. I don't know if there's a danger in how Myra is acting, but for me, I know that when I allow one element within me to take over the others, I am out of balance, and bad things happen."

"Like your seizure?" Tama guessed.

"Yes. I know that Ted and Maggie and all my teachers, really, keep a close eye on me to make sure that doesn't happen again. But when it comes down to it, I'm responsible for my own balance and whatever part I have to play in balancing the elements externally."

"Are you scared?" Tama continued.

Emily had to pause to consider her answer. "I don't let fear dictate how I interact with the elements if that's what you're asking. But there are a lot of things that still scare me in this world."

"You are very well-spoken, Emily. I could tell without being told that you have indeed begun the Awakening. You see, I have an adopted granddaughter your age. I can't have a conversation with her without a minimum of ten eye rolls." Tama smiled and patted Emily's hand. "I'm glad to have had this opportunity to speak with you. Breakfast is available in the main house if you're hungry. I'm sure we'll talk again sometime." The woman stood and walked back up toward the main residence.

Emily sat and stared out at the water again. She wondered why Tama asked her questions about Myra. And she also wondered how she managed to come up with the insights she had to explain their differences. Regardless of whether Myra was dating Brandon, Emily knew she didn't want to be like her beautiful classmate anymore.

"Nice morning, isn't it?" Ted walked up behind her and sat in the seat Tama had recently vacated. "I passed Tama, and she mentioned you were down here. I'm sorry you were left alone all night."

Ted looked exhausted, and she wondered if he'd slept at all. "It's fine. I'm an only child. You get used to wandering off and amusing yourself when you're surrounded by adults all the time. I'm actually very comfortable and wouldn't mind spending more time here," she admitted.

"I wish we could, but I have duties at the Academy, and you have classes," Ted said. A little bit of his exhaustion seeped into his words. He stifled a yawn, but it was clear Ted needed to recharge.

Emily nodded sadly. "Yeah," she said. "Do you think I have a little time to explore some more? I'd like to take a walk in the trees before we leave."

"Of course. The Elders are eating breakfast and having another discussion before voting. There's nothing left for me to do except wait for their decision. It will probably be a few hours before we head back to North Shore."

"What are they deciding?" Emily asked.

Ted thought about it and then decided to share it with Emily. "As the world changes and grows, we are given more opportunities because of advancing technology. Basically, they are deciding whether or not we can be true to the elements and maintain balance if we pursue certain avenues that have opened up to us through technology."

Emily's features twisted in confusion. "It sounds complicated. In this one situation, I may have preferred one of your non-answers."

Both chuckled before Ted stood and returned to the meeting. Emily was granted a few more hours to acquaint herself with the elements around Tama's estate.

CHAPTER SIXTEEN

E ven though it was night when they returned to North Shore Academy and it wouldn't be until morning when she'd have to interact with others at school, Emily was still struggling with a sense of dread in her stomach. The entire school was aware Ted whisked her away the day before, and there were probably many theories about why. Not only did she have to deal with that attention, but it would also be Valentine's Day. While she wasn't jealous of Myra anymore after her conversation with Tama, she did miss Brandon. His friendship alone was such a big part of her life for months. Between her mom's death, the beginning of her Awakening, and reading the journal at Tama's, she felt a deep ache because of his absence in her life.

"How'd the vote go?" Emily asked as the helicopter circled around the landing spot.

"The majority of the Elders agreed with me, for the time being. It seems that whatever you and Tama discussed gave them a perspective that they hadn't considered. I'm glad you were there," Ted said with a tired smile.

Emily's mind quickly went over the conversation she had with Tama. "Was the vote about Myra and me? Do they want to kick me out of the Academy?" she asked.

Ted shook his head with a chuckle. "You aren't being threatened with expulsion, Emily. Just this once, please simply accept my gratitude for your help and don't overthink it. Yes, I can practically smell that brain of yours in overdrive. But please know you are exactly where you're supposed to be."

The travel companions parted after stepping out of the helicopter. Ted walked toward his office while Emily meandered around the nearly-empty campus for a while. It felt good to stretch her legs and appreciate the elements unique to the Academy. Emily knew Ted was right; this was where she belonged.

Emily passed by a girl taking down one of the posters for Valentine's Day roses. "Did you guys give up on selling flowers?" Emily inquired.

"Not exactly. We ran out," the girl admitted. "It's great news for our planned garden expansion, but we're going to be so busy delivering flowers tomorrow. Thankfully, Gaia told us we could do it during classes."

"Congrats, I guess," Emily said with a shrug and continued walking.

Outside was peaceful and quiet, a stark contrast to what Emily found inside her residence hall. The common room was crowded and loud, with girls buzzing about Valentine's Day. Emily *almost* slipped by without being noticed, but then Ashley yelled from across the room, and every eye turned to her. Emily wiggled her fingers in greeting and then was rushed by her water elemental family, receiving hugs and condolences from them all.

"I'm so sorry," several girls said.

"I lost my grandma last year," another chimed in.

"My dog died over Christmas break," a fourth-year student said with a sniffle.

"Alright, ladies," Greta intervened. "Your sentiments are very sweet, but let's allow Emily to breathe a little."

"Thank you," Emily said to everyone. "I'm just a little tired and really want a shower and to relax in my bed."

There was a chorus of "definitely" and "of course" as the girls parted and made a path for Emily to exit down the hall.

Emily could hear girls laughing and talking in the common room when she exited the shower but was able to slip unnoticed into her room. While nothing had physically changed since she was last there two days prior, a part of her felt like everything changed.

Ashley slipped quietly into the room and gave her friend a long hug.

"I guess everyone knows about my mom," Emily said as her roommate walked to her bed with her.

Ashley nodded while the two girls sat. "With the way you left—which was really cool, by the way, flying away in that helicopter—they told everyone the truth, so you weren't bothered with people talking about you when you returned." Ashley shrugged. "Did you get to see her, I mean, before she . . . you know."

"Died?" Emily asserted. "It's okay to say it. Yes, I saw her, but she couldn't speak." Emily considered showing Ashley the note her mother wrote but then decided to keep that to herself for now. "It was almost like she was holding on just so I could tell her goodbye."

"That's very sweet and sad," Ashley admitted and squeezed her friend's hand. "How's your dad doing?"

Emily scoffed immediately. "He cared more about some stupid basketball game on TV than he did about his wife dying or me being there. I'm sure his church is helping him out, but I won't go back there again."

"Ever?" Ashley asked in surprise.

"I don't care about my things. My old friends ditched me. And my dad hates me. So no, I don't see myself ever going back. I'll talk to Ted as the school year ends. Maybe they'll let me stay here and work over the summer or something. Or maybe I'll ask Elder Tama if I can stay in the spare house on her property." From there, Emily launched into telling Ashley all about the beautiful estate, the conversation she'd had with Tama, and the journal.

"Wow," Ashley replied in astonishment. "Whose journal was it?"

Emily shrugged. "I never found out. But I did realize something while I was there."

Ashley tilted her head in curiosity.

"I miss Brandon," she admitted. "Not being his girlfriend, but I miss my friendship with him."

"Are you going to tell him?" Ashley asked.

"I thought maybe I'd buy one of those roses and send it with a note, but they were taking down the posters when I arrived. The girl said they sold out, so I'll have to think of something else." Emily shrugged. "Did you get one for Xander?"

Ashley's eyes sparked back to life after the solemn conversation they'd been having. She spent most of the rest of the evening gushing about her relationship and catching Emily up on random gossip from when she was gone.

Emily could definitely tell that life at the Academy had gone on in her absence. The dining room at breakfast was filled with excited energy and more coupled people. With Emily's blessing, Ashley ate breakfast with Xander at their usual spot. Emily sat at the end of a table near the window, appreciating her own peaceful solitude. *Maybe today won't be too bad*, she thought while finishing her omelet.

Her mood soured slightly in healing class when the rose deliveries began trickling in. It appeared that Greta and Lir shared her frustrations because their lesson kept getting interrupted.

"We're going to spend the rest of the class silently reviewing the research on water memory," Lir explained after the fifth interruption of his demonstration.

Emily glanced over to Ashley, who was huddled with Xander, likely thanking him for the two roses she received. The two other girls in the class were giggling about something while the boys mock-sword fought with the rose that each had received. Even Greta and Lir received roses, presumably from admiring students. Emily wished she was back at Tama's estate.

On the upside, the information about water memory was really fascinating. It was a new concept to the school, and they would get to be the first ones to test out Lir's theory on manipulating the water memory to promote healing and balance.

"Feeling up to working with me for a bit?" Lir came over to Emily and crouched down next to her without her realizing it.

Emily shrugged. "Sure," she said and looked around the classroom. Usually, their tutoring took place outside of class. While she was completely comfortable working with Lir, she felt a little awkward with having onlookers.

Lir seemed to sense her hesitation. "Why don't we go down to the lake to work until lunch?"

Emily nodded and gathered her things. "Okay."

"How are you feeling?" Lir asked as they walked together toward the lake.

"I'm okay, I guess," Emily replied automatically. "It still feels a little surreal," she admitted.

"I understand completely. Two years ago, my oldest brother died by suicide," he said as the two walked out onto the wooden dock at the lake. "It was my last year here. We had plans to go to Ireland over the summer. Despite already having experienced the Awakening, it was difficult for me to accept."

Emily felt the tears form in her eyes, and at that moment, realized she hadn't yet cried about her mom's death. "I'm so sorry," she said as a tear fell down her cheek.

Lir offered a small smile. "It's funny how we as a species feel the need to apologize for a pain which isn't tied to actions that we have any control over, but yet we have to make huge efforts to apologize for things we did to cause someone else's suffering." He tossed a small rock from the dock into the water. "It's just like throwing a pebble into a large body of water. The ripples near the drop point are dramatic and contain a lot of energy. As the ripples fan out and the energy dissipates, the water becomes less connected to and less affected by the disturbance. I think people act in very similar ways. It's difficult to feel things correctly and react appropriately when you're so connected to the situation."

"Wow," Emily said in awe. "I've never thought about it like that before, but you're right."

"I spend a great deal of time theorizing. Water is the center of my being. It's a part of me more than just the percentage that's physically in me. The way I honor and bring balance to my element is through understanding it and bringing that knowledge to others." Lir spoke very humbly.

"Can I ask you a question?" Emily said while nodding to affirm that she had been listening to everything Lir was explaining.

"Fire away," he joked. "Wait, it doesn't involve actual fire, does it? You didn't discover you have a fourth affinity while you were gone, did you?"

Emily giggled. It felt almost unnatural for her to be both crying and laughing at the same time. "No, no. Of course not. I did get burned by fire at Elder Tama's house, but that's a boring, unimportant story. What I wanted to know is what the Awakening is like. I mean, when I looked into my mom's eyes, something inside me came to life. I have these distant memories that I can't quite see, like trying to remember a dream once you woke up. People keep telling me they see the change in me, but I really just feel like myself, only a little more confused."

Lir chuckled. "You saw your mom's soul just before she died. Our souls," he explained while motioning between the two of them, "have existed for lifetimes. What you felt, and what you feel is a little bit of awareness of everything your soul has experienced." Lir paused for a moment. "I probably shouldn't tell you any of this. Ted is much better at giving vague answers."

"No, you're a great teacher, Lir. These bits and pieces of internal and external information are what I need to figure out who I am. I honestly don't know how everyone goes around with partial knowledge and seems perfectly okay with it. I crave to know. I want to know this person everyone expects me to be."

"You are braver than you believe, stronger than you seem, and smarter than you think." Lir leaned to the side to nudge Emily.

"Did you just quote Winnie the Pooh to me?" she said with a giggle and nudged him back.

"And what if I did?" Lir teased. "That little bear and his friends have it all figured out."

"Oh? How's that?" Emily asked.

"For example, a quote which helped me a lot when I was an Abecedarian was 'Rivers know this: there is no hurry. We shall get there someday.' Maybe you should write that one down and remember it when you start to get frustrated at not having all the answers," Lir teased her. "The river knows."

Emily giggled. "You are as funny as you are smart and cute," she accidentally blurted out.

Lir raised a brow at Emily, shook his head, and laughed. "I don't think I've met a student brave enough to say that to me. See? Pooh knows. You *are* braver than you believe."

It was nice that Lir didn't make a big deal about Emily's slip up, but it didn't stop her from blushing. "I didn't mean it like that," she tried to explain.

"No? How did you mean it then?" Lir brought his hand to his chin in a thoughtful pose.

"Now you're just torturing me. As if you didn't know by all the roses you got today that practically every girl at the Academy has a crush on you." Emily rolled her eyes.

"Did you send me a rose?" Lir continued to tease.

"Nope," she replied plainly while folding her arms across her chest. "Didn't even cross my mind."

"Wow. Inflating and then deflating my ego in under a minute." Lir shook his head in mock sadness.

"I'm sure you'll recover almost as quickly."

"You're probably right," he admitted. "So, who *did* you send a rose to?"

Emily shook her head and looked down at her hands. "No one. And no one sent one to me, either," she said confidently.

Lir looked her over suspiciously. "If you had to send one to someone, who would it have been?"

Emily crinkled her nose. "If I say you, will you drop these questions?"

"If you had said it was me, I'd know you were lying. Although . . . you *did* admit you think I'm cute."

Emily rolled her eyes again. "You're not going to let me forget that, are you?"

Lir shook his head. "No, but you're dodging the question."

"What happened to being like a river?"

"Touché. Now answer."

Emily huffed. "Fine. I *should* have sent one to Brandon. But not because of love or romance or whatever we're supposed to be celebrating today. I just . . . I miss his friendship."

Lir nodded. "Do you think he misses yours?"

"Probably not. He's pretty involved with Myra." Emily shrugged and was glad she didn't get to send one to him. It probably would've only made their non-friendship even more awkward than it already was.

"What happened that you're not friends anymore?"

Emily couldn't see where Lir was going with these questions but answered anyway. "He unintentionally—apparently—said something that offended me. I got mad, and that's how things ended."

Lir nodded thoughtfully. "So, you're telling me you're basically a ripple of water that's too close to the disturbance. I see."

Emily sighed. "I get your point. This is something I directly affected, and I need to apologize, right?"

Lir shrugged. "You have to make that choice for yourself. But from where I'm sitting, saying I'm sorry is better suited for this situation than it is for apologizing to someone who lost a loved one." He stood up and looked down at Emily. "It's time for lunch. This was a very enlightening lesson, Emily. Thank you for opening up to me."

Emily gazed up at her teacher. "You're less cute when you're right about things I don't want you to be right about." She smiled and added, "Thank you for the lesson."

With Ashley spending the day with her guy, Emily decided to skip lunch and visit with Maggie. She needed to thank her for helping her pack, but also kept in the back of her mind that Ted told her to have a conversation about "choices" with Maggie.

Emily found Maggie in the garden picking herbs. "Hello," she said.

Maggie stood immediately and embraced Emily in a hug. "It's good to have you back. How are you feeling?" She noted that Maggie didn't apologize for Emily's mother's death.

"I'm a little sad, a little relieved, a lot grateful, and . . . umm . . . yeah, I think that about covers it."

Maggie smiled. "That sounds exhausting. Come and sit with me. We'll talk and snack on the apples I brought out here with me."

Emily didn't know where she should start, so she did what came naturally to her and began with a question. "Ted urged me to talk with you when we got back. So, what can you tell me about choices?"

Maggie's face screwed up in confusion. "That's a broad topic. Care to fill me in on the conversation that led you here?"

Emily explained about the hospital, her asshole of a father, and her mother's condition when she arrived. "She wrote this to me."

Maggie looked at the note Emily's mom wrote and nodded. "You saw something in your mom, didn't you?"

After briefly explaining the confusing memories, Emily continued the story. "I thought maybe my mom had a gift like me, and my dad forced her to deny it. That's when Ted told me it's not how affinities work, and I should talk to you about choices."

Maggie set down her apple and pressed her hands together in her lap. "Do you remember asking me why I can't manipulate an element?"

Emily nodded.

"It hasn't always been this way," Maggie began. "When I was little, I knew there was something different about me. I would spend hours walking through the fields at my house while my sisters and friends would be inside playing with dolls or coming up with new dances to perform. Being inside and interacting with artificially made things upset me. My parents thought there was something wrong with me when I ignored the puppy they bought and sat in the garden talking to the flowers instead. So, they took me to see many doctors. I was too little to understand the various diagnoses. Nothing any of the doctors did or said helped, though. When I was ten, I discovered I could make the rose bushes that bordered our house bloom by interacting with them. I was so excited and showed my sisters."

"How did they handle it?" Emily asked.

"Not well. They told my dad, and I willingly showed him what I could do. Needless to say, he was horrified, afraid I was a witch or had the devil inside me. He declared that I needed to be baptized. I was a child who grew up in a religious house. My sisters were all baptized, so I didn't think much of it. I went to the classes at the church, and one Sunday, it was time for me to accept Jesus into my life, which I did dutifully and willingly as they poured blessed water over my head." Maggie paused for a moment and stared into the garden.

Emily thought she saw tears building in Maggie's eyes and placed a hand over Maggie's in silent consolation.

Maggie's breath was shaky as she breathed in and continued. "When I got home that afternoon, I changed into my play clothes and went outside to enjoy the roses. But when I tried to make them bloom, nothing happened. I tried for weeks to affect them again, but no matter how hard I concentrated, no matter what I said or did, I couldn't make them bloom again."

Emily gazed around the gardens Maggie took care of. They were flawless and beautiful.

"I became enraged. Finally, when I was fourteen, I ran away from home. My parents had the authorities bring me back the first ten times, but either they grew tired of chasing me down, or they just stopped caring—I don't know. By sixteen, I was living on my own. I slept in parks, in forests, in open fields . . . it didn't matter as long as I was outside. I stole food from convenience stores and from dumpsters outside of restaurants as I wandered from place to place. I walked and hitchhiked from Oregon to New Orleans in my travels, and that's where I met Lucas." Maggie paused, and the smile returned to her features. "He was like me in many ways and understood losing touch with his element. Unlike me, though, he filled the gap left in him by working with food in normal ways, although I will always believe his talent with food is anything *but* normal. I found myself spending so much time with him in the kitchen where he was employed that they actually thought I worked there, too. It was so different than being outside, but I came to understand that earth is everywhere."

At the mention of Lucas, Emily was dying to ask more. She was practically shaking with enthusiasm about this element of Maggie's story.

Maggie was aware of Emily's curiosity, so she added, "Yes, Lucas and I were very close and dated. That seems like another life, though." She trailed off, then continued. "Darius approached Lucas after work when he and I were walking down the street. I don't think you've met Darius. Anyway, he's very intuitive about people and tasted something in the food that clued him into Lucas having an affinity. The three of us talked for hours that night. I told Darius my story, and that's how both Lucas and I ended up here."

Emily allowed the story to sink in and then slowly asked, "So being baptized took away your ability to manipulate your element?"

"The simple answer is yes, but as I'm sure you're aware by now, there's always a more complicated answer. You'll take a class in your third year that goes in-depth about how religions and our elemental affinities work together and against each other, and how that all fits into the Awakening."

"And if my dad had forced me to be baptized?"

Maggie nodded. "You would have lost your ability to manipulate your elements. But I promise you; we would've done everything within our power to have prevented that. It really does come down to you, though. If you had wanted it, and if you believed in what the baptism stood for and accepted that for yourself, you would've taken a different path. Who knows? You could've ended up here teaching like me."

Emily finished her apple in quiet contemplation while Maggie returned to her herbs in the garden. She tried to imagine how it would feel to not be able to work with her elements anymore. While Maggie was obviously still gifted, she could no longer affect her element in the same way. Emily wondered what Maggie would be doing if she'd never lost her elemental ability.

"I'm assuming you have plans to go to the dance tonight?" Maggie said as she plucked a mint leaf from the plant.

Immediately, Emily wrinkled her nose. "I wasn't aware they were doing a dance. But no, I'm not going. I'd prefer to be a wallflower among actual flowers than to have to be witness to a bunch of happy couples making goo-goo eyes at each other all night."

"I think you should go," Maggie encouraged her. "The journey you've been on can take you to very dark and lonely places. Being around positive energy is best for you, regardless of whether or not you have a date."

Emily replied with a shrug. "I'll think about it." She added her apple core to the compost pile. "I wish I could've seen you with your powers, but I'm happy you're here. I think you're one of the most powerful people I've ever met."

Maggie smiled softly at Emily. "I'm glad you're here, too."

Emily started to leave when she noticed a single bud on one of the rose bushes. "Would you mind if I took this? I promise to donate to the earth elementals' garden fund."

Maggie looked over at the rose bush and at Emily. "You may have it if you promise to go to the dance tonight."

Emily sighed. "Fine," she said and gently removed the bud.

As Emily entered her class early, she pulled out a piece of paper and wrote a quick note. Emily was grateful there were only a few other Abecedarians in the classroom, and she hurried to place the flower and note on the desk where Brandon always sat. Closing her eyes in concentration, she made the flower bloom into a beautiful yellow rose. Satisfied with her work, she returned to her seat and waited.

Emily left quickly after class, not bothering to look at Brandon to see his reaction to her note. She merged between several exiting students and broke into a jog until she was safely inside her dorm.

Ashley was surprised to return (much later than Emily) to find her roommate trying on outfits for the dance. "Does this mean you have a date?" she asked hopefully.

"No," Emily said sourly. "It's a penance."

Ashley quirked a brow at her friend and started to get ready herself. "Did you take out a building with a gust of wind?"

Emily laughed. "No, I took a rose."

"That punishment seems rather severe. I mean considering how opposed to this dance you've been," Ashley pointed out.

"I agree. But I needed the rose, and the earth affinates said they sold out, so what choice did I have?"

Ashley blinked. "Now the important part . . . what did you need the rose *for*?"

"What if I'm giving it to you?" Emily asked mysteriously, avoiding directly answering the question.

The girl looked around her room and shrugged. "I don't see anything here for me. Besides, I don't believe you. Try again."

"I gave it to Lir because we're having a torrid affair?" Emily suggested.

"Nope. While that would be hot, I'm not buying it." Ashley assumed her serious pose—hands on hips, head tilted forward, and eyes narrowed to slits. "The truth."

"Fine," Emily sighed. "I gave it to Brandon with an anonymous note telling him his friendship means the world to me."

Ashley smiled. "Now that I believe. So, did you guys talk?"

Emily shook her head. "No, I escaped back here too quickly after class. I guess I chickened out."

"Maybe you can talk to him tonight at the dance?" Ashley suggested.

"Yeah, or maybe he doesn't want to talk. Either way, I promised I'd go tonight. What do you think about this outfit?" Emily held up a sheer dark shirt to a pair of black jeans.

"I'd say that was great if you were going to an emo dance." Ashley dropped her outfits on her bed and dove into Emily's closet. "I like the top, but let's add some color to your outfit." She pulled out a crimson red skirt that was hiding in the very back of Emily's closet. "Try this," she insisted.

Emily grumbled but tried on the selected outfit. "How's this?" she asked unenthusiastically.

"That looks amazing. I wish I had your figure," Ashley admitted. "And I have a pair of knee-high boots that'll go perfectly."

Emily joined Ashley and several others from their house as they walked to the dance. The girls were talking the entire way excitedly while Emily fell slightly behind and remained completely quiet. The others thought she was feeling sad about her mom, which she was to a degree, but was mostly in deep contemplation over the two conversations earlier with Lir and Maggie.

Several groups of students rushed into the dance ahead of them. Emily noticed almost everyone was wearing red and black and wished she hadn't let Ashley talk her out of her all-black outfit. Even from outside, the muted sounds of trumpets and saxophones could be heard.

"Did they hire a live band?" Emily whispered to Ashley.

Ashley responded with a mischievous grin. "I guess we're about to find out."

Emily wasn't sure what Ashley's response was supposed to mean but quickly found out as she stepped inside. There was indeed a live band, a jazz band like the ones common in New Orleans. There was the usual banner draped across the middle of the room as there had been for the other dances, although this one read "Celebration of Life." There were dozens and dozens of roses decorating the room, which made it smell and look beautiful.

When everyone stopped and looked at Emily as she walked in, she felt tears forming in her eyes. "Is this—" she began and choked up.

"Because of you? Yes. And the flowers were donated by everyone who received them today," Ashley boasted.

The band paused after the song they were playing so Ted could say a few words to the group. "I'm told there was much debate in my absence about holding a dance today. The faculty looked at all the pros and cons and put a lot of consideration in whether we would hold our first ever Valentine's Day dance. Some students and faculty members came together and proposed we instead host a Celebration of Life dance out of respect for Emily and her recent loss. As many of you know, our view of death is that it's not a final destination, but rather a transition. Like many other cultures around the world, we choose to celebrate all life when someone we know passes. I want to thank you all for creating and donating to this wonderful event." Everyone clapped and whistled while Ted cued the band to continue.

Emily was a wreck. All the crying and all the emotion she'd bottled up came bursting out when Ted was speaking.

"This is supposed to be a happy thing," Ashley whispered and nudged Emily.

Ted smiled supportively as he approached Emily. "Just because we celebrate life doesn't mean we don't grieve for those who have gone. Life and death, joy and sorrow . . . they are all a part of the balance of life." Ted gave Emily a hug before moving on to talk to other students and faculty.

Emily wiped tears from her eyes. She was touched by the event and by everyone surrounding her. "Thank you, Ash. You are an amazing friend," she said as she sniffled. "You should go enjoy your night with Xander, though." Emily gave her friend an encouraging smile.

"I will be back to check on you," Ashley warned. "I hope you end up joining me out there dancing." Ashley gave her friend a hug before disappearing onto the crowded dance floor.

"How are you doing now?" Lir asked as he stepped in to fill the space Ashley vacated.

"Grateful, sad, happy . . . pretty much all over the place," Emily admitted.

Lir smiled in understanding. "Do you think you could settle on one or two of those emotions for a few minutes while we dance?"

Emily eyed her teacher. "If this is a pity thing, you don't have to. I'm okay. Really."

"Does it look like I'm offering pity? I'm offering a dance."

Reluctantly, Emily tucked her arm into Lir's, and the two joined the other students enjoying the jazz music on the dance floor. "Did you choose to apologize to your friend?" Lir asked as he danced with Emily, his head seeming to move in Brandon's direction.

"Yes. Kinda," Emily admitted. "I tested the waters, really, to see if he'd be open to being friends again."

"So the real answer is no, you didn't apologize." Lir nodded. "It is always your choice, Emily." He reached into the inside pocket of his blazer and pulled out a white rose. "I know you indirectly received all the roses in the room, but I wanted you to have one just for yourself." He handed Emily the rose with the attached note, bowed slightly, and said, "I only stopped to check on you. Enjoy the rest of your night, Emily."

Emily looked suspiciously after Lir as he left. She couldn't help but chuckle to herself as she squeezed her way through the dancing students and took refuge against the railing on the porch. As she looked around, she breathed in the rose's scent deeply, enjoying the moment before she read Lir's note. *Anything you lose comes around in another form ~ Lir.*" Emily didn't know what the quote was from, but she didn't think it was Winnie the Pooh this time. She smiled as she read it over again.

"Ahem." Someone standing near Emily cleared their throat.

When she looked up, she saw Brandon standing nearby, watching her. "Secret admirer?" he asked, motioning to the rose and note Emily was holding, sounding a little uncertain on how he should talk to his old friend.

Emily laughed quietly. "No, not at all. Just words of advice from a friend." She shrugged at Brandon. "You look nice. Are you enjoying the dance?"

"Yeah, it's very lively. I just wanted some fresh air while Myra got drinks." Brandon tucked his hands in his pockets. "Didn't mean to bother you, though. I'll head back inside."

As he neared the door, Emily called out, "Wait! I mean, can you please wait a second?"

The expression on Brandon's face was a cross between relief and concern, as if he wanted Emily to stop him, but he also didn't want Myra to see him. "Yeah?" he asked as he turned back to Emily.

Emily twirled the white rose between her fingers. "I sent you that yellow rose," she began.

"I know," he interrupted.

"I just didn't want you to get the wrong idea, but I wanted you to know I miss our friendship and that . . . well . . . I'm sorry for ruining everything." While she managed to keep her voice steady through the speech, tears welled up in her eyes as she was saying it.

"I'm sorry, too," Brandon admitted. "Things got really complicated really fast, you know?"

"I know. I don't know why, but you're right." Emily bit the inside of her lip. "Are you happy now, at least?"

Brandon nodded. "For the most part, yes. But I miss you and Ash, too."

"Ash misses you, too. She's a loyal friend and didn't want to hurt me or be in the middle of our awkwardness. I'm sure she'd be happy to see you if you wanted to go talk to her. She's with her boyfriend on the dance floor."

"Yeah, I heard about her and Xander. Sounds like they're a good match," he said distantly. "How are you doing, Em? I mean, with your mother dying and stuff."

"I'm surviving. Apparently, I need a good cry and probably have to get really angry or something. You know those stages of grief. But I'm okay. I have distractions."

Brandon nodded slowly. "Like Lir?"

Emily looked confused for a second and then laughed. "Lir is my teacher. He's really like an older brother I never had, but that's it. And yes, he has been helping me out a lot with my abilities."

"Oh. Because I saw you guys dancing and the rumors and all."

"At least you know now," Emily replied with a shrug. "Myra seems really great. She's very determined. It's interesting to have a class with her." Emily thought back to the conversation with Elder Tama about Myra. Emily didn't feel threatened by the bi-affinate anymore after realizing the two of them wanted different things. "We certainly have different approaches to our affinities."

"Yeah, she's really gotten good with her fire abilities. She pushes herself hard to master everything." While Brandon sounded supportive, he didn't seem excited about the direction his girlfriend was heading.

"I burned myself with fire the other day. It made me think of you and how you'd probably laugh at me for it," Emily admitted.

"Why were you playing with fire?" Brandon asked with concern.

"I wasn't playing with it; I just wanted to light the fireplace. The good news is I succeeded," Emily smiled proudly.

It *almost* felt like things were normal again with Brandon . . . and then Myra showed up.

"Did the party move out here?" Myra asked as she handed Brandon his drink and planted a kiss on his lips like she was trying to lay claim to him.

"I just needed some air," Brandon replied and took hold of Myra's hand with his free hand.

"You know I'm always happy to give you some extra air and then take your breath away," Myra replied to Brandon with a wink, acting like Emily wasn't there.

"I think I'll go find Ash. Thanks for the chat, Brandon. Have a good night, you two," Emily said and slid past the couple.

Myra was too busy kissing Brandon to say anything to her. Still, Emily saw Brandon's eyes follow her as she went back inside to join Ashley on the dance floor.

CHAPTER SEVENTEEN

The days slowly grew longer, and a hint of warmth returned to the breeze that blew in off the lake. Even her friendship with Brandon had rekindled a bit, although with Myra discouraging him from spending any time with his old friends, it felt more like he was an acquaintance than one of her best friends. Emily and Lir, however, spent a lot of time working on her affinities out by the water.

"Like this?" she asked her new mentor as she created a tiny twister on the surface of the water.

Lir was fascinated by the tri-affinate's abilities to balance the elements and control them. "Not bad, Em. Now, do you think you could control three elements simultaneously?"

Emily thought for a moment and then allowed the water-spout to dissipate into the lake. "You know, the only thing I could think of was to create a puddle in the dirt and then hurl mud balls at you with the wind."

Lir's laugh echoed off the lake. "You would've gotten sprayed by the splatter, though."

Emily shrugged. "Might've been worth it."

"You'll figure out how to use them together eventually. I have no doubt," Lir replied with a reassuring nod. "Any luck on finding clarity to those memories you saw with your mother? You've been working with Maggie on that, haven't you?"

"Yes, she's been helping me with a meditation technique, but nothing is obvious yet," Emily admitted glumly.

"Okay, we're going to try something today," Lir said as he faced Emily. "Look into my eyes and practice your breathing techniques, like this." He inhaled deeply while looking at Emily's eyes.

With a shrug, Emily complied. She took up the cadence of Lir's rhythmical breathing and looked into his stunningly blue eyes. "Like this?"

"Almost. Don't look *at* my eyes. Look *through* them."

Emily tried again, shifting her focus from the beautiful irises to the dark centers of his eyes. As she was about to give up on the exercise, something changed inside of her. While she couldn't *see* it, she could *feel* it, an intimate familiarity with Lir, but again, it was like a dream she couldn't quite recall. The hairs on her arms stood up as her skin prickled while she focused and tried to grab hold of the image hidden behind his eyes.

"What do you see?" Lir's voice seemed like a whisper in the back of her mind. Emily wondered if he even spoke the words.

And then there was a brief moment of clarity. "Stones . . . in a green field surrounded by trees. It's cold, maybe late spring after a long winter. I'm running to catch up with a boy . . . or a young man. Yes, it's a young man. He's wearing a skirt. No, it's a kilt with long socks that reach his knees and an off-white shirt with sleeves tied in the middle of his forearms. My long skirt is also plaid but wraps up around my shoulders where it's pinned. It's peacefully quiet. As we reach a group of round stones, he lets me catch him, and we wrap our arms around each other and laugh. '*Mo ghràidh, mo ghràdh,*' he says." Emily closed her eyes for a moment and recalled the images before opening her eyes up to Lir again. "Wait," she blinked at him in surprise. "It was you?"

"Was it?" he asked with a grin.

Emily shook her head slowly. "It didn't look like *you*, but I remember that—if that's even possible."

"That," he began, "was another life. There was a river we were sitting by until I splashed you. You chased me by the stones," Lir reminisced and then returned to the present. "But like I said, and like you *know*, it was a different lifetime."

"Why can't I remember more?" Emily asked with furrowed brows.

"Because you're not ready to remember more," Lir replied kindly.

"Do you remember?" she inquired.

"I do, but it doesn't interfere with *this* life. It's a soul memory," he explained.

Emily nodded, not completely understanding. "Were we . . . ?"

"Married? No," he said with a hint of sadness. "We loved each other, yes. But we were then as we were always meant to be."

"Which is?" Emily prodded.

"Important to each other," Lir said mysteriously. "And now it's time for you to focus on this life and getting to your next class." He stood and offered Emily a hand to get up.

Emily once again remained seated, staring at him with confusion and fury. "I'm just supposed to go about my day as usual after you show me that?"

"I didn't show you anything. You awoke a memory that's yours." Lir's hand was still extended for Emily.

"You're evil," she said and crossed her arms defiantly, unmoving from her seated position.

Lir laughed. "Evil is a bit harsh, don't you think?"

Emily proceeded to roll her eyes at him. "How long have you known I was this other person?"

Lir lowered his hand and resigned to sitting beside her again. "It's difficult to explain, but once you've completed your

Awakening, it'll make sense. But for your benefit—and to get you to stop looking at me with daggers in your eyes—I will tell you that you have been familiar to me since I first saw you."

Emily blinked in surprise. "So, people here really *do* know me? How many others do you know?"

Lir shrugged. "I don't keep count of all the people I meet in this life who I've known before, but there are a lot. Think of it like this . . . why do we live in cities and communities around other people?"

Emily shrugged. "Because that's where our houses are?"

"Yes, but why do we build houses near others? Not everyone does, that's true, but the majority of humanity lives around others and at a very minimum, interacts with others. Why?"

"Safety?" Emily guessed. "Convenience?"

Lir nodded. "Yes, those are two reasons, but at the core of humans, in our souls, is a need for connection to each other. And for the most part, we desire comfort and familiarity. Souls who have a connection tend to find each other in other lives."

"Like soul mates?" Emily inquired.

"Yes, but soul mates aren't always romantic in nature. I suppose it can be literally translated to soul friends." Lir smiled. "Now, are you satisfied enough with that answer that you can get to class?"

"Soul friends. I like that. Are there soul enemies, too?" Emily asked as she finally stood.

When Lir laughed, it sounded like the laugh she'd heard in her soul memory. "Do you think souls have vendettas and seek each other out to cause misery through the ages?" Lir considered this for a moment. "I'm sure it's possible, but *most* people are called to what gives them peace rather than strife. But if there's anyone in this life who I know could seek out a soul enemy, it would definitely be you."

"You're hilarious, Lir," Emily said sarcastically. "I'm a student of balance, not war, remember?" She didn't wait for him to respond and hurried off to her History of the Academy class.

It was hard for Emily to focus in class because she kept trying to recall more soul memories. She wanted to know more about her past lives with Lir and what he meant when he said they were important to each other. The one memory she was able to recall with him made it seem like they were more than friends. If she was honest with herself, it felt nice to feel someone loving her again. But something inside her that she couldn't tap into yet questioned whether their connection was romantic. She thought the world of her water elemental teacher and was often awed by his insight and theories, but Emily wasn't sure she was attracted to him like that—like she had been to Brandon.

Emily glanced over at Brandon, whose hand was intertwined with Myra's as they listened to Adamina's lecture, and she wondered if there was a soul memory of him. Her eyes scanned the room, wondering the same of the other Abecedarians, but there were no revelations during the class.

When Adamina's class ended, Emily left to join Gaia and Rai in the field outside for a combined earth and air class with Myra. This was Emily's favorite combination class because she was able to learn how to balance and control both elements that she didn't have usually get to focus on as much.

"It isn't about dominance, Myra," Rai explained in response to the girl's question about why Emily's element in this class seemed to cause chaos with her earth element.

"It doesn't seem balanced, though," the older girl complained. "Emily's wind sweeps through and does whatever it wants to my earth. I don't get to fight back."

Emily saw Gaia and Rai exchange glances and knew they were probably sensing what Emily had known for a long time—Myra believed everything was a power struggle. "The earth indeed relies on wind and water to move it, but without earth, what would those elements be?" Gaia asked in a soft voice.

"Wind and water need earth for connection, to ground them," Emily explained. She knew from her own experiences the truth in this. She felt Myra should've known this, too, because everything they had been taught revolved around the balance of all of the elements. "Everything, including the elements, desires connection," she indirectly quoted what Lir had just explained to her earlier that afternoon.

"Doesn't that exploit the elements' weakness, though?" Myra asked. "Being independently strong seems more . . . desirable . . . than being weakened by reliance and balance. I mean, it seems like there's a lot of potential energy wasted in obtaining the balance."

"Do you feel your affinities are balanced within you, Myra, or is there a struggle for dominance?" Rai asked.

"I feel my fire is more powerful than my earth affinity. Since waking up with two affinities, I guess I naturally favor the stronger one." Myra shrugged like her preference was natural.

"What about you, Emily? Do you favor one of your affinities over the other?" Gaia asked.

Emily shook her head. "I have so much more practice with water, but I find myself constantly appreciating how they work together." She could practically feel Myra roll her eyes at her. "Today, Lir was having me create things using water and air together. The water was stagnant and in balance on its own, but when I had the wind swirl the water, it allowed the water to expand and move and experience something beyond the stillness."

Both Gaia and Rai nodded at Emily.

"When Brandon and I work together with fire, you can feel the strength and energy it has on its own." It almost sounded to Emily like Myra was challenging her.

"Okay, for the next time we meet, I want you to explore both sides of this debate. Emily, you should focus on a single element and try to understand Myra's perspective of energy and power. Myra, I would like for you to focus on both your elements and see if you can appreciate how by working in harmony with each other, they create a different strength through balance."

The two girls nodded and left their teachers in the field while they went to eat dinner.

"I still think I'm right," Myra snapped as the two walked toward the dining room. "You'll see."

"You really believe you have it all figured out, don't you?" Emily spat back, the pleasantries from the class fading. "Maybe you should think about the reasons why you feel like you're better than everyone else. Perhaps your desire for power over balance comes from your own insecurities."

Myra turned and faced Emily, fury behind her blue eyes. "I *am* more powerful and better than everyone else. The only thing they teach here is weakness and submission. I mean, listen to yourself. Balance is power. It's total bullshit, and you know it."

Emily stood blinking in surprise as Myra stormed ahead. "Wow," she whispered to herself.

Ashley agreed with Emily's sentiment after hearing the recap from Emily at dinner. "What a bitch. I mean, besides the stupid rivalry between the elemental houses, no one *really* believes they're better than the others, do they?"

Xander shrugged. "Not really, I guess," he said. "But I kinda get what she's saying. When we," he continued, pointing between himself and Ashley, "work on elemental stuff, it really does seem stronger to combine our gifts."

"I think Em's point is we're not trying to take over the other elements, though. We're trying to maintain the balance of them," Ashley asserted while squeezing Xander's leg.

"Exactly," Emily burst out. "I think she's dangerous, and I think the Elders might see that, too." She didn't mean to say the last part aloud and regretted it as soon as she saw her friends' shocked faces. "Forget I said that. I don't know anything. I'm going to go try to find answers for myself by doing things *her* way."

Emily left before dessert was served. She walked through the garden, hoping to find Maggie there, but she had no luck. She went back down by the tree by the lake, considering how she would work with each element individually to test out Myra's assertion.

"Hey." Brandon walked up behind Emily and squatted down next to the trunk of the tree.

It would've been so easy for Emily to go off on Brandon about how ridiculous his girlfriend was, but she opted for a more peaceful route. "Hey," she replied.

"It's been a while since I came down here. There really isn't much for my element by the water," he said.

"Yeah, it's been a while. Nothing's changed here except a few dandelions are growing now."

"I remember picking those as a kid and giving them to my mom like they were flowers," Brandon commented with a chuckle. "Everything was simpler."

Emily grunted. "Yeah, I suppose."

The two remained in silence for several minutes. There was a weird tension between them, but Emily didn't know if it was because this had been their special spot or if it was because of the Myra thing.

"Myra seemed pretty upset after your class today. Everything okay?" Brandon was treading lightly on the subject.

"Shouldn't you be asking *her* that?" Emily reflexively asked, but then sighed. "Sorry, I didn't mean that. Everything is fine."

"Even I know that fine coming from a girl means exactly the opposite. Want to talk about it?" Brandon offered.

"I don't have anything nice to say, so you should probably just accept my answer," Emily said.

"That's the thing . . . I don't want to accept that answer. So, let me have it—the good, the bad, and the ugly."

Emily had to decide if she wanted to waste the energy in a likely futile attempt to have Brandon agree with her. Finally, she decided to test the waters. "You and Myra spend a lot of time working with your fire affinities, right?"

Brandon settled into a seated position and nodded. "I've worked with her to help her understand it since she's new to it."

"We're all new to this, Brandon. But that's not the point. What I want to know is, do you think you are doing good by creating a powerful joint affinity?"

Brandon scratched his head. "I guess I never saw it like that."

"Your girlfriend does. She thinks balance is a weakness and is quite focused on being stronger than everyone with her fire affinity." Emily purposefully left out the part where Myra told her she thinks she's better than everyone else.

"Huh," he replied. "She's never said that to me."

"She said it very plainly to me and Gaia and Rai. But she's also tried to prove her power and dominance over me and my affinities in every class we've had together."

"Maybe she's just trying to prove to everyone that she's capable. I mean, you make it all look so easy with how you balance your affinities." Brandon shrugged.

"It's not easy for me, Brandon. I have to work really hard to figure out how to balance them and then completely hide one of them from everyone," Emily admitted. "Why haven't you told her about my earth affinity, by the way?" She was fishing to see if maybe Brandon *had* told her.

"Because it's your secret to tell, not mine," he admitted. "I honestly never really understood why it had to be a secret in the first place, but I haven't told anyone."

"It has to be a secret for now because of people like Myra who see our gifts as powers to dominate instead of a burden to maintain balance. Besides that, people were already scared of me because of my two affinities."

"You can be really scary, Em. I don't blame them," Brandon said with a smirk.

"That isn't helping," Emily replied but felt the corners of her mouth stretch upward. "How are you doing with your Awakening?" Most of the Abecedarians had begun their Awakenings.

"Everything's still hazy, I guess you could say. Mostly, I feel things but don't know what they mean. Myra doesn't understand because she hasn't entered the Awakening yet, so I can't really talk with her about it."

"I'm here, so talk to me," Emily offered. "It's what friends do, right?"

Brandon leaned his back against the tree and looked out at the white clouds floating by. "Well, what was it like for you?"

Emily thought back to her mom at the hospital and closed her eyes as she explained. "I saw myself as an unborn child in my mother's womb. A brother was there with me, a twin," she began. "I felt him become a part of me when he died. I also saw a lot of things I did as a child with my mom, like they were pieces of her memory she wanted to give me. But mostly, it was like a dream I couldn't remember clearly, like I could feel the emotions from, but couldn't put pictures to the stories they told."

Brandon nodded. "Yes, feelings without the pictures to go along with them. That's it exactly. It's almost like *déjà vu*, too. Like right now, I feel like we've talked like this before, only I can't quite place the conversation."

"We have talked like this before. It was about five months ago, right here," Emily teased.

"Ha, ha. That's not what I mean," Brandon chided. "Maybe it's because Myra hasn't started the Awakening, but I don't feel things like that about her."

Emily raised a brow and looked over at him. "You feel things about me, though?"

"Not *things*. I mean, I don't think it's things like you're suggesting. But then a part of me feels like I've felt those things about you from the day we met, only they were buried too deep."

"Like an itch that you can't seem to scratch?" Emily suggested.

"Yeah, like that," Brandon agreed.

"Fantastic. I'm now akin to an annoying itch that you can't get rid of. I'm so flattered," Emily said sarcastically, but playfully.

"I'm not even going to deny that, Em." Brandon chuckled. "I should probably get going. I'm supposed to be studying with Myra."

"Ah, yes. Well, have fun studying," Emily replied, putting air quotes around the last word.

"Thanks for talking with me. I really mean that. I miss this place and you," he added.

Emily tried not to read anything into his words. "Hey, before you go, I have something you can try to help bring clarity to some of those feeling memories." She quickly explained the breathing and eye gazing technique she'd learned, although strangely left out it was with Lir.

"Thanks again. I'll try with Myra. See ya!"

Try it with me! Emily wanted to scream at him but decided just to let him go study with his power-hungry girlfriend instead.

CHAPTER EIGHTEEN

"How'd it go?" Emily asked as Brandon strolled over toward where Emily was sitting. She'd caught him out of her peripheral vision as she'd been finishing her Saturday brunch under the tree. "The memory exercise, not the studying. I really don't want to know about the studying," Emily explained. It had been a couple of days since their last conversation in that same spot.

"Why'd you accuse Myra of acting like she's better than everyone else?" Brandon started.

"Glad to hear it went so well," Emily said sourly.

"Just answer the question, Emily," Brandon demanded.

Emily cringed when he repeated her full name. "Because it's the truth," she sighed. "She proceeded to tell me that she *is* better than everyone else."

Brandon looked stunned.

"Oh? Did she leave that part out? I can see why. You might've taken it badly, and then who would she have to enable her to be the fire queen?" Emily blinked furiously at Brandon. She could see his jaw tense and expected him to yell at her or just walk away.

But he stayed and looked down at Emily with a sad expression. "I don't get it, Em. She's never treated me like that." He sat beside the tree with a frown.

"Maybe because she needs you for her own purposes," Emily began, but when she saw Brandon's expression darken, she added, "Or maybe because she loves you."

"To answer your question, it didn't go well," Brandon said flatly. "She was mad when I suggested we try it."

Emily wrinkled her nose. "Did you mention it was my suggestion?"

Brandon shrugged. "Maybe, but that's not the point. You and I didn't try it. It was a great suggestion. I just . . . I just—" He sighed. "I don't understand girls."

"It could also be she's frustrated with not starting the Awakening yet," Emily offered, surprising herself by coming to Myra's defense.

"Why should that matter? Shouldn't she want to help *me* with the things that are important to me, too, and not just do the things that benefit her?"

Emily could see his point. "I would hope she'd want that. You know her better than anyone, though. Does Myra really want good things for you, too?" She wasn't trying to insinuate anything.

"I really don't know. We've spent these last four months focused on helping her with her new affinity. I've never asked her for anything." Brandon buried his face in his hands.

"Well, the only thing I can say is you have to figure it out for yourself. You can choose to approach her with this, or you can choose to keep it to yourself and continue forward with doing things only for her." Emily offered her friend a shrug. When he stayed silent, she added, "I'm probably not the best person to give you advice on this, though."

Brandon looked up from his hands with confusion. "Why wouldn't you be a good person to give me advice? You probably know *me* better than anyone."

"That was true once, but we've changed in these months apart," Emily explained.

"Maybe we've become more of our true selves," Brandon countered.

Emily opened her mouth to say something but closed it again with the thought unsaid.

"What?" Brandon prodded and elbowed Emily.

She held her hands up in surrender. "Nothing. I swear it." Emily cleared her throat and looked out at the water. "It looks like glass today. There's no wind at all."

"Okay, fine. Just answer me this. Have you successfully done that meditation thing you suggested I do with Myra?"

"First off," Emily began, "I never suggested for you to do it with her. I simply told you a way you could maybe unlock a soul memory with *someone*. Secondly, yes, I have."

"A soul memory? Huh. Okay, so who did you want me to practice with if it wasn't Myra?" Brandon inquired.

"I didn't have anyone in mind," Emily lied.

Brandon looked wearily at Emily. "Fine, I'll let it drop. But if you ever wanted to try with me— "

It was really all Emily could think of doing since the soul memory with Lir, but she couldn't make herself admit it aloud. "Are you sure you want to try it with me? What if it changes your perspective on things?"

"What could it change?" he asked.

Emily licked her lips as she tried to decide the best way to approach the topic. "I saw a shared memory with the person who helped me. We loved each other in that life, and although he says we weren't married, it still has impacted how I see him in this life." Emily could see Brandon struggling with the vague details she was sharing, so she continued. "I know he's important to me, but not how. I don't know if or how that will change us in this life, but I know I don't love him now. My point is, though, it was only a brief glimpse at another lifetime, and without knowing the whole story, someone's perspective might be misleading."

"It was Lir, wasn't it?" Brandon asked, his jaw clenching.

"Why does it matter?" Emily genuinely wanted to know why her past life would upset Brandon.

His shoulders slumped, and he sighed. "I guess it doesn't matter. You're probably right in thinking we shouldn't try this. But I just feel like there's a memory that's yours." Brandon rose to leave. "I've felt it since the day we met but didn't know what it was."

Emily stood. "If it helps, I feel that, too. I would like to explore it someday with you, but I don't think now is the time." She offered Brandon a small smile.

"I should get going. I have some things I need to think about. You're really a good friend, Em. I'm sorry for how I've been acting."

"You're a good friend, too, Brandon. Sorry, I refuse to call you 'Bran' like Myra does."

Brandon chuckled. "I've never been fond of it either. Reminds me of that crippled kid in that one show."

Emily smiled and nodded. "Exactly. And hey, I'm always around if you need to talk or just need a friend."

"Thanks. And you, too." Brandon waved and retreated toward his residence hall.

Emily could feel an ache in her chest. She wanted nothing more than to share a soul memory with him and was mentally kicking herself for letting the opportunity pass her by. "It was the right thing to do," she told herself aloud and decided to sit under the tree for a bit longer.

"If it makes you feel any better, I think you did the right thing, too," Maggie said as the two sat in the garden eating apples.

"It doesn't make me much feel better," Emily admitted. "Thanks for trying, though." Emily had caught Maggie up on all the things that had been going on over the past few days.

"And about Myra . . . she isn't familiar to me except in this life, at this school. I wish I could tell you not to worry about her, but I think it's good for you to at least see her perspective and understand how her ideas fit—or don't fit—in with your current life. Perhaps you are the balance she needs."

"Myra's not familiar to you . . . but I am?" Emily didn't understand how Maggie's experience was different than hers.

Maggie nodded. "Yes, our souls know each other."

"Did you experience the Awakening and can see soul memories?"

"No, since I was baptized, I didn't experience the Awakening like you are. It took a lot of work to understand why I felt that faint tickle at the back of my mind when I met someone I knew," Maggie explained.

"So, if you can't see soul memories, how do you know my soul?" Emily asked with innocent curiosity.

"When Lucas and I first met Darius, he helped us discover pieces of our past lives through past life regression hypnotherapy. I imagine going through that was probably very similar to how you feel now. You know things and people are important, but you can't really access the soul memories."

"How did you fill in the gaps? I mean, I'm assuming you did since you keep telling me I'm important," Emily enquired.

"I read lots and lots of books, journals, diaries, and pretty much everything I could get a hold of. Ted and Darius were both extremely helpful. And now I have most of those books and journals in my office to refresh my memory when I meet someone I once knew," Maggie explained.

"Am I in any of those books in your office?" Emily was shocked by this revelation.

"Yes. I see that look in your eyes. No, you can't read the books. Your Awakening needs to occur naturally."

Emily screwed up her face in dissatisfaction. "Not even a tiny glimpse?"

"Nope. No peeking," she warned.

"Hmmm . . . well, could you at least tell me how I'll know I've completed the Awakening?" So much effort had been put into helping the Abecedarians recognize they *started* the Awakening, but no one shared how it ended.

"You will know your soul's name. That's when you will have passed to the end." Maggie finished her apple and tossed it in the compost pile.

"My soul has a name?" Emily asked in astonishment.

"Of course, it does. All of the affinates use their soul's name after the Awakening. You'll just have to trust me about this. I promise it'll all make perfect sense when the time comes."

"They told us it could take over a year to get through the Awakening. Is it really going to take that long? I think I'm going to go insane with all the bits and pieces of information I have," Emily whined.

"You have progressed quickly, Emily. I don't think you'll achieve full insanity before you make it through," Maggie teased.

Emily wasn't as confident.

"*Mo ghràidh, mo ghràdh,*" Emily whispered to herself as she sat in front of a computer in the library. "How do I even spell that?"

Others around her looked over, wondering who she was talking to. Days after her first soul memory with Lir, she still didn't have any more insights or answers, so Emily decided to figure things out the old fashion way—research. She phonetically spelled out the words she could still clearly remember, trying different ways of spelling until she came across a site which referenced Scottish Gaelic. As she went through her memory, it made sense that it was Scotland. "What does it mean?" she asked aloud.

"My darling, my love, loosely translated, of course." Lir had crept up behind her.

Emily was startled but craned her neck to peer up at him. "I was figuring it out," she said sharply.

"You could've asked me," Lir suggested.

"And risk getting a vague answer? No, thank you. I managed fine," Emily responded defiantly. "What are you doing here, anyway?"

Lir stared blankly at the girl. "I didn't realize this had been renamed the Emily-Only Gallery of Knowledge. But since you asked so politely, I'm doing research." He shrugged and continued along his original path to the bookshelves.

Emily stared after him with furrowed brows and then decided to follow him. "What does that mean? 'My darling, my love?' "

"I thought you were using Google as your main source of all knowledge now," he said while thumbing over some book titles on the shelf. Lir dropped his hand to his side and sighed. "If you're so determined to know, maybe we should see if we can awaken another soul memory."

"Or you could just tell me," Emily said playfully as the two left the library.

Lir gave her a look and shook his head. "I'm not going to bother replying to that."

Emily shrugged. "It was worth a try." She followed beside Lir as they walked to the building where the dances always took place. Last time Emily was there, the room was filled with roses in a celebration honoring her mother. "What are we doing here?"

Lir opened the door for Emily to enter and followed behind her. The tables were spaced evenly throughout the room but weren't set. The only light illuminating the room was from the sun, which was about four hours from setting. The warm glow was welcoming, but Emily felt a subtle hint of sadness. In the corner by the glass wall, a black grand piano had been placed, presumably for an upcoming alumni event.

"Soul memories can be triggered in many ways," he explained and motioned for Emily to sit on the piano bench. Lir sat to her right and began fingering the keys. "Do you know how to play the piano, Emily?"

She shook her head. "I might remember how to play 'Mary Had a Little Lamb,' but I only had a few lessons when I was five."

Lir nodded and began playing notes in the middle of the keyboard. The slow melody was sad and beautiful.

Emily felt his arm brush against hers as he reached for the lower keys. "When did you learn to play?" she asked in quiet awe.

"Shhh," he said gently. "Close your eyes and listen."

Emily listened as the music filled the room and allowed each note to vibrate within her being. At the crescendo, just as the tempo increased, Emily felt a tingle in her heart, and pictures began dancing in her head. She saw a man seated at a piano in front of a paned window in a room that was lined with dark wooden shelves. The ceiling was accented with crown molding and a chandelier of unlit candles hung in the center of the room. The window looked out over a field of tall grasses with evergreen trees in the distance. Emily sat on a maroon velvet lounge in a light blue satin gown and was lulled by the music.

"Clair de Lune," Emily whispered to Lir as he continued the piece. "It was a humid summer afternoon, but I always forgot all the discomforts when you played for me." She retreated further into the soul memory. "You weren't playing for me, though. You were playing for you. You were . . . sad." Emily swallowed the sorrow she felt. "You were angry with me that day," she continued. She had to wait for the memory to become clearer, but she knew she'd hurt him. "I told you

Paxton proposed to me," she said. She couldn't see the other man, but she knew his name and knew it hurt Lir.

As Lir concluded the melody, Emily opened her eyes and looked at him. She could see the same sorrow in him there as she'd seen in her memory. "Why were you sad?" she asked softly.

Lir smiled, but it was one of those smiles that didn't reach his eyes. "In all the lifetimes that our souls have found each other, I have always been grateful for your presence. We have helped each other out in ways you'll remember eventually, and my soul has always loved yours."

"How many times have I hurt you?" Emily asked, feeling the truth in his words as much as hers.

"It's not important. I have loved and will love others, so this isn't the tragic story you think it is." Lir placed his hands back on the keys. "Another thing with soul memories is the abilities from past lives you can pick up again. Rest your hands on the keys," he instructed.

Emily looked at him curiously but hovered her fingers over the lower keys.

"Relax your hands. You're not trying to smack the keys."

Emily looked at Lir's fingers and tried to imitate him.

Apparently, it wasn't a good imitation because he chuckled. "Listen to the music again and let your fingers remember the notes." Lir began playing a song Emily remembered hearing in a *Peanuts* Christmas show.

Emily couldn't help but giggle until Lir elbowed her, and she refocused. The tune was familiar, and within moments, Emily heard the lower notes of the song join with the higher ones Lir was playing. She looked down and saw her fingers skillfully accompanying her teacher. She could feel the joy and fun she'd had with Lir in another life.

As the short piece came to an end, Emily had a huge smile on her face. "I can't believe I can do that!" she exclaimed.

Lir was smiling a real smile again, too. "Okay, one more. See if you remember this." He cleared his throat and began a melody that sounded like the 1920s in New Orleans.

Emily didn't accompany Lir on this song but found herself tapping her foot along to a distantly familiar tune.

"I'm gonna sit right down and write myself a letter . . . and make believe it came from you," Lir began singing as he played.

"I'm gonna write words oh so sweet, they're gonna knock me off my feet," Emily joined in. She didn't know she could sing or even knew the song. She wasn't aware Lir had a nice voice, either. However, having experienced those soul memories with him, it seemed almost obvious.

"Do you remember," Lir began after they finished their jazzy song, "the flat in Jackson Square where we spent hours drinking and playing cards before going to—"

Emily cut him off. "Le Petit Theatre du Vieux Carre?" She spoke the French words like it was her native language. "That woman . . . what was her name? Ruth?"

Lir blushed a little. "Yes, Ruth. I remember her quite well."

"I'm sure you do," Emily said, enjoying Lir's reaction.

Lir and Emily reminisced about that lifetime and the fun they shared. "See? I'm not the pathetic fool-for-love you thought I was."

"Fair enough," Emily replied. "Can I ask you a question, though?"

"I think you just did. But go ahead and ask another," Lir teased.

"Have I ever known how you felt about me in those lives?"

Lir wrinkled his nose just like Emily remembered from her soul memories of New Orleans. "A few times, yes."

Emily frowned. "I'm sorry," she said. "I don't think I'd ever want to hurt you like that."

Lir shrugged. "Patterns usually repeat until we learn the lesson. Thankfully, in this life, I'm your teacher, and you're far too young for me to think about you like that . . . for now," he added slyly.

Emily rolled her eyes at him. "You're hilarious. Truly. But really, I don't want to see that sadness in you like I did when you were playing the piano."

"Ah, Emily. What is happiness if you don't know sorrow? Everything is about balance, even emotions," Lir explained and stood from the piano. "I really should get back to my research. Do you have enough answers for today, or are you going back to reclaim the library as your own again?"

"I think I'm going to stay here and see if I can remember any more songs on the piano. Enjoy your dusty books, though," Emily said.

"Enjoy your memories, *mo ghràidh*." With a wink, Lir turned and left Emily alone in the empty room.

"Oh my god, Em. That's incredibly romantic. I can't believe you and Lir have spent lifetimes together . . . and he *loves* you," Ashley gushed after Emily shared her afternoon with her.

"C'mon, Ash. His soul loved mine, and nothing has ever come of it in any lifetime," Emily explained. "Besides, he's my *teacher*, and I don't think either of us wants that."

"I dunno. Dating an older guy would be hot," Ashley said dreamily. "Oh, but speaking of which, Xander and I shared our first soul memory."

Emily listened enthusiastically to her roommate's memory. She was happy Ashley was progressing in her Awakening. "So you basically met in World War I when you were his nurse after he'd lost a leg? That's insane. I can't imagine how weird it would feel to remember a life where I was missing a body part."

"I know, right? But it was such a sweet memory," Ashley sighed happily.

"Do you think Brandon and Myra have soul memories together?" Emily asked.

"Ick. Do you really want to think about that?" Ashley recoiled.

"Not the details, no, but Maggie told me she doesn't know Myra's soul. And since we tend to seek out souls who we've connected with previously, maybe they have been soul lovers for lifetimes." Emily crinkled her nose at the thought.

"To be fair, Myra was kinda thrust on all of us, so she didn't really seek any of us out," Ashley offered. "And her working with Brandon is only a result of him being stuck here over winter break. Who knows? She might've been mentored by Adamina if Brandon hadn't set fire to that building."

"True. I guess we all have unique circumstances that brought us together here." Emily smiled and nudged her roommate.

"Speaking of which . . . ready to conjure another soul memory with me?" Ashley asked.

CHAPTER NINETEEN

"As we enter our last month before the summer break, I wanted to remind you all of the upcoming ceremonies for our graduates. As most of you know, our graduation is a festive event honoring our elements. For those of you who have reached the conclusion of your Awakening this year, you will also be invited to formally announce your soul name during the celebration. We admire the changes everyone has gone through this year and look forward to all of your continued work with your elements." Ted concluded his announcement in the dining hall, and breakfast was served.

Students chatted excitedly amongst themselves about the final ceremony of the year.

"Do you think we'll know our soul names by then?" Ashley asked as she cut her banana into perfect slices.

Emily shrugged. "Doesn't seem like it. I don't think any of us ABCs know our soul names yet."

"I overheard Julius telling a third-year student in the common room that he knew his soul name," Xander offered.

Ashley and Emily looked at each other with the same frustrated expression. "No fair," Ashley complained.

Emily, while anxious to reach the end of her Awakening, was actually enjoying discovering her soul memories. "I think the more I try to figure it out, the more my soul fights me. I've been trying to take Lir's advice and be patient like the river."

"Hey, guys," Brandon said as he slid into the vacant seat next to Emily. "Mind if I join you? Myra's in the infirmary with a headache," he explained.

Emily and Brandon had had a few conversations by the lake after the one about Myra and the soul memory exercise. He apparently concluded he would work on his soul memory recollection with his other fire elemental friends and didn't bother to bring it up again with his girlfriend. Emily thought it was sad he couldn't share that with her but had vowed to stay out of that business between Brandon and Myra.

"That sucks," Xander said with half a mouthful of muffin.

Ashley nodded in agreement but opted to keep her mouth closed until she swallowed. "Are they worried about her coma thing? I remember how scared they were with Em after her seizure."

Emily remembered that, too, but mostly she remembered how Brandon barely left her side while she was in the infirmary.

"They want to keep an eye on her, but they seem to think it's just a normal headache. She's been doing a lot of work with her earth affinity lately and probably just overdid it or something," Brandon explained vaguely.

"I hope she's okay," Emily finally added.

Brandon shrugged and nodded. "So, are you guys talking about your soul names? Have any of you discovered yours yet?"

The four friends chatted casually as they ate their meals.

After breakfast, Ashley and Xander went to the library to look up something they'd seen in one of their shared soul memory quests.

Emily rose from her seat. "I think I'm going to go for a walk before class," she said to Brandon.

"Would you mind company?" he asked.

With a shrug, Emily invited him along. "Is everything okay?" she asked when they stepped outside. "I thought you would've gone to see Myra before class."

"She didn't want me there," he said flatly while staring off toward the distant lake.

Emily's features were marked with concern. "That seems odd."

The two walked silently toward the lake and the tree where they always sat. "I've never appreciated this spot like I think you do," he remarked while placing his hand on the tree. He ran his fingertips over the bark, studying it. "What is it like to have multiple affinities?"

While Brandon studied the tree, Emily studied him. "Some days, it's frustrating. It feels like I'm being pulled in multiple directions all at once. But mostly, it's peaceful. I am surrounded by all the things that make me whole no matter where I go." She watched him be mesmerized by the tree for a moment and then tugged on his arm. "Brandon? What's on your mind?"

"I asked Myra that question. She told me it made her feel powerful. I didn't think much of it at the time, but then I saw her use her affinities together. It was destructive, and I realized that when she said powerful, she meant *real* power, not something that made her whole."

Emily's frown deepened. "What was she doing?"

"As she explained it," Brandon began, "earth is inferior to her fire, and its purpose is to fuel the fire. It's not like I'm a great person to tell her she's wrong since I spent many years using fire for destruction."

"Doesn't that make you the perfect person to tell her? You've learned it can't be the way things are, haven't you?" Emily recalled the story of the deadly fire Brandon started. "And it's not just because of what happened, but because a part of you knows that fire is part of the elemental balance, right?"

Brandon nodded. "I know that now. I don't know if I can help Myra understand that." Brandon withdrew his hand from the tree truck and showed Emily the inside of his forearm. "She did this . . . intentionally."

Emily looked at the red, blistered skin and then back up at Brandon's face. "Holy crap, Brandon. Why?"

"When I saw what she was doing, I told her to stop, that it was wrong. When she didn't stop, I tried to stop her. She scooped the flame into her hand and hurled it at me like she was throwing a baseball at me. It was so sudden, so unexpected that I didn't have time to deflect it." There wasn't a trace of anger in Brandon's voice, only sadness or maybe an unexplored regret.

"I can fix the burn, but you need to fix the situation with Myra. Have you told Ted what happened?" Emily motioned with her head for Brandon to follow her to the water.

"No. This sounds stupid, but a part of me wants to protect her. And then there's the other part of me that's completely embarrassed. I mean, how many fire affinates get burned by their element?" Brandon sighed but followed Emily toward the lake.

"I don't think you have anything to be embarrassed about. I mean, I trip over rocks and tree roots almost daily," Emily said, trying to lighten the mood. "I've even been known to erupt in coughing fits when I failed to drink water correctly."

Brandon flashed Emily a small smile as the two squatted on the lake's shoreline.

"This might hurt a little, so sorry in advance," Emily warned. She pressed the palm of her hand against Brandon's and focused on feeling the imbalance of water in his damaged tissues. She placed her other hand on the surface of the water, allowing it to float. After a minute of focus, she brought her wet hand to Brandon's burned arm, allowing drops to fall onto the red skin.

Brandon flinched as the first couple of drops hit the sensitive tissue, but when Emily placed her wet hand on top of it, he could feel the coolness ease the pain.

Emily concentrated on manipulating the water to heal Brandon's skin. And then it happened.

The blue of the sky was quickly being overtaken by dark, rumbling clouds. The wind picked up the dust, giving the clouds something to chase. The horses' nervous whinnies only intensified the energy in the air.

"It's almost here," she said as the palo verde trees seemed to tremble in the gusty breeze.

"Are you sure you don't want to try to reach the town before the storm hits?" he asked, less confident of their safety than his companion.

Both could smell the water as it struck the parched earth in the distance, but she could feel it, her elements coming together. There was nowhere else she wanted to be at that moment. "We are safe here," she said with confidence.

He took her hand as they stood next to the fire he'd created and waited.

The horses calmed as did the air, and within moments, they could hear the sound that was creating the clean smell the wind had gifted them. The muted thuds of water hitting the thirsty desert floor sounded like the crescendo of an audience's applause.

She tilted her head back and laughed as the wetness peppered her face like hundreds of kisses from a lover while he stretched out his free hand to protect the fire. There was nothing as invigorating as the elements existing in this chaotic harmony. It was how she always felt when she was with him, their polar affinities so powerful, yet peaceful together.

"This is magnificent!" she shouted up at the clouds, which responded in kind with a clap of thunder.

He smiled at her, thinking the same thing. Dropping his protective hand from the fire, he wrapped it around her waist and pulled her against him. Her cool, wet lips met his fiery kiss with the energy of the thunderstorm surrounding them.

As the fire danced beside them with the rain, the two seemed to melt into one and made passionate love amidst the turbulent elements.

Both Emily and Brandon recoiled from each other simultaneously. The burned flesh was forgotten. Slowly, Emily's eyes drifted from staring at his heaving chest and met his gaze.

"Did you?" Brandon started.

"Was that?" Emily continued.

They both knew, though. It was a soul memory.

Emily was the first to look away, quickly searching for a distraction from what she just saw and felt. "Your arm is healed," she said, still feeling breathless from their memory. She could feel where he'd been wrapped around her in the memory. She felt the tingling excitement of how their bodies moved together while they made love, and the rain soaked them. She could even taste his lips. Emily's heart was racing.

"I, um, should get to, ah, class," Brandon stuttered and then walked hastily away.

Emily remained crouched, staring after him, stunned, and then crumbled to the ground. She rested her hands on the damp shoreline ground and tried to balance herself by using the elements.

The campus grew quiet around her as all the students began their morning classes, but she remained unmoving, still processing the memory. She remembered months before longing for him to kiss her like that, craving that connection between them, which always seemed to be buried just below the surface. She felt rage boiling inside her thinking about how hard she'd tried to let go of her feelings for Brandon. Angry tears fell down her cheeks as she stared down at her shaking hands.

Without thinking about it, Emily rose and marched with purpose toward the infirmary. She passed Maggie in the hallway but didn't respond to or even look at her friend. Emily was unaware that Maggie followed her, stunned.

Gaia was in the room when Emily burst in to confront Myra. "I'll be with you in a moment, Emily," Gaia said, unaware of the storm that carried Emily in.

Emily didn't hear Gaia, just as she didn't hear Maggie in the hallway. "Next time you need to prove to yourself how powerful you think you are, come find me," she spat at Myra, who looked unaffected by the verbal assault.

"I think you should calm down, Emily," Maggie said from the doorway behind Emily.

"Myra has a migraine. You need to go quietly," Gaia warned.

Emily and Myra had locked eyes, though Myra had a calmness about her that only infuriated Emily more. "What? So you can blow my hair in my eyes as a distraction? Please," Myra taunted with an eye roll.

Emily raised her hand and seemed to command the air to leave the room with the closing of her fist. Gaia, Maggie, and Myra immediately grabbed their throats and started gasping while Emily stared wildly at the girl in the bed. "Don't. Fuck. With. Me." Emily spat out just before Maggie lunged at her, breaking her concentration.

The air returned to the room, and the three were breathing heavily, trying to replenish the oxygen of which their bodies had been momentarily deprived.

Maggie yanked Emily out of the room while telling Gaia, "I've got this. Make sure Myra is okay."

Emily couldn't recall the walk to Ted's office or anything Maggie said during that time. She suddenly was aware that both Maggie and Ted were staring at her, either waiting for her to explode or to say something. But she remained quiet.

The sensation from her soul memory was gone, and she sat in Ted's office feeling dazed and numb.

"We're waiting on an explanation, Emily," Ted said with a hint of impatience in his tone.

"What would compel you to attack a student like that?" Maggie added, although her voice was filled with concern.

"You're asking the wrong student," Emily said harshly, folding her arms across her chest.

"What are you talking about?" Ted asked as he leaned forward.

"Little miss victim in there attacked Brandon with a fireball. Oh, yeah. Your sweet little miracle student burned her own boyfriend to prove how powerful she is and how much better she is than anyone here. I just had to heal him. I am done working with her. I will not be the pillar of balance for her only to have to turn around and clean up after the harm she does."

"No, you clearly won't be working together anymore," Ted explained. "And I'm not sure you will be working with anyone for a little while until I'm confident you can control yourself." He sighed. "I thought we were finished with your elemental attacks after the incident with Titus in December."

Emily felt shame for abusing her affinity like she had, but she didn't regret it. Myra deserved much worse than a headache and a little asphyxiation for all her elemental imbalances. "Fine," the girl finally replied. "Throw me in isolation or ship me off somewhere, but you're allowing a dangerous person to go unchecked. *I'm* not the problem here. But whatever."

She didn't want to be sent away, so Emily was relieved by Ted's response. "We don't send our problems away, Emily. For the foreseeable future, likely the remainder of the school year, you will be removed from your classes and will not be allowed to attend school events, including eating in the dining hall." Ted massaged his forehead with his fingers. "Please return to your room in your residence hall, and for the love of the elements, don't destroy anything or anyone along the way."

Maggie touched Emily's arm as the girl stood to leave. "I'll be there to see you in a bit," she said quietly.

Emily nodded and left Ted's office.

On the walk to her room, Emily realized how much she'd changed since the start of the school year. Instead of being that girl who was packing her things up after failing the first meditation exercise, she felt strongly now about staying at the school. Her anger had subsided, although she could feel it faintly under the surface. Mostly she desired to retreat to her room and revisit the soul memory she shared with Brandon.

The residence hall was empty and quiet. Emily entered her room and closed the door behind her, securing her sanctuary from any unexpected chaos that might enter the dorm. Immediately, she walked to her window that looked out at the lake and opened it up. The warm breeze embraced her, and she let out a sigh that felt like she'd been holding in for hours. Positioned on the windowsill, halfway inside and halfway outside, Emily sat and appreciated the calm. She reached out and caressed a low-hanging leaf from the tree planted just outside her room.

It was a while before there was a soft knock at her door, and Maggie entered. Maggie sat on Emily's desk, which had been pushed away from the window before Emily opened it up.

"What are they going to do to me?" Emily asked, still running her thumb against the texture of the leaf.

"*To* you?" Maggie was confused. "*With* you might be more appropriate, but either way, you'll do just as Ted said. Lir and Adamina will work with you privately, and you'll be doing research in the library while the other students are in class." Maggie paused for a brief moment. "What possessed you to lash out at Myra like that? I completely understand that she hurt your friend, but this seems like a bit of an overreaction."

Emily spoke softly as she stared out the window, almost like she was talking to the lake instead of Maggie. "When I healed him, I had a soul memory. When it was over, I felt so many things, but what came out was a protectiveness, I guess."

"An intimate soul memory?" Maggie guessed.

Emily nodded. "I think I was angry because I've worked so hard to be okay with my platonic relationship with Brandon. Those emotions—and deeper ones—overtook me, and all I wanted to do was to hurt the person who hurt Brandon." She finally shifted her focus away from the scenery and looked at Maggie.

"I'm sure you're angry with yourself, too, for rekindling those buried feelings," Maggie concluded.

Emily nodded with a shrug. "If Myra hadn't burned him, I'd be happily ignorant and sitting in Lir's class, pretending he was singing his lecture."

"They are all your memories, Emily. We don't get to decide what we did in other lives, but we certainly control our actions in this one. Just because you experienced something with Brandon in another life, doesn't mean you should let it change things now."

"Easier said than done. I'm pretty sure it freaked Brandon out as much as it did me—maybe more." Emily returned her gaze outside. "It's probably good for him that I'll be locked away now."

"First off, you're not locked away. Secondly, I'm almost certain that Brandon, will at the very minimum, want to talk to you about it after he's processed it."

Emily closed her eyes for a moment and sighed. "What's going to happen to Myra?"

"She will be watched closely and have some extra tutoring to help her control her elements," Maggie explained.

Emily grunted in response but said nothing.

"I spoke with Lucas before I came to see you. He's agreed to prepare meals for us to eat in my office. So, you won't have to eat alone."

It helped Emily to have Maggie care about her so much. She turned back to Maggie and smiled. "That doesn't sound like a horrible punishment."

"You're not a horrible person, so it's a fitting consequence." Maggie hopped off the desk and rubbed Emily's arm. "I'm going to talk with Ashley, let her know what's happened and about your new situation, although I'm sure you'll share with her all the events in glorious detail later."

"Thanks. Yeah, I pretty much tell Ashley everything. You and she have been my constants since I've been here."

CHAPTER TWENTY

The isolation was lonely, but Emily adjusted as best as possible. Besides spending a lot more time with Maggie in the gardens and her office, Emily got a rundown of the day each night after dinner from Ashley.

"He really misses you, Em," Ashley said. In the week that had passed since the soul memory between Emily and Brandon, he had filled in the gap Emily had unintentionally vacated in their friendship circle. In contrast, Myra had melted comfortably in with some of the other fire affinates. "I really think you should talk to him."

"I'm not allowed to talk to anyone except you, remember?" Emily said. "Besides, this punishment enables me to be a coward about the whole situation without looking like a chicken. He's better off without me screwing up everything in his life."

"You don't screw up his life," Ashley said with a dramatic eye roll. "I think he's simply a magnet for destructive people."

Emily threw a pillow at her roommate. "Gee, thanks."

"Anytime," Ashley replied happily and threw the pillow back.

"So, what did Lir teach in class today?"

Emily heard rumors of more and more students—mostly second years—who discovered their soul names. But the idea of Emily accomplishing the same, not to mention the nearly impossible task for her to achieve in her isolation, wasn't her focus at the moment. When she was assigned to study in the library, she spent most of the time trying to find the specifics of the few details from her memory with Brandon. Her obsessive idea was to find a way to convince herself that the glimpse didn't represent the larger picture.

The only thing she had to show for her research, though, besides the numerous paper cuts on her fingers, was a vague location and timeframe.

"The cacti, the trees, the cracked ground . . . it had to be in the Southwest. I can only assume by our transportation and clothing that it was the mid-1800s," Emily explained to Ashley one evening.

Ashley yawned as she listened to Emily prattle on about places and events that she wasn't able to connect with. "I think you should let this research obsession drop and just go talk to Brandon."

"What would I even say? 'Hi, I'm obsessed with thoughts about that time in another life where we did it by the fire. Oh, and sorry that I almost killed your girlfriend.' " Yeah, that's a conversation I plan to avoid. Forever."

"So, what if those two are back to talking to each other again. I've seen him looking for you."

"Nope. I've got two more weeks before everyone leaves for the summer. I can easily avoid seeing him," Emily said.

"Speaking of summer, have you figured out what you're doing yet?" Ashley was grateful for an opportunity to change the topic. She loved her roommate, but her stubborn obsession and avoidance of the obvious grew tedious.

"Maggie said there are usually a few students who remain over the summer, and she doesn't think it will be a problem if I stay. I have to meet with Ted and officially request it. Something about legal documents that have to be filled out and approved. I don't know."

"You could always come along with me on my magical family vacation around remote Alaska," Ashley rolled her eyes. Despite being a water affinate, Ashley preferred limited time out in places where she lacked electricity and cell phone signal.

"Pass, but I wouldn't mind taking that trip with other affinates someday. It sounds beautiful. Besides, Lir mentioned something about taking a trip to New Orleans. I think it would be really cool to see a place I lived in a past life. Who knows? Maybe that would be when I discovered my soul name," Emily said. "Speaking of which, I'm supposed to meet Lir for a lesson tonight. Something about using the energy of the full moon or something." Emily shrugged.

"Sounds romantic, if you ask me," Ashley teased.

"Ha! You know, if he was our age, I might agree with you," Emily admitted as she checked her hair in the mirror.

"I honestly don't know how you do it."

"Do what?" Emily asked innocently.

"Spend so much time with a man who admitted he's loved your soul for lifetimes. Ugh, it's just so tragic!"

Emily shrugged as she neared the door. "He's loved others. Besides, I'm already on thin ice around here. If I had a torrid romance with a hot teacher, I'd be kicked to the curb for sure."

"And he'd end up in jail," Ashley said with a grin.

Emily rolled her eyes and laughed. "That, too. Although," she paused, "since my soul is much older, maybe it's a loophole." Emily shrugged, but she enjoyed teasing her roommate a little. "I'll see you later."

"What exactly do you mean?" Emily blinked in horror after Lir told her the plans for their lesson.

233

"I thought I was speaking a language you knew. Let me try this again, slower. You. Boat. Get in. Middle of the lake. Comprende?"

"There's no motor or oars, genius," Emily fired back. She often mused about how she spoke to Lir and how never in a million lifetimes would she speak to Adamina or even Greta in the same way. But Lir was different. They were behaving more and more like soul friends rather than teacher-student.

"Did someone baptize you and make you forget we're both water affinates?" Lir shook his head at Emily. "Now get in. I don't have all night."

"What? You have a hot date?" Emily teased as she attempted to balance the wooden boat and get in while not falling into the lake.

"Maybe," Lir replied with a shrug and skillfully sat down facing Emily.

"Seriously? When were you going to tell me?" Emily huffed.

"Since when do I tell you all about my personal life? And I didn't say I did, just that I might."

"I kinda know a lot about your lives now and about some very private parts of those lives, too." Emily rolled her eyes, but mostly she just enjoyed making Lir crazy. "I feel like I have access to my very own Cinemax-after-hours shows."

"Just wait . . . I know some things about you in your past lives, too, that would make that pretty little face of yours turn shades of red that haven't been invented yet."

Emily flashed him the evil-eye. "I think you're full of crap. But fine, I'll drop it. What are we going to do?"

"Why I've put up with you for umpteen lifetimes, I'll never know," Lir grumbled. "Okay, get us to the middle of the lake." He stared at Emily with arms folded across his chest.

"Seriously? That's the big lesson?" Emily touched the tip of her middle finger to the water. She created a current in the water, which drifted them to the center of the body of water, at which point, she withdrew her finger from the lake. "Easy peasy."

"Great job," Lir said sarcastically. "You've graduated out of the first week of water elemental class. Now can you please take this seriously?"

"I don't know. This kinda feels like that scene from *The Little Mermaid* when Prince Eric is trying to woo Ariel." Emily snapped her fingers, wondering if she had some unknown magical powers to make the animals begin a chorus of "Kiss the Girl."

"I think this isolation sentence of yours is making you even crazier." Lir rubbed his forehead with his fingers.

"Sha-la-la-la-la-la-la-la." Emily was singing quietly.

"Emily! Would you *please* take this seriously?" A hint of frustration entered Lir's voice.

"Sorry," Emily said through giggles. "That happens to be my all-time favorite childhood movie."

"Get out of the boat," he instructed.

"What? You want me to hop into the lake?" Emily asked, the playfulness gone from her voice.

"I didn't say that. I said for you to get out of the boat. If you don't want to go for a swim, then figure out a way to not get wet."

"Wow, I think I'd like it better if you were a singing crab," Emily grumbled and tried to adjust herself to safely get out of the boat.

"I think I'd prefer you to be a mute redhead, but here we are." Lir smirked at Emily's shocked expression. "What? You didn't think I knew the cartoon?"

Emily sighed in exasperation and looked around for her solution to get out of the boat without getting soaked. "Ice?"

Lir shrugged. "It's your call, but I'm going to start rocking this boat in a second, and it won't be long before we're both in the water. One, two, three—"

"Okay, okay. Give me a sec."

"Four."

Emily placed her hand on the water and felt her energy manipulate it until crystals formed on the surface. Meanwhile, Lir started rocking the boat back and forth, breaking the ice crystals she'd just formed. "I'm working on it!" she scolded and kicked Lir in the shin.

"Ouch! Hey! Why so violent? I guess that's why you're stuck in isolation," he jested.

"I swear to the elements if you make me fall into this water, I'm taking you with me," Emily warned.

"Better hurry then." Lir's rocking motion was getting more dramatic, and the water was beginning to slosh into the bottom of the boat.

Emily plunged her hand in the water, which instantly started hardening. Within two sways of the boat, it had become entirely trapped in thick ice. After another moment, Emily stood and stepped out onto the ice. "Happy?" she asked, circling her arm at her accomplishment.

"Not yet," Lir said and placed his hand on the ice, melting it just as quickly as Emily had formed it.

She didn't have time to say anything but allowed her instincts to take over. The trees on the far side of the lake rustled violently, and suddenly Emily was floating above the water in a whirlwind of air.

Lir sat back and watched Emily control the wind, noticeably impressed. "Not bad at all, Ariel," he said, obviously still making fun of her for the *Little Mermaid* reference.

Emily seemed to float back to the boat and was set down gently by the wind that came to her aid. "That was a mean trick," she pouted.

Lir offered a half-hearted shrug. "You rely on your water affinity too much. I wanted to see if you had it in you to expand your mind."

"So, all that stuff about the full moon and being stronger was total BS?" Emily asked, still a little miffed.

"It sounded good, didn't it?" Lir smiled. "The truth is the moon does affect the elements, but it's not about power, it's about learning to understand them and achieve balance when the elements are in a heightened state."

"What would you have done if I didn't succeed, and you tipped the boat?" Emily asked.

"Gone for a swim, I suppose." Lir grazed the water with his fingertips. "It's been warm, and the water feels nice." Once he retracted his hand, he untied his shoes.

"What are you doing?" Emily asked as she watched Lir remove his shoes and socks and empty his pockets.

"Going for a swim." He proceeded to take off his shirt—something that Emily was sure would make the entire female student population swoon—and jumped into the water. When he resurfaced from his impromptu dive, his dark hair was slicked down. Drops of water glistened on his muscular shoulders and arm as he held out a hand to her. "Are you coming in?"

Emily looked up at the moon and stars as if searching for an answer.

Lir splashed water at her. "Well? Do you have something better to do?"

With a groan, Emily took off her shoes. "Aren't you going to be late for your hot date?"

He splashed her again. "I never said I had a date. You just presume the worst of me."

"With good reason," Emily fired back as she struggled to stabilize herself in the shifting boat.

Lir sent a medium-sized wave in the direction of the boat. "Stop overthinking and jump in."

It was all Emily could do to not fall in, but Lir was actually right. She had been overthinking everything too much lately. With a deep breath, she took a leap of faith and plunged into the water.

Lir was right again; the water was the perfect temperature, and it felt so natural to be surrounded by the element. Her long, brown locks fanned out from her head like seaweed.

She must've been under the water for a while because Lir's hand reached down, grabbed her arm, and forced her to the surface. "I hate to break this to you, but you're not a real mermaid," he said while Emily gasped for some much-needed air.

Her hair was stuck to her cheeks while her clothes billowed around her small frame. "You're full of useful information tonight," she said as she tried to free one side of her face of the stringy hair.

Lir reached out and brushed aside the hair from the other side of her face, his fingers caressing her cheek for a brief moment. "In one of these lifetimes—" His words, full of regret, faded away as his hand moved from her face.

"Yes, I know. I'm just an impetuous child who hasn't even had a real kiss," Emily huffed. She long ago discounted the kiss she shared with Brandon because, in her mind, it might as well not have happened because it was a hasty, impromptu kiss that was never followed up by a real one.

"You are far from just a child, Emily. And I know you know that. Your soul is old and beautiful." It was one of the sincerest things she'd ever heard Lir say to her.

If this had been any other situation, if she was physically older or him younger or maybe even a different lifetime, Emily believed he would've shown her what a real kiss felt like. She could feel the desire like it was an instinct in her. Maybe it was true she had an old soul, and perhaps that's what governed her at that moment, but she slowly lifted her hand and—

"What do you mean, you splashed him?!" Ashley was furious with her roommate. "I thought you were going to tell me a tale of forbidden love, of passion, and desire fulfilled. I feel like *I* need to take a cold shower after that. What did he do?"

"After the initial shock of getting a face full of water, he splashed me back. The weird tension between us disappeared, and we were back to just being ourselves, laughing, and joking around. I even teasingly told him that his being shirtless was making it difficult for me to remember who I was in this lifetime. I suppose that was the truth, but it was completely playful," Emily admitted as she ran her brush through her tangled, damp hair.

"Uh-huh. And if he's moping in class on Monday, I know who's to blame." Ashley pointed at Emily.

"He's fine. Besides, it would've made the trip to New Orleans really awkward." Emily shrugged.

"Or extremely romantic. I worry about you, Em. It's so obvious to everyone that he feels something for you that goes beyond a teacher-student relationship. Even Brandon sees it."

"What do you mean, Brandon sees it? First off, there's nothing to see, and secondly, how would you even know what Brandon sees?"

"I don't know, just a hunch. Whenever Xander and I are talking about something Lir taught in class, Brandon's right eye twitches. I think he's jealous of Lir."

"You're all insane. Brandon has his own girlfriend, so it really shouldn't matter who I do or don't have a relationship with. But most importantly, there's nothing relationship-y between Lir and me." Emily threw herself down on her bed in a huff.

Several girls walking in the hallway outside Emily's room giggled.

Emily covered her face with the pillow and screamed into it.

"I know what would fix that frustration," Ashley teased.

Emily looked out from under her pillow, thoroughly unamused. "Do you think it's too late for me to request a new roommate?"

"Ouch," Ashley replied while holding her heart and feigning hurt.

CHAPTER TWENTY-ONE

"The concept is fundamentally flawed. You're taking a natural process and forcing it through technology." Ted's voice echoed down the hallway as Emily approached. She wasn't spying. She was scheduled to meet with him. "Dammit, Eli," Ted hit the desk with his fist, startling Emily.

Emily took it as a sign that she needed to make her presence known and knocked on his door.

Ted motioned for her to enter. "I will have to call you back. I *am* trying to run an Academy here." Ted hung up the receiver forcefully and invited Emily to sit. "How are you doing today, Emily?"

The girl shrugged. "I'm okay. That sounded intense," she said cautiously.

"I've been accused of being too caught up in old ways. It's not always easy to be a champion for an unpopular opinion. But that's not why you're here. Let me find the paperwork for you." Ted flipped through manila folders on his desk until he found what he was looking for. "Here we go. Now you have two options: you can either have your guardian sign the papers authorizing you to remain here for summer instruction—"

Emily wrinkled her nose and was already shaking her head.

Ted chuckled. "I suspected that. The other option is for you to file for emancipation. This process is a bit more complicated because you won't be thirteen for another month. Even at thirteen, though, it's difficult to get approved. What I would suggest is we jointly file for guardianship and emancipation, naming one of the faculty members as your temporary guardian until you turn sixteen. How do you feel about that?"

"You mean my dad wouldn't have a say in anything in my life anymore?" Emily blinked in surprise. That was a much better outcome than she anticipated from this meeting.

"That's exactly right. I thought that—"

"Maggie," Emily interrupted. "I'd like Maggie to be my guardian. I mean, if she wanted to."

Ted nodded. "We were thinking along the same lines. I talked with Maggie about this already, and she would be delighted to do this for you."

"And when I turn sixteen?"

"Provided the court agrees, you would be legally responsible for yourself."

"Do you think they'll agree?" Emily asked, not really understanding the legal system.

"Depends on you, I suppose. If you can manage to stay out of trouble, I wouldn't see there being any issues preventing emancipation. But that means you can't go around threatening other students or causing mass destruction of Academy property," Ted warned.

"I haven't destroyed anything," Emily offered with a shrug. "Am I ever going to be released from this isolation sentence?"

"We're going to continue as-is for the rest of the school year, Emily. Allowing you time to focus on control and your Awakening is the best thing for you right now."

Emily frowned. "Will I be allowed to attend the end of the year celebration?"

"I haven't made any decisions on that yet. Now, if you're ready to sign these papers, I will send them to our attorney and get them filed with the court this afternoon." Ted slid the thick set of papers toward Emily.

"Isn't it a beautiful day?" Emily asked Maggie as the two sat down for lunch in the garden.

"It's usually lovely here this time of year," Maggie said with a smirk. "I'm guessing you signed the papers in Ted's office this morning?"

Emily nodded enthusiastically. "I can't believe I really won't ever have to see my dad again." Emily's leg swung as she took a bite of her sandwich. "Thank you, by the way."

"For what?" Maggie asked.

"For agreeing to be my guardian."

"It seemed only natural, and I'm happy to do it," Maggie explained. "Don't forget, I know a little bit about not wanting to be around parents. I'm glad I can allow you to have an easier time than I did."

Emily nodded sadly. "I wish Darius had found you sooner."

Maggie smiled. "I don't regret the adventures that brought me here. You shouldn't regret yours, either, no matter how uncomfortable it may feel at the time."

"I have a laundry list of regrets," Emily said sadly, "and I don't think they're all from this lifetime, either."

After spending most of the afternoon in the garden with Maggie, Emily decided she needed some time alone to think about the things she regretted. Brandon was at the top of that list, although she didn't know whether she was regretting things ending with him or beginning with him. Mostly, she regretted that once again, he wasn't a part of her life. Lir was next on her list of regrets. She felt deep remorse for all the lifetimes she'd hurt him and wondered if her actions in the lake added to his hurt like Ashley suggested.

Emily snuck into the banquet hall and sat down at the piano. The air in the room was still and calm, and the ordinarily bright room was shaded by drawn curtains. Her fingers brushed over the entire keyboard as she tried to recall her ability to play the instrument. A melody from a distant memory entered her mind. After she figured out the starting notes, the melancholy tune filled the room. Emily closed her eyes and focused on the soul memory. She allowed her hands to take her on a journey through time.

She remained with her eyes closed as the somber melody came to an end but was startled into the present by the sound of soft clapping. She turned around to see Lir walking toward her.

"A beautiful rendition of 'Moonlight Sonata,' " he said. "I saw you heading over here and wanted to make sure you were okay."

"Yeah," Emily said, with an air of sadness from the music still lingering. She invited Lir to sit and patted her hand on the piano bench beside her.

Lir sat beside her, and she instinctively rested her head on his shoulder.

"I should be happy," she began without prompting. "I signed papers to start the emancipation process. Maggie is going to be my guardian until I turn sixteen," she explained.

"That sounds like pretty good news. Why do you seem sad then?" he asked, adjusting his body to allow Emily to rest more comfortably against it.

She shrugged, but then answered. "Exploring regrets."

"I can't believe you've piled up too many in this lifetime . . . and the past is the past. It can't be changed or rewritten, no matter how much control over the elements we have. It is the universe's rule that we live, learn, and grow, or else we repeat mistakes."

"Why do you continue to love my soul after the lifetimes of heartache I've caused you?" Emily positioned her hand in his and held it.

She could feel a slight shift in his posture, but he didn't pull away from her. "Some pain is worth it," Lir replied. "Sometimes the pain reminds us we're alive."

Emily thought about that while she continued to hold onto Lir. "Would you have kissed me the other night if I hadn't splashed you?" she asked and then quickly realized that could easily become another regret.

"Does it matter?" he asked in return. "I'm nineteen, you're almost thirteen. While there was a time when you would be preparing to get married to someone my age, this is neither that time nor place. What we *want* isn't always what we get."

Emily wasn't certain what answer she was hoping he would say, but the non-answer left her feeling the full force of regret as they sat in stillness together.

"A part of me," Lir said several minutes into the silence, "wanted—and still wants—nothing more than to gift you your first kiss." His thumb caressed the top of her hand.

"And the other part?" Emily asked as she watched his hand interacting with hers.

"The other part repeats to me that pain can help remind you that you're alive."

Emily lifted her head from his shoulder and looked at him. "Who's overthinking things now?"

Lir's focus shifted from their joined hands to meet her gaze, where he stared deep into her eyes. "Damn you, *mo ghràidh*." He squeezed Emily's hand while his other hand moved to her cheek. His fingers gently curled at her jawline, tugged and brought their lips together.

Lifetimes flashed through Emily's mind as her eyes closed, and it took everything in her to keep herself in the present. She wanted to experience *this* kiss, *this* moment, not the hundreds or thousands of others kisses they may have shared. Emily could feel the love his soul had for hers as his lips moved with hers, as he held onto the moment just as she was.

Emily's heart raced as his hand released hers only to caress her face with both of his hands, never allowing any space between their joined lips. She moved her hand over his chest, feeling his quick heartbeat through his shirt, until her hand clasped onto the back of his neck, holding onto what felt like the essence of life itself. The still air of the room came to life as the two kissed, dancing around their bodies while her skin tingled all over, like a gentle mist falling on it.

And when the kiss finally concluded, Lir rested his forehead against Emily's, and his thumb caressed the lips he'd just tasted. There were no words to be said, no witty remarks to be made; there were only two people trying to figure out what would happen next.

About the time Emily's heart rate had returned to normal, Lir softly kissed her forehead and withdrew from their embrace. "There was another reason why I came here," he began.

Emily let her hand fall from his neck, coming to rest on her lap. She could feel sadness engulfing her before he even began.

"I am leaving the Academy," Lir said and quickly placed his hand on Emily's, hoping to stop her from interrupting the speech he'd planned. "No, it is not because of you, so get that thought out of your head right now."

Emily nodded and allowed him to continue.

"I have been asked to join a group of the top water elemental affinates on a research project in Greenland. My instinct is and always will be to protect and help you in the ways I can, but now that you're thriving in your Awakening and are on your way to mastering your previous two elements *plus* a new one to this life . . . well, I think it is time for me to allow you to find your true self, your true place in this life, and for me to explore the opportunities presented in this life, as well."

It sounded like news they should both be celebrating, but Emily couldn't stop the tear that fell down her cheek, and Lir didn't sound as excited as he should be. Before Emily could wipe the tear away, Lir brushed it with his thumb. He kissed her forehead again and stood up.

"When are you leaving?" Emily finally managed to ask as she tilted her head up to look at him.

"Tonight," he said and offered her a sad smile.

Emily nodded. "Can I ask you one last question?"

"You just did," he replied with a smirk. "We will see each other again. I have no doubts about that. But what was it you wanted to ask?"

Emily felt ridiculous for even thinking it, let alone actually asking it. But to prevent another regret from being added to her long list, she said, "Am I a good kisser?"

Lir considered for a moment how he would answer that and then said, "A kiss can't be truly enjoyed if one of the two isn't a good kisser. So now I ask you, did you enjoy your first kiss?" He already knew the answer because while he didn't say it to her, it was one of his favorites of their lifetimes of kisses. "*Gus a coinnich sinn a-rithist, mo ghràdh* . . . until we meet again, Emily."

CHAPTER TWENTY-TWO

E mily opted against telling her roommate or anyone else about the kiss with Lir, so she made up a story about not feeling well to avoid the probing questions about why she didn't want to leave her room for the remainder of the week. Before Lir's plane took off, he texted her a link to his YouTube channel of classical piano pieces. In her solitude, Emily listened to the songs and allowed herself to get lost in soul memories.

Maggie came in with meals for Emily, but not even the blueberries she loved so much could snap her out of the melancholic mood she'd spiraled into. "Ted's agreed to let you attend the end of the year celebration," Maggie told Emily on the Sunday after Lir's departure.

Emily offered a sad but grateful smile. "I'm not really feeling up to celebrating, but thanks," she replied.

"You have a couple of days. Maybe you'll feel better by then. What did Gaia say about your illness?"

"I didn't go see Gaia," Emily admitted.

Maggie sighed and nodded. "I see." She paused for a moment. "I know Lir has been and is important to you. While I don't understand your relationship as a teacher and student, I know it's been hard for you since he left. As I'm sure you know from your soul memories, goodbye is never really goodbye." Maggie stood and squeezed Emily's shoulder. "I really hope you'll reconsider."

Emily knew there was truth in what Maggie said. Still, in her days cooped up in her room, she'd ruminated so much that she actually believed she was the kiss of death to relationships. First, she kissed Brandon, and that relationship ended without another kiss. When she finally got over him, she let herself get caught up in a romantic tragedy of a man who deserved so much better than to be caught in a cycle of loving the unlovable Emily . . . and then lost him, too, after one kiss. Is this what Lir had meant when he said live, learn, and grow or repeat past mistakes?

That evening, the girls of the water elemental residence hall were having a party in the common room. Their excitement for the end of school, the celebration, and the anticipation of learning and sharing all the soul names led to a high-energy evening that everyone except Emily chose to be a part of. With her earbuds tightly in her ears, she could barely hear the noise over the volume of her own music, which made it even more difficult for her to hear the rocks hitting her window. Someone was outside and trying to get her attention, but she remained oblivious to it . . . until a big enough rock was thrown hard enough to break her window.

Emily jumped up from her bed and rushed to see what was happening outside. She saw Brandon standing there, waving his arms at her. She pushed the window up, careful not to cut herself on the broken glass. "What the hell's wrong with you?" she shouted down to him.

"I needed to talk to you. Can you just come down here, so I don't have to shout for the entire Academy to hear?" Brandon sounded frustrated, which, in Emily's opinion, was never a good sign.

But perhaps exploding a little at Brandon would be enough to snap her out of her mood. "Fine," she said and carefully sat on the windowsill with both legs hanging out. She hadn't dressed in days and was wearing rubber ducky pajama pants and a white V-neck shirt. Her hair was pulled up in a two-day-old messy bun with strands of hair flying out randomly. Using her air elemental gift, she slowed her drop to the ground two stories below. She landed gracefully with her bare feet in a grassy area by the tree. "I'm here. What?" She stood with her arms folded across her chest, staring at Brandon.

Brandon frowned for a moment at her less-than-friendly-greeting but continued anyway. "I was *going* to talk to you at the end of the year celebration, but Ash said you weren't going."

"I'm not going. I'm not really in a celebration type of mood."

"Not in the mood to celebrate. Got it." Brandon nodded. "What about a walking mood? Would you mind if we went for a walk?"

Emily looked down at her attire and her bare feet and then back at Brandon. She knew she was acting difficult, so she nodded without putting up a fight.

The two walked in silence toward the lake for a bit until Emily felt compelled to be cordial. "How's your arm?" she asked.

Brandon waited for a few more steps before responding. "That's kinda what I wanted to talk to you about."

"Did it get infected? Did something happen to reverse the healing?" Emily frowned. She might not be good for relationships, but she was damn good with her elements.

"No, no. Nothing like that. It's perfect. It's just—" Brandon paused as they were about halfway to their regular spot by the lake under the tree.

"The memory," Emily said.

"Yeah," Brandon said. "I didn't want to leave for the summer without talking to you. You know, like how we left things over winter break?"

Emily nodded, feeling a little ashamed for being so chicken about talking with him and not having the same forethought to do so.

"It's just . . . I shouldn't have run off. I wanted to say I'm sorry for that."

It still hurt Emily deeply that he treated that soul memory like she had murdered his puppy. "Why did you run away then?"

"I don't know," he admitted. "It freaked me out a little. I've never *felt* something that intense in a memory before."

"You should probably get used to it. I've lived many lifetimes and have remembered all sorts of crazy, wonderful, stupid, and embarrassing things. I guess I've always been grateful for the memories I can feel so deeply because it means I lived rich, emotionally rounded lives."

"How many soul memories have you seen?" Brandon asked, somewhat changing the topic. Despite everything, he really did miss Emily's friendship and the ease of talking with her.

Emily shrugged. "Too many to count. I've seen lifetimes dating back to the building of the pyramids. I don't think that was the beginning, but it's harder to touch on the really old ones, I guess."

"Wow," he said in astonishment. "I was talking with Adamina about her lifetimes. I was impressed when she said her first lifetime was the mid-fifteenth century during the War of the Roses."

"Huh," Emily replied. "I guess I assumed we'd all lived around the same number of lives."

"I hadn't put too much thought into it," Brandon responded with a shrug. "But getting back to our lives now, I want you to know I really enjoyed that shared memory."

Emily was sure if there was more light, she would've seen him blushing. "Me, too," she replied softly. "It doesn't have to mean anything, though. I mean, for all we know, we were struck by lightning just after that memory, and it was just a thing that happened at that moment."

Brandon chuckled. "I don't really believe that, but fine. We can leave it at that if you want."

Emily didn't want to leave it at that, but she also didn't know what she *did* want, either. "What other options do we have? There's enough that's happened in this life, in less than a year of knowing each other, to put a strain on our relation—, err, friendship. I've never done anything like that memory in my life now, and I can't see how having that as part of our dynamic will ever amount to any good." Emily unloaded a lot of the pent-up emotions from the last several days onto Brandon. She turned away from Brandon and faced the lake. "I'm tired of driving the people I care about away."

"I'm here now, aren't I?" Brandon reached to rest a comforting hand on Emily's shoulder but then withdrew it before he touched her.

"Yes," Emily muttered, aware now that Brandon was hesitant to touch with her. "But you're too scared to make any kind of physical contact with me now, and your girlfriend is like my mortal enemy. Did you happen to mention to her anything about our soul memory?" She turned back around to face him.

"No, of course not," Brandon stated.

"See?" Emily pointed out. "You were too embarrassed or afraid. or something—I don't know what—to admit to her that you and I had an amazing connection in another lifetime."

"It was something private and personal and special to me. I didn't want to share it with anyone. Besides, she's not my girlfriend anymore. I kinda draw the line with attempts to set me on fire."

"Oh," Emily replied. "But you still talk to her."

"I still talk to you, too." Brandon flinched as soon as Emily shot him a hateful look with that remark. "Okay, let me rephrase that. Actually, I'm not going to rephrase that. Yes, I talk to her. Yes, I talk to you. She shares my affinity, so we have classes and things in common. You were one of my best friends whom I still miss every day, but you barely talk to me, and when you do, it's rarely without this anger in your voice. I regret how things have been between us for most of the last five months, but I don't, nor will I ever, regret that soul memory with you."

Emily was about to say something when both of their expressions changed. "Do you smell that?" she asked, looking around with concern.

"Fire," Brandon said, and they both took off running toward the wooded area that the school backed up against. A small orange glow illuminated the moonless night while the gentle breeze carried the smoke away from the school.

Before the two could get within a hundred yards, they could feel the intense heat and slowed. "Why is it so hot?" Emily said with a frown. She could see a couple of trees that had fire eating their trunks, but it looked like the fire was on the ground itself. "It's okay, I can get water to it from here," she continued while Brandon studied the fire.

No longer was he the child mesmerized by the fire, but he was using his elemental instincts to determine what kind of fire was this. As soon as Brandon realized, he turned to Emily and said, "Don't use water!"

But it was too late. Emily had already called on her element and carried enough water over on the wind to extinguish the moderately sized fire. When the water contacted the hot fire, it triggered an explosion that sent both Emily and Brandon flying backward about twenty feet.

"It's a metal fire," Brandon explained as he regained his footing and offered Emily a hand to help her stand.

"Metal can catch on fire?" Emily was a little dazed from being tossed around like a rag doll but otherwise appeared uninjured.

"Yes, and water can't put it out." Brandon was moving closer to the fire again.

"Obviously," Emily said, but then caught up with Brandon. "What are you doing? You can't put it out with your body."

"Actually, I can. But I need your help." Brandon looked around at the dozens of new trees that had caught fire. "Can you pull the air from that area?"

Emily shook her head. "I can't do that out in the open, but I can create a vortex around the fire to keep it from spreading."

The explosion got the attention of other students and faculty. To prevent another water elemental affinate from causing another explosion, Brandon yelled out, "Stay back! No water. We've got this."

Emily stretched her arms out in front of her with her palms pointed at the fire. In a mere moment, a vortex whirled around the area of the fire, containing it. But the metal continued to burn hot enough that Emily felt sweat dripping down the sides of her face.

Brandon slowly walked toward the flames despite people yelling at him to stay back. The flames on outlying trees seemed to jump to him as he approached, but he showed no signs of catching on fire.

He's absorbing the fire, Emily thought in quiet awe. She focused more of her energy on creating a cooling barrier with the wind, trying to shield Brandon from the immense heat he was approaching. As he somehow managed to take in all of the flames, he collapsed down to the charred ground.

Emily dropped her vortex and joined the others as they ran to help Brandon.

"Stay back!" Ted yelled at the students while the head teachers of the four elements circled around Brandon and began trying to balance his body.

Nearly half of the student population stood in worried wonderment as they witnessed their teachers trying to heal Brandon. Emily noticed someone on the far side of the trees where the fire had been, seemingly watching everything that had happened. It was too dark for her to see if they were male or female, or even be able to guess approximate age. She suspected it was whoever had set up the fire. She started to move around the circle of students toward the mystery person when Ted caught her by the arm and pulled her to his office.

Emily had heard Ted get angry over the phone, but she'd never seen him angry nor had been the focus of his fury. He slammed his office door closed and confronted Emily. "I'm trying very hard to find a reason you and Brandon were experimenting with fire. I haven't thought up with any excuse for this that I can accept. So please, enlighten me."

Emily watched Ted as his anger settled some. "We didn't start the fire," she said calmly. "Brandon and I were talking and smelled smoke. When we ran over there, the fire was hot and intense. I tried putting it out with water, but Brandon yelled at me too late to not use water. When the water touched whatever was burning, it exploded. He said it was metal." Emily reached back to feel a small bump on the back of her head that she must've gotten when she was thrown back. "Everything we did was to try to stop the fire someone else set. They created it purposely so water would have a devastating consequence for whoever tried to put it out." Emily's voice was extremely calm as she explained the situation. Maybe it was her soul-self emerging a little more, or perhaps it was because she was exhausted and worried. Maggie entered the office as Emily continued. "I saw a person in the trees watching after Brandon collapsed. I couldn't tell you who it was; it was too dark. I was going to go after them, but you pulled me in here." Emily looked at Ted with sad eyes. "I don't know how you could think I would ever do something like that."

"I believe her," Maggie inserted. "I thought I saw someone, too, but couldn't catch them before they disappeared. Huo is continuing the search. Rai, Adamina, and Greta have gone with Gaia to the infirmary to treat Brandon there. The students have returned to their residence halls. Is there anything you need me to do?"

"Is Brandon okay?" Emily interrupted.

"I don't know, Emily," Maggie replied honestly.

"I tried to protect him," Emily said as a tear rolled down her cheek.

Maggie looked at the back of Emily's elbow. "You're bleeding. You should have Gaia look at this."

Emily shrugged. "I'll be okay."

"Maybe you should have it looked at anyway," Maggie encouraged. "You might be able to check on Brandon if you do."

Ted watched the interaction between the two and ran his fingers through his hair. "Do we believe this was a student, or do we have outsiders trespassing?"

Maggie shrugged. "I haven't heard of any threats from outside the campus, but it's a possibility since I can't imagine one of the students would do something like this."

"Myra would," Emily said quietly.

"That's a serious accusation. I thought you said you didn't see who the person was?" Ted questioned her.

"Everything she's done with me in these months has been testing her powers, her abilities against mine. That fire . . . tell me someone with a fire affinity who knew how to get power over other elements didn't start that. Give me a reasonable explanation about why an outsider would start a fire which was purposely set to be stronger than water could put out." The anger in Emily was rising. "You have all chosen to turn a blind eye to her, to punish *me* for everything she's done. And still, she walks around, free from even a doubt that this miracle girl who arose from a coma with a new affinity could be anything except good." Emily started toward the door.

Ted grabbed her arm and spun her to face him. "There are things at play here you couldn't possibly understand. Those very things you say I turn a blind eye to are what I have fought tirelessly with the Elders about. Before you go wild with your accusations, you need to be absolutely certain about what you're talking about. I see your true self in your eyes and know it's bubbling under the surface. But you are still a student in my Academy, and you still have a whole lot to learn."

Maggie put her hand on Ted's arm, and he released Emily.

"I *am* sure about this," Emily replied and angrily left Ted's office.

Emily had calmed down some on her walk to the infirmary. Despite not wanted her wounds to be looked at, she knew Maggie was right, and she'd get to check on Brandon without being pushed out.

The faculty in the infirmary hovered around Brandon's body. He was unconscious, or at least was in some sort of deep sleep. The smell of burnt hair and flesh filled the air, making it almost unbreathable.

"Is he going to be okay?" Emily asked as she entered unnoticed.

"You shouldn't be in here, Emily," Greta said as she stood to meet Emily.

Emily showed her the wound on her elbow and shrugged. "I hit my head in the explosion, too. Maggie said I should have it looked at."

Gaia responded from where she stood beside Brandon. "Greta, I need you over here to continue cooling his body. His temperature is still over one hundred and nine degrees. Emily, have a seat over there, and I'll get to you when I can."

Emily nodded and sat down on the bed next to the one where they were treating Brandon. "Can I help any? I healed his burn the last time," she offered.

"Thank you, Emily," Rai responded. "Greta has this under control."

Emily watched as Greta moved her hands along Brandon's bare chest, trying to bring balance to his core, which had absorbed way too much fire. She wondered if Brandon had felt this helpless when it was Emily lying in that same bed unconscious after her seizure.

The pain from the bump on her head was starting to radiate out, causing Emily to feel dizzy and nauseated. She laid her head on the pillow and was able to have a clear view of Brandon's face. "Please be okay," she whispered just before she passed out from exhaustion.

Emily awoke the next morning to a bright and nearly empty room. Only one person was hovering over Brandon, and it wasn't until Emily rubbed the blurriness of sleep from her eyes that she realized who it was.

"Should've known you'd be in here," Myra said gruffly to Emily, although she didn't look over at her.

"Get your hands off him," Emily demanded and sat up too quickly, causing her to feel dizzy.

"I'm helping him while you're just in the way playing victim or martyr or whatever it is you are today."

Despite Emily's extreme dislike of the girl, it looked like Myra was actually helping Brandon. She decided to take a stab in the dark about her theory of Myra setting the fire. "I saw you in the woods last night," Emily began innocently.

"There were a lot of people there last night," Myra shrugged and moved her fingertips across Brandon's damp forehead.

"Why did you set that fire?" Emily decided to take the direct approach.

Myra feigned innocence. "Why would I start a fire?"

"Because you have some stupid notion that you have to prove yourself to be better than . . . well, better than me." Emily was still wearing her rubber ducky pajamas. She realized she probably didn't look like much of a threat to the older girl who always looked like she stepped out of the pages of a fashion magazine.

Myra laughed. "I didn't need to set a fire to prove what we both know." She shrugged. "But it was epic watching you fail with your elements and nearly blow yourself up." Myra continued to stroke Brandon's face. "I didn't expect him to get hurt, though. But it's nothing I can't heal."

Emily didn't get the full confession she wanted, but it was enough to cancel any doubts she might have had about Myra's involvement. "I have lived thousands of lifetimes and don't need to set traps to know how strong I am with my elements. There are volumes of books in Maggie's office alone that are evidence of that. What do you have, hmm? Parlor tricks?" Emily rolled her eyes. "You are an insecure child who only knows how to destroy." Emily laid back down on the bed.

Myra wasn't quite so cavalier about what Emily had said. She rose up and pulled fire from Brandon's overwhelmed body to create a ball of flames in her hand.

She probably would've hurled it at Emily, too, if Gaia hadn't walked in. "What is going on here? Myra, that's enough. You're not supposed to be in here. Leave this instant."

The fire dissolved in Myra's hand while she sneered at Emily. "I was only trying to help," she said innocently. "I think you'll find his temperature is down now." After throwing a fake smile at Emily, Myra left the infirmary.

"She's right," Gaia said as she was checking on Brandon. "His temperature is almost back to normal, and he appears stable. He should be waking soon." Gaia moved around Brandon's bed to check on Emily. "How are you feeling this morning?" she asked as she was feeling the bump on the back of Emily's head.

"I still have a headache, and I got dizzy when I sat up too fast. I'll be okay, but maybe I could rest here a little longer? It's not like I have anywhere else I need to be."

Emily must've fallen asleep. One minute she was watching Brandon sleep, and the next time she opened her eyes, he was sitting up in bed, talking with Ted and Gaia.

"That was a stupid thing you did, absorbing that much fire," Ted was saying, "but also very brave. Thank you, Brandon."

"Emily helped," he said, and the three of them looked over at Emily. "You're finally awake," Brandon said with a tired smile.

"I could say the same for you," she replied.

"You need to get some rest, Brandon," Gaia interjected.

Ted nodded in agreement. "Gaia told me you should be up and around in time for the end of the year celebration tomorrow. I hope to see you both there." Ted gave Emily a long look and then turned and left.

Gaia followed Ted out of the room to discuss something, leaving Brandon and Emily alone.

"How do you feel?" Emily asked and slid over to sit on Brandon's bed.

"I imagine it's how lobsters must feel when they're being cooked," Brandon said with a laugh.

"Myra snuck in and did something that helped bring your temperature down. She seemed slightly concerned that you were cannon fodder in her plans."

Brandon quirked a brow. "She started the fire?"

Emily shrugged. "In not so many words, she took credit for it."

"A month ago, I would've thought you were insane to make the accusation. But I believe you now," Brandon resigned.

"My sanity is questioned a lot," Emily replied playfully.

Brandon rested his hand on Emily's. She could feel from his touch that he was still hotter than he should be. "Maybe insanity is a part of living as many lifetimes as you seem to have," he teased.

It was nice for Emily to feel Brandon's touch again. There were no surprising soul memories that surfaced. Maybe it was a sign that things could actually get back to normal between the two. "I can't believe you were able to do what you did," Emily said with a humble quality to her tone. "When did you get so strong with your fire?"

Brandon considered his response, speaking aloud to himself. "Hmmm . . . do I pretend to be offended by that, claiming I've always been strong, or do I admit I didn't know I had that in me either, that something woke up inside of me and I just knew what to do?" Brandon stroked his chin as he gazed off in thoughtfulness.

Emily laughed and nudged him. "I almost forgot how ridiculous you are."

"Does that mean you might actually join me . . . and the rest of the Academy, of course . . . at the celebration tomorrow?"

"We'll see." Emily shrugged. "But I really don't think it is a great idea for me to be in the same room with Myra. I don't think she's finished trying to prove me to be inferior to her."

"I doubt she'd do anything in front of the whole Academy," Brandon replied with a yawn.

Emily was fighting the urge to yawn, thanks to Brandon. "You look like you need more sleep before you're in a celebrating mood. I think I'm going to head back to my room. I have to explain away a broken window, and I need to talk with Ashley." She squeezed Brandon's hand before standing. "Need anything before I go?"

Brandon considered for a moment. "Actually, a glass of ice water sounds really good right now."

Emily laughed and poured a glass of water from the pitcher beside Brandon's bed. As she handed it to him, ice cubes formed in the clear liquid. "I'll see you later."

CHAPTER TWENTY-TWO

"Bye, Em."

The glass was cleaned up, and the window was repaired when Emily got back to her room. She was glad Ashley was there, but it seemed the girls had somehow swapped moods. Ashley was packing her room and sobbing while listening to sad pop songs on her phone.

"What's wrong, Ash?" Emily said and was instantly at her friend's side.

Ashley's face was red and moist. She must've been crying for a while. "Xxxanddder and I . . . hhhheee—"

Ashley could barely form words, but Emily got the gist of it. "You guys broke up?" she asked.

The sad girl nodded and blew her nose into a tissue and then tossed onto the mountain of used tissues next to the trashcan. Ashley took a deep breath and tried to calm herself enough to get most of the story out before she started bawling again.

"Oh, sweetie," Emily comforted and held her shaking roommate in a tight hug. "Boys are stupid. Xander is stupid. I don't understand why not seeing you for the summer should mean that you have to break up. Maybe he'll change his mind."

Ashley withdrew from her friend's embrace and shook her head. "He finished the Awakening and said it's better to end things now."

Emily plopped down onto Ashley's bed with a frown. "Oh." Emily knew from her conversations with Lir and from her own soul memories that there were a lot of patterns in their soul lives, and not all of them were good.

"He said we have different paths to take. What does that even mean?" The shakiness in Ashley's voice and the quivering of her lip suggested she was on the verge of another meltdown.

"Live, learn, and grow, or repeat the same mistakes. That's something Lir was trying to get me to understand before he left. I know this hurts now, Ash. Hell, look at how I've been acting over the past week, and it wasn't even my boyfriend who left."

Ashley sniffled and nodded. "Honestly, you've been a miserable, depressing mess," she said.

"I have to believe you are destined for something greater, Ash, and Xander must've known it, too. Someday, you might even look back on this and appreciate what he did." Emily shrugged. She considered what would've happened if someone had told her that same thing a week earlier and was grateful her friend had a calmer reaction.

"Maybe," Ashley replied and wiped the tears off her face with the back of her hand. "At least now I won't have a reason to worry about not having a cell phone signal."

Emily thought that was an odd conclusion but let her friend have it if it helped her feel better. "Do you need any help packing?"

CHAPTER TWENTY-THREE

Most of the students had packed and put their bags outside the main hall. They would be leaving shortly after the end of the year celebration had concluded. Emily helped Ashley pack up her things but stayed behind when she went to take her suitcases and join the others in the hall for the start of the celebration.

"I'll be there in a bit," Emily promised with a pinkie swear to her roommate.

But despite feeling better about things, Emily still didn't feel like celebrating. She sat in her half-empty room and stared across at the abandoned bed that would be her roommate for the next several months. Emily felt the ache of loneliness and decided to listen to Lir's music.

When she picked up her phone, she noticed she had a text message waiting.

I just heard about what happened. Are you okay?

Lir's text from a few hours earlier had gone unnoticed until now. She felt a little less lonely, knowing that Lir was still looking out for her from what felt like halfway around the world.

You know me. Pissing people off, putting out fires, surviving explosions. All a typical day for me, she texted back.

Emily waited for a reply back for about fifteen minutes and then gave up, tossing her phone onto her pillow. "He's busy living his own life," she said aloud, trying to convince herself it was for the best. She'd already done the math the week he left and knew there was only a three-hour time difference between them. It was late morning for her, so maybe he sent the text during a break and was working. She shrugged and realized it didn't matter. Lir left to allow them both to explore their own lives. Emily sighed as she ran her fingers across her lips, still feeling the ghost of his kiss.

"This is stupid," she said suddenly and forced herself up. "I have to live my life, too." She walked with purpose to her closet and began searching for something to wear to the celebration.

Eventually, she decided on crop pants and a loose-fitting pink tank. She was admiring her reflection when her phone rang on her bed.

Every thought she'd resigned herself not to have about Lir went out the window as she rushed to answer it. Excitement tingled inside her when she confirmed it was Lir calling. "Hey," she said, trying to sound casual.

"Hey, yourself. What do you mean 'explosions?' "

Apparently, Lir hadn't heard the whole story of what happened. Yet, he seemed less surprised about the situation with Myra than she would've thought.

"Ted's right, Emily. A lot is happening that you don't know about. Just tread lightly for a bit, please?"

"That sounds a lot like you're telling me to cut off my right hand and try to continue on like nothing happened," Emily replied sourly. Just once she wanted someone to side with her.

Lir laughed. "I don't think either of us wants you hacking off limbs. You wouldn't be able to play the piano anymore."

Emily wandered out of her room with Lir in her ear and sat on the steps outside of her residence hall. "Yeah, well, it feels like you're part of the conspiracy to protect her instead of stopping her. That fire could've hurt a lot of people and burned the Academy down." Emily sighed. "But fine, I'll play nice for the next few hours until she's gone with everyone else for the summer." Emily had been watching the students migrate toward the main hall and also noticed Lucas leave the dining hall and get into a car. She watched the car drive off campus and disappear. "What can you tell me about your research?" she asked in an attempt to keep Lir on the phone for a little longer.

It worked, too, because, after an hour of talking about anything and everything, Lir finally admitted he had to go. "I'm adding some new music to my YouTube channel. It's called 'Dream Trance.' I think you'll like it. We'll talk again soon, Emily. Try to be good until then," Lir said and hung up.

Emily immediately opened up YouTube on her phone and started listening to the dreamy, yet upbeat music Lir had added. She finally had hope that she wouldn't be moping around all summer to the classical pieces that had filled her time during the previous week.

In the distance, she could hear Ted speaking on the microphone in the hall and knew the celebration had started without her. Emily was tempted to forego it entirely and spend the afternoon enjoying this new music Lir introduced her to, but then reluctantly resigned to keep her promise to Ashley and started walking to join the other students and faculty in the main hall. She had to admit, she was curious to see and hear the students who completed their Awakening, and especially interested to see if Xander sounded different. She'd found herself reflecting in the past months on how the Awakening would change who she was.

The sound from the hall grew eerily quiet as Emily approached, but it wasn't until she opened the door that she knew something was terribly wrong. The smell of smoke was strong, but she didn't notice it filling the room because all she saw was everyone who had gathered for the celebration lying unconscious on the floor.

Emily quickly knelt down at the first person she came to and felt for a pulse. Relief washed over her when she felt the boy's heartbeat in his neck. "What's going on here?" she asked in stunned disbelief as her eyes scanned the room. She saw Ted, Maggie, and Adamina at the front of the room, the microphone dropped in front of them. Ashley was on the far side of the room, lying beside Brandon. "No," she whispered and began running toward them.

"Yes," a disembodied voice entered the room.

Emily was suddenly halted in her tracks. She looked down and saw she was rooted—with actual tree roots—to the hardwood floor. It didn't take long for her to realize the culprit, and only a second passed before she had confirmation.

The slender blonde girl rounded the entryway from the hallway into the main room where their classmates and teachers all lay unconscious. "Myra."

"This looks like it was one hell of a party," Myra said casually and kicked the microphone, causing it to generate an ear-piercing squelch.

Emily struggled to free her feet from the earthly grasp *without* resorting to using her elemental gifts. After the surprise explosion from Myra's last calamity, she was determined to be cautious and mindful of her actions and reactions. "What did you do to them?"

Myra shrugged. "Nothing that can't be undone, I'm sure. It's a pity, though. I was hoping you'd be caught up in the festivities, too." She arrogantly strolled over to the table with the food and beverages and held up a cup of punch. "Care for a drink? Or maybe a taste of these delicious desserts Lucas prepared specially for the event."

Emily's thoughts raced to Lucas leaving earlier. "He wouldn't have hurt them," Emily said while shaking her head.

Myra smiled and set the cup back on the table. "We all need something, Emily. It just so happens that I have something that intrigued our dear chef."

The tree was growing upward on Emily, encompassing her legs and reaching for her hands. She struggled in her current predicament but remained reluctant to use her elemental gifts until she knew more about what Myra was planning. "Let me guess," Emily taunted, "setting the world on fire? Or perhaps you'd rather bore the world to death with your egomaniac mind?"

Myra flicked her finger, and the vines tightened around Emily. "Do you know why my fire affinity is so strong?" She slowly paced toward Emily, stepping over the bodies in her path.

"Hmm . . . Brandon is strong, so I'm guessing you managed to siphon some of his gifts." Emily recalled how seamlessly Myra had absorbed some of the fire within Brandon to create the fireball in the infirmary.

"He is delightfully strong," Myra mused. "But sadly, no. I thought I could convince him to join me, but once again, *you* got in the way." Myra looked up at the smoke filling the ceiling. "It seems like we're quickly running out of time here. The flames will be following this smoke shortly, I would imagine."

Emily looked up and used her air abilities to try to clear the room. Without the use of her hands, though, it wasn't as powerful. "Tell me why you're strong," Emily demanded. She hoped that by stalling Myra, she'd put out the fire herself.

"My fire affinity was a gift," she said as she circled Emily and moved the vines up to encircle her throat. "I don't think your precious water or air is going to help you this time. You see, even if you manage to put out the flames which, seeing how pathetic you are without the use of your hands, seems highly unlikely, the smoke alone inhaled by these poor unconscious people, is going to cause quite a lot of problems. Not to mention if they don't receive the antidote soon . . . Well, you get the picture. And that still leaves you with the little problem of being slowly swallowed by the earth itself. Maybe I was too harsh on my native element. A slow, painful death through squeezing and suffocation is really quite powerful."

"What . . . do you want . . . from me?" Emily struggled to ask.

"Seeing that you possess both of the elements I don't, I simply want your soul. With you dead, I can use the technology that gave me the soul with the fire affinity and absorb you. Of course, I didn't have a choice when they gave me the other soul while I was in a coma, but I'd seem ungrateful if I complained." Myra shrugged.

Suddenly, it all made sense: Ted's phone calls, the questions from Tama, the warning from Lir . . . Emily felt like a fool for thinking the Elders weren't cautious with the monster they created with Myra. "You're . . . insane." Emily gasped.

Myra smiled at Emily. "I'll be back for you . . . well, you'll be dead before I come back to take what's mine." She wiggled her fingers at Emily and walked over to Brandon's body. "I think I can give you one more chance. Who knows? When I absorb Emily's soul, you might become quite attached to me." She lifted Brandon's feet and started to drag him out of the room.

Emily didn't want to give away the secret of her third affinity, but the charade had gone on too long. It was seeing Brandon being dragged away that snapped something powerful inside her. She called upon the soul power of her lifetimes, and instantly the plant retracted from her body. With barely a flick of her wrist, a vortex of air surrounded Myra and suspended her in the air.

Myra gasped for air and flailed, but Emily paid only enough attention to her to keep her trapped.

She scanned the room quickly for someone to help the students. The heat from the growing fire was barely tolerable. In the back of the room, Emily saw Gaia's body and ran to her. There was no time to try to figure out what the poison in their systems was, so she did what she saw Brandon do with the fire and used her water and earth affinities to absorb it from Gaia's body.

The older woman's eyes fluttered as she pushed herself to seated and saw the horror scene around her. "What's going on?" Gaia demanded. Emily knew she didn't have time to explain now that the poison was in her.

"They've been poisoned. The food, the drink . . . we need an antidote *now*," Emily commanded. "Myra did this," she continued as she pointed to the girl in the air. "Don't let her escape. I'm going to stop the fire."

Emily didn't wait for the teacher to say anything before she was hurrying toward the hallway. After taking a quick glance at Myra, she realized once the poison took effect, Myra would be free of the vortex. Emily did the only thing she could think to do in that split second. She hurled Myra through the air into a wall, knocking her unconscious.

Myra's limp body slid to the floor with a trickle of blood coming from her nose.

The fire consumed half the hallway, and it looked like it originated at the far end. "Maggie's office," Emily breathed. She used the wind to push the smoke and flames back toward their origin, but she needed water—lots of water.

As Emily followed her wind down the hallway, she pushed the office doors ajar and broke the windows inside with gusts of air. She stumbled several times but managed to access the water through the broken windows. Within moments, water droplets from the lake flew in and got caught up in the air current down the hall. "Please don't let this be a metal fire," Emily whispered as the water made contact with the burning wood, creating steam and white smoke throughout the narrow passage.

Three-quarters of the way to Maggie's office, Emily fell to her knees and couldn't stand up. The adrenaline in her system was keeping her conscious, but her fast heart rate also meant the poison was quickly overtaking her.

With no other options, she crawled the rest of the way to Maggie's office just in time to see the water overwhelm the fire. The office was ruined, but at least the fire was out. With that knowledge, Emily crumbled the rest of the way to the floor, watching the ashes of burned books slowly cascade toward her.

Gaia rushed to the nearest student to see if she could understand the makeup of the poison without having to siphon it from a student like Emily had done to her. Once she discovered it, she rushed to the infirmary to gather the needed ingredients. She would have to administer the antidote intravenously to Rai and Greta so they could work together to move the medicine through the air. It would take time for the students to wake up, and they were all likely going to have extreme headaches, but Gaia believed this was the best course of action.

She returned to the hall with three syringes: one for Greta, one for Rai, and the third for Ted, who obviously needed to be conscious when the students were revived. Upon returning, Gaia administered the shots and then went to check on the injured Myra; she might have done a horrible thing, but Gaia didn't discriminate with her healing. Myra, however, was nowhere to be found.

Ted, Greta, and Rai were quickly caught up to speed on everything that had happened.

"We'll get right on curing the students," Greta said, and without hesitation, she and Rai got to work.

"Myra was missing when I returned. Emily managed to knock her out before running out of the room, but she must've come to and run after I went to the infirmary," Gaia explained to Ted.

Ted nodded. "I have some people I can call to help find her, but I have a very good idea of where she's running."

The students started waking up, each of them groaning and rubbing their heads. Ted took the opportunity to address them (without the microphone), and soon the older students took charge of helping to heal the remainder of the symptoms.

Ted returned to Gaia. "Where did Emily go? She's not in here. I know she didn't eat or drink anything because I specifically looked for her among the students."

"She healed me and then ran off down the hall. Oh, Ted. She absorbed the poison in me. We have to find her."

Ted grabbed Maggie, and the two went running down the charred hallway. Coughing because of the lingering smoke in the air, they glanced at the destruction caused by the fire and Emily's elemental intervention, but they were mostly focused on getting to the girl.

"Is that her in the doorway of your office?" Ted asked Maggie.

They ran and arrived to find Emily covered in burned pages and barely breathing.

"Tell Gaia to get to the infirmary *now!*" Ted ordered as he scooped up the limp child.

CHAPTER TWENTY-FOUR

*S*ilence and darkness surrounded Emily almost immediately. If she could've felt anything, it would've been fear. The lifeless void that had a grip on her was unlike anything she'd ever experienced. Perhaps if she needed a space to yell when she was angry, this might be ideal. But when she tried to talk, there was nothing.

And then things slowly started coming into view. Her soul was communicating directly to what remained of her conscious, dying mind. Maybe it was a defense mechanism, the soul's desire not to lose all it had done and learned before the current body expired. Or perhaps this was just what Emily needed to be able to process so much information.

Emily saw, felt, heard, and tasted lifetime after lifetime of her soul's existence. First, she witnessed everything that happened in her current life—from the power of her using the elements to defeat Myra, to the kiss with Lir, to her mother's death all the way back through her receiving her brother's soul in the womb. She watched as her soul's lifetimes were played out for her. She danced in the rain and mud at Woodstock and sat beside Ava in a country house after World War II as she died her last death. Emily's soul had seen and done so many good, bad, strange, and *wondrous things all over the world. So many souls she knew in so many lives were all revealed to her.*

Further and further back, the memories took her from loving princes to fleeing witch hunts to curing people of diseases. Druid, healer, priestess, witch, friend, lover, wife, sister . . . she'd worn so many titles, yet none and all somehow seemed to fit her.

Emily's soul was speaking to her as only a soul could—and it didn't want Emily's life to end. Her soul drew from her origins, a small community of farmers who lived along the Nile River at the origins of the civilized world and provided her twelve-year-old body with enough strength from the elements to keep her soul attached.

"I don't know why she isn't awake yet," Gaia explained to Ted.

It had been two days since the fire and the almost massacre at the school. All of the students had recovered and continued on with their plans to return to their homes for summer break. As soon as Ted carried Emily into the infirmary, Gaia had administered the antidote. The heads of the elements at the school healed Emily's body back to balanced, but the girl wasn't showing signs of waking.

"I talked to Lir," Greta said. She, Ted, Maggie, and Gaia stood around Emily's bed. "He's catching a flight back right now. He says he thinks he knows something that will help and wants to be here for it and for her."

Gaia shrugged. "She's completely stable and free of the poison. It isn't going to hurt her to remain asleep. I'm sure her body is just exhausted from everything she went through."

"We still don't know the entire story, though, including why Myra did this," Maggie said with a frown. Her office and all the historic records inside were completely destroyed.

"I haven't had any luck locating her yet, but Elder Eli has also gone missing. I fear the two of them may be conspiring to do what the Council has been hesitant to approve," Ted explained.

"Where are they going to find affinates willing to do this?" Gaia shook her head. "I'm with you and the Elders on this one, Ted. There's no place in our world for this."

Everyone in the room nodded in agreement. "It has its appeal to the newer souls in our ranks. I've listened to the arguments for this for almost a year now." Ted paused and shook his head. "I think the events here during this past week should quiet most." Ted sounded exhausted.

"Ted, you should go and rest," Gaia said and rested her hand lightly on his forearm.

"Yes, I know. But I still have some concern that Myra might return. We need to have someone in the room with Emily at all times until she's awake," Ted explained.

"I have some inventory to do, so I'll take the first shift," Gaia said.

"I can take the next one until Lir gets here," Maggie said.

"We'll schedule more watches after his visit if needed," Greta added.

Emily retreated far into her soul memories. She was fascinated by all the lives she'd lived but spent a considerable amount of time—which was separate from the passage of time in the real world - learning about her first life. Everything was about survival, and the lessons learned in that lifetime were the foundation of her character in every lifetime. She was a survivor, a provider, a healer, and very attuned to her elements. She was intrigued to find out she was initially a water affinate and that her earth affinity didn't become a part of her for thousands of years after her first life.

Another part of her journey was to discover all the lifetimes she'd had connections with Lir. It was during the early Roman Empire when they first met, and in every lifetime following, they found each other. Watching the evolution of their connection help Emily understand why they were important to each other. Despite their shared importance, there was always something that prevented them from being more than soul friends, like the elements themselves disapproved of an imbalance their union would cause. Sometimes the complication was as simple as having different skin colors while others were the necessity to marry a person of value. Emily was married off by her father in multiple lives. It wasn't until the mid-eighteenth century when Emily found a soul who she could love and could love her back over lifetimes. It never stopped her and Lir from being close, though, nor did it help with his inevitable heartache. That deep hurt and sadness were a part of her soul, too.

It was a little after six that evening when Lir arrived back at North Shore Academy. Greta and Ted greeted him as he exited the car he took from the airport. After the small talk had run its course, they talked about Emily's condition.

"We've really done all we can. It's up to her to wake up now," Greta explained.

"As I explained on the phone, I think I know what will help. I'd like to go see her now."

The three walked to the infirmary, where Maggie was talking to the unconscious Emily. Upon seeing Lir, Maggie stood and gave him a big hug. "We lost all your records in the fire. I'm beside myself that I didn't keep them somewhere safe."

Lir returned Maggie's hug. "Maybe I'll spend my retirement years writing everything down again." He smiled as he spoke to Maggie, and there wasn't a hint of anger in his tone.

"I appreciate your kindness and willingness to help. We will leave you alone with Emily. Let us know if anything changes."

When the room was cleared, and Lir was alone with Emily, he placed a bouquet of heather beside her pillow and took her hand in his. "I wouldn't put it past you that you have been

278

pretending to be asleep just to get me to come back here." He chuckled quietly. "You know I'm just kidding, but I swear you are the most stubborn soul I've ever known. Only you would think to absorb poison out of someone and then run off into literal flames." He lifted Emily's lifeless hand and pressed his lips to the back of it while singing an old Irish love song.

Lir continued talking to Emily after he stopped singing. "Do you remember when Ava made everyone except me leave the room before she Ascended? I've never told another soul what she said to me. She said, 'It does not matter how slowly you go as long as you do not stop.' I later found out she quoted Confucius. It figures, huh?"

"She told me the same thing," Emily whispered, though her eyes were still closed.

"How long have you been awake?" Lir asked, feigning surprise.

"I'm pretty sure this is still a dream. You're in Greenland," she said.

Lir chuckled. "You've got everyone pretty worried about you. How long have you been faking?"

"Would I ever fake something so horrible that kept me inside?" Emily turned her head to the side and groaned, but still refused to open her eyes. "How long have I been in this bed? I hurt all over."

"It's been two and a half days since our phone call," Lir explained. "Why aren't you opening up your eyes?"

"I told you; this has to be a dream, and I'm not ready to wake up from it yet."

"Alright. I'll play along for a bit. Tell me more about this dream you're having."

"A dear old friend of mine thought it would be proper to introduce me to a bottle of Atholl Brose. There was something about pretending to be a cat and chasing a mouse. Then I found myself in a field of heather down by the loch."

Lir laughed at Emily's dream. "Did I ever tell you that there never was a mouse?" He continued laughing at the memory.

Emily finally opened her eyes and wrinkled her nose at him. "No, you left that part out even after the whole town made fun of me. I was called 'Catty Ady' for the rest of that life!" Emily grabbed the heather from beside her head and hit Lir with it.

He continued laughing and then stopped suddenly. Lir grabbed Emily's arm and demanded her attention. "Look at me," he said.

Emily slowly blinked and turned her eyes to his. She gazed deep into his familiar eyes and knew exactly what he saw. "Yeah, it's me, Adya." All it took was nearly dying for Emily to finally know her soul name.

EPILOGUE

August 9, 2013

I promised Maggie I would spend more time documenting my lives, but there's so much that happened over seven thousand years, it's going to take more than one summer to complete. Besides, I may know where some of my old journals have been stored, but that's a trip that will have to wait for a time when I have more than a few months of free time. Regardless, my young body craves new experiences more than reliving past ones.

I spent a lot of the summer working on and off with the Elders on the Myra issue. It was confirmed that Elder Eli disappeared with Myra, and while some appear relieved that there was no activity from either since the attack on the Academy a few months ago, there are some of us who can practically feel this is the calm before the storm. They both seem to be on some quest to create super-affinates.

Outside the Myra-super-villain business, my summer has been filled with enjoyable activities. I spent several weeks visiting some old (soul) friends around the country. Yes, I even took a week to go with Lir to New Orleans, although he treated me like his kid sister most of the time—an annoying fact seeing that I'm a couple thousand years older. Eventually, he had to return to Greenland to continue his research. I look back on that week I spent moping in my room after he first left and roll my eyes at myself. He and I share connected lifetimes, and there is plenty of time for us to see how our relationship would evolve in this lifetime after it is socially appropriate for us to explore a relationship together. The advice Ava gave us both on her Ascension bed was true; as long as we remained true to ourselves—to our souls— it didn't matter how slowly it happened, as long as we didn't stop loving each other in whatever ways we were able. Yeah, I'm paraphrasing.

Brandon and I have exchanged texts and talked on the phone a few times, but I'm very cautious with how I interact with and influence him before he completes his Awakening. Besides, he started dating a "normal" girl back home. I am truly happy for him. Maybe in this lifetime, having something different is what his soul needs.

As I get ready for the new school year to begin and for new Abecedarians to join us at the Academy, all I can do is hope I can meet the challenges the year will bring with the grace, beauty, and knowledge gifted to me by my everlasting soul. May we honor our elements and ourselves in the changes to come.

~Adya

True Self, the second novel in Anne Williams's compelling Soul Magic series, will be available for purchase soon. Join Adya as she determines how her soul lives fit into her current one, the true meaning of balance and power, and how love can take lifetimes to discover. Read on for an exclusive preview.

PROLOGUE

Perspective is how we see and judge the world based on our own experiences. It is, in essence, a person's truth. It is also how we identify our "self." Rene Descartes spent a portion of his life devoted to understanding truth outside perspectives. What is truth, and hence what is permanent in a world that was fluid and forever changing?

People with old souls see the world differently, and perhaps *have a better grasp of what it means to be truly oneself. After all, it is the ones with old souls that have experienced many different perspectives and can call upon them all to judge people and circumstances. However, when you've lived hundreds of lifetimes and had so many experiences, you tend to believe your perspective is a universal truth rather than an opinion. More often than not, though, when you try to force people to live up to your view of them and your truths about the world, they will fall short.*

Let's return to Descartes and his famous "I think; therefore, I am" statement. It becomes difficult to accept personal perspective as truth and apply it fairly to one's identity in the world no matter the age of the soul or how many—or few—lifetimes they've existed. So how does one identify their true self? Is it the diligent worker who dots their I's and crosses their t's, or is that same person who drinks too many beers after work and yells profanities at his wife and children? How can different versions of the same person all be labeled as "true"?

When an affinate completes the Awakening, they face these conflicting thoughts. How can you live the life of the mortal body when your soul has an opposing perspective? How can you be suddenly thrust into the world as a mortal being and be expected to abide by its laws when your soul tells you that you're so much more? It's utterly exasperating, to be honest. I said it before and I'll say it again—being a teenager sucks but being an Awakened affinate teenager comes with a whole new definition of suckiness—and maybe a few really cool perks.

CHAPTER ONE

"**I** don't know," Ashley said hesitantly. Her right eye narrowed and twitched slightly. "It's going to be weird calling you Adya. I mean, you still *look* like Emily."

The two roommates took time to catch up after their summer apart while the new Abecedarians were getting placed in their elemental residence halls. Ashley had written Emily letters during the summer, but since she was in the wilderness of Alaska, Adya didn't have a way to write back.

Adya laughed. "You can call me Ady; it's close to Emily. I promise I won't hold it against you if you slip up occasionally. Besides, I still *am* Emily, just more now than she was."

"I wish I could've stayed for you after you-know-who did those awful things. You looked dead when I saw you last." Ashley frowned.

"This isn't *Harry Potter*, Ash. You can say Myra's name." Adya laughed.

"Yeah," Ashley said. "It makes me want to vomit to say her name, though."

Adya rolled her eyes and laughed. "Speaking of vomiting—or hopefully not—we have a new kitchen staff this year, including a woman head chef, Chef Caroline." Adya filled her roommate in on the Lucas situation, how he made a deal with Myra to poison the students at the End of Year Celebration in exchange for presumably getting his affinity returned. "Yeah, apparently she was former Elder Eli's chef. When Eli disappeared with Myra, the remaining Elders went through his house and belongings. That's when she requested to remain in the service of affinates. Ted immediately offered her the position here."

"Do you think she'll let us sneak in for snacks?" Ashley asked.

Adya fondly recalled the memories of visiting with Lucas in the kitchen and felt his betrayal and loss deeply. "She seems cool, but I haven't needed comfort food lately."

"Speaking of the need for comfort food. . . did you talk with Brandon over the summer?" Ashley hung up her last shirt and sat on the edge of her bed, perched to hear real gossip.

"Yeah, we talked a bit. Brandon's dating this girl back home now. But things are good between us. We're back to being just friends," Adya said with a smile.

Ashley furrowed her brows and frowned. "That's it? So, you didn't have any wonderful soul memories of past lives with him? No hot affairs?"

Adya laughed. "Well, you know about the one in the desert. His and my life have touched many times in the past. Things between us may change when he finishes his Awakening. For now, I'm grateful for Brandon's friendship in this life, regardless of whether he and I end up together."

Ashley stewed in silence. She was both jealous and dismayed by her roommate. Adya seemed noticeably different than the Emily she knew before her Awakening, coming across so mature in thought for a thirteen-year-old. Ashley would've been devastated to learn that Xander—now known as Calder after he completed his Awakening and broke Ashley's heart just before the end of the school year—had a new girlfriend, let alone a non-affinate girlfriend. "Fine," she resigned. "What about Lir? Have you heard from him?"

Adya still hadn't told anyone about her kiss with Lir, but Ashley had always been aware of "something deeper" between her and their water elemental healing teacher. "He flew back when he heard about Myra's attack. He was there when I woke and was the first one to see me after I completed the Awakening. We spent some time together, but it was mostly talking about how we could help restore all the knowledge in the books destroyed in the fire in Maggie's office."

"Ugh!" Ashley protested and threw her hands up in the air. "You've gone full-on boring. Give me Emily back."

Adya scrunched her face. "Gee, thanks. I don't know what you want me to tell you. I've been working with the Elders and doing things by myself all summer. There wasn't much opportunity to even think about dating."

"Fine," Ashley submitted. "Can you at least reassure me that we've always been best friends?"

"You know I can't tell you about *you*, but I know you already know we have a deep-rooted friendship." Adya smiled and skillfully changed the topic. "So, tell me all about Alaska."

Ashley sighed and rolled her eyes in dramatic exasperation, but as she told her stories—some of which she'd already shared with Adya in letters—her eyes lit up, and her voice became animated. No matter how much Ashley detested roughing it, being in nature for the summer suited her well.

"It's almost time for dinner, ladies," Greta interrupted as Ashley was nearing the end of the story about a momma bear and her two cubs.

"Thanks," Adya replied. "How many new water affinates do we have this year?"

"Just one in our house," Greta said with slightly slumped shoulders, sounding somewhat deflated. "So, I'm sure she could use some water elemental friends." She motioned to someone outside the girls' room. A girl with dark brown hair, big glasses, beautiful ebony skin, and braces appeared beside Greta. "Girls, I would like you to meet Sierra. Sierra, this is Adya and Ashley."

"Nice to meet you," Ashley said with a warm smile.

The girl smiled shyly. "Hi," she said and then immediately looked down at her well-worn sneakers.

"We're about to go to dinner. Want to join us?" Adya asked as she stood from her bed.

Sierra shrugged and looked up at Adya briefly. "Sure."

Greta's shoulders relaxed, and she breathed a small sigh of relief when they offered to help the new Abecedarian. "I will see the three of you later," she said and continued down the hall to let the others know it was dinner time.

"So, what do you think of it so far?" Brandon asked Sierra as the four friends ate their first course.

"It's nice," Sierra replied.

Everyone nodded in agreement. "Yeah, and in case you were wondering, all the residence halls are elemental themed," Brandon added astutely, obviously remembering the previous year's humiliation by Titus.

"Oh," the girl said.

Adya couldn't tell if Sierra's short responses were because she was intimidated by Brandon, was attracted to him, or if she was just timid.

"I remember how nervous I was last year," Ashley said. "I'd never been away from home before, at least not without my family."

Sierra nodded. "Yeah, I've never even gone on a vacation before," the quiet girl admitted.

"This feels like a resort, at least when you're not in classes, but you have to wear uniforms," Brandon added.

"If she's never been on vacation, how would she know what a resort was like?" Ashley interjected.

Like Sierra, Adya remained mostly quiet during the meal. She found herself struggling with how to interact with the three who hadn't completed their Awakening. It felt like she was an outsider, like when she went home for the previous winter break and tried to hang out at the mall with her old friends. Having been caught up in her thoughts, Adya suddenly interrupted her friends mid-conversation. "How's your girlfriend, Brandon? Angela, isn't it?"

Ashley and Brandon raised a brow in surprise by the seemingly random question while Sierra remained quietly picking at her dinner.

"Yeah, Angela," Brandon said and shifted in his seat uncomfortably. "She's okay, I guess."

"How'd you meet her?" Ashley asked enthusiastically, preparing herself to hear some good gossip finally.

"Dad got me a job at the country club for the summer. She was there with her family a lot. We just got to talking, and it was cool." Brandon shrugged. He glanced at Adya, presumably to see her reaction about talking about Angela, but Adya gave no indication that she was unhappy or uncomfortable hearing about his new girlfriend.

"Aww, that's sweet. It sounds like it should be a movie," Ashley gushed.

Brandon chuckled uneasily. "It wasn't that interesting. We had fun together over the summer. Don't know how well a long-distance thing is going to work out, but we said we'd give it a shot." Brandon glanced at the clock on the wall. "Speaking of which, I need to go call her. It was nice meeting you, Sierra."

The Abecedarian flashed a shy smile as Brandon left.

"How rude," Ashley said as soon as he'd walked away. "He didn't even say it was nice to see *us* again. Boys," she huffed and rolled her eyes.

When Sierra was called to the library for orientation with Adamina and the other Abecedarians, Ashley returned to the common room in their residence hall. Adya decided it was a beautiful night for a walk. She didn't have a specific destination in mind, but she needed to get a grasp on her out-of-place feeling.

Adya was passing by the old main hall—which was still under reconstruction from the fire—when Calder unexpectedly jogged up beside her. "Hey."

"Oh, hi," Adya said as the boy's pace slowed to match hers. "Is everything okay?" She looked to make sure Ashley wasn't around. Despite not having any hard feelings towards Calder, she knew it would hurt Ashley's feelings for Adya to be chatting with him.

"Yeah, I mostly wanted to thank you for saving us at the celebration and apologize for making you feel like you were insane about your dislike for Myra," Calder explained.

"You're welcome, and it's okay." Adya smiled. "Although 'dislike' is putting it mildly. I have a question for you, though."

Calder shrugged. "Sure, what is it?"

"Why did you end things with Ashley?"

Calder's eyes widened, and his cheeks flushed subtly. "Because she—"

Adya held up her hand, cutting him off immediately. "Don't feed me the bullshit you fed her. I know you, and I know what you two have meant to each other in past lives. Tell me the truth."

The boy paused, looking thoughtfully into the distance. Finally, he looked back to Adya and said, "Why haven't you told Brandon the truth?"

Adya narrowed her eyes, replying somewhat defensively. "He deserves to make his own choices no matter what lifetime it is. I didn't see any good that would come of me telling him before he completed his Awakening."

Calder nodded. "My reasons were similar. I didn't want Ashley to feel manipulated. I want her to decide where her future lies and with whom. Besides, you know that I've hurt her many times. Maybe it's time she doesn't suffer."

Despite Adya knowing intimate details of Calder and Ashley's past lives—both the good and bad—she couldn't help but turn his words internally. She felt the sting of the suffering she'd caused Lir for lifetimes. "You've also been responsible for lifetimes of her happiness. Pain is always a part of life, and it's the reason why we can appreciate the love and happiness so much. I don't think the struggles of your past lives with Ashley are enough to break ties with her completely in this life, but I do understand what you're saying," Adya added. "Can I ask you another question?"

Calder nodded. "Sure."

"Did you feel out of place among all the people who hadn't completed their Awakening yet?"

"A little. Seeing people for who they've been for lifetimes when they don't know who that is yet is a bit of a mind fuck," he admitted.

"How do you cope with it? I mean, I've been around Awakened people since it happened. Seeing everyone again and knowing who they are without them knowing is harder than I imagined," Adya admitted.

"Lir helped me out before he left. He reminded me that the un-Awakened version of ourselves is still us. I don't know. It made a lot of sense when he said it." Calder shrugged. "It was more difficult when I was at home for the summer because my family expected me to be the same Xander as when I started school. I just had to learn how to be both. I guess that's why we have a class on being Awakened this year."

Adya hoped the class would help. "Thanks for talking with me, Calder. I think I just needed to talk with someone else who's dealing with in this weird limbo of Awakened and un-Awakened people."

"No problem, Adya. See you in class tomorrow," Calder said as he walked towards his residence hall.

"See ya," Adya replied and continued her thoughtful stroll. She hadn't seen Maggie in a few days and decided to join her in her new temporary office.

"Do you think she'll try another attack?" Adya asked Maggie as they drank some tea in her closet-turned-into-an-office. It felt unnatural to be in the windowless room, and she knew Maggie didn't like being so out of touch with the earth.

"I wish I could tell you, Adya. From what we understand of Myra and Eli's plan, it seems more self-serving than vindictive. We have people keeping an eye out for the three of them."

Adya could see the pain in Maggie's eyes that remained after her old lover helped Myra poison them. While they never had a conversation about Lucas specifically, Adya knew from the depressed energy around Maggie that her legal guardian felt the loss deeply. "If there's anything more I can do, I'm happy to help."

"You've done more than anyone could've ever asked of you already. Until we can locate them, we just have to keep our guard up." Maggie reached into the drawer of her desk and pulled out a large envelope. "Lir sent me one of his old journals. He said you guys uncovered it in New Orleans along with a faded picture. Since these are partially yours, too, I wanted you to read through it before I scan it into the new digital archive."

Adya took the envelope with a soft smile. "Thank you. I'll read through it tonight and let you know tomorrow. I'm sure it'll be fine, though." There was some comfort for Adya to be able to escape from her current life—even if only for the night—before she was thrust in full force with the start of classes the following day.